ONLY CHILD

BOOKS BY CASEY KELLEHER

The Lucy Murphy Series

No Escape

No Fear

No Going Back

The Byrne Family Trilogy

The Betrayed

The Broken

The Forgotten

Standalones

The Taken

The Promise

I'll Never Tell

Mine

Rotten to the Core

Rise and Fall

Heartless

Bad Blood

ONLY CHILD

CASEY KELLEHER

bookouture

Published by Bookouture in 2022

An imprint of Storyfire Ltd.
Carmelite House
50 Victoria Embankment
London EC4Y 0DZ

www.bookouture.com

Copyright © Casey Kelleher, 2022

Casey Kelleher has asserted her right to be identified as the author of this work.

All rights reserved. No part of this publication may be reproduced, stored in any retrieval system, or transmitted, in any form or by any means, electronic, mechanical, photocopying, recording or otherwise, without the prior written permission of the publishers.

ISBN: 978-1-80314-424-5
eBook ISBN: 978-1-80314-423-8

This book is a work of fiction. Names, characters, businesses, organizations, places and events other than those clearly in the public domain are either the product of the author's imagination or are used fictitiously. Any resemblance to actual persons, living or dead, events or locales is entirely coincidental.

For Emma & Vicky
My Gladstone Girls

AUGUST

My mother thinks I'm dead.
    But being dead is not the worst thing.
    Being here is.
    Being his prisoner.

PROLOGUE

'Ninety-eight. Ninety-nine. One hundred. Coming! Ready or not!' Ethan Hegarty shouts, his tone giving a firm warning to his friends as he finally turns from where he's been standing.

His eyes scrunched closed, his head resting against the bark of the thick oak tree that stands so proudly in the middle of the woodland's clearing, Ethan is aware how childish he sounds as soon as the words have left his twelve-year-old mouth, and how stupid he'd look if anyone else from school was here to see them playing a kid's game like Hide 'n' Seek.

Anyone else other than Christopher and Louis that is.

They don't always play stupid games when they come here though. Sometimes they do other things. More grown-up things, like build dens and start fires. Once, Christopher had even stolen a cigarette from his mother, and the three boys had taken turns with it. Coughing and spluttering out the fumes each time that they'd accidentally breathed the smoke down too quickly and deeply into their lungs.

Today they are happy here just playing games, having some fun, like they used to do when they were younger.

Ethan scans the dense woodlands for any sign of his two

friends, determined to win. He is good at this. Too good; Christopher and Louis know it too. They'll be crouching down somewhere, quiet as mice, as they hold their breaths and stifle their giggles, waiting for him to pounce.

And he will pounce.

Today will be no different, he thinks as his gaze sweeps across the thick line of trees ahead of him. He grins, watching, as a stream of autumnal leaves blows across the wet, muddy ground like a trail of burning fire all reds, oranges and yellows.

He listens then, tentatively, certain he can hear the sound of sniggering: a giveaway sign. Only the sound is gone so quickly, picked up with the wind as it whistles loudly, sweeping through the dense branches as they sway abruptly against the breeze.

Then nothing. Silence.

Ethan starts walking. Further into the woods. Creeping slowly, carefully. Trying his hardest to keep his steps light, to suppress the sound of twigs as they snap beneath his footfall.

He is close. He can feel it.

And he is ready. Ready to sneak up on them. Ready to use the element of surprise to scare them both. Peering around the next lot of trees, he screws up his mouth when he sees it is empty. His friends aren't there.

Doubt has started to creep in. What if he can't find them this time? What if this time they had finally managed to outsmart *him*? He keeps walking. Much further into the woodland, further than he's ever ventured before on his own.

He is starting to feel on edge. He doesn't want to admit that even to himself, but being here in the woods like this makes him feel suddenly creeped out. Maybe they have left him here. In fact, the more Ethan thinks about it the more he is convinced that's exactly what his friends have done. They have run off and left him here, to walk around the thick, dense woods all alone.

They might be back home by now. Both of them laughing in

hysterics at his expense. Feeling so clever with themselves at how they had mugged him off.

Because they did that sometimes. All three of them to be fair, him included. They played stupid pranks and tricks on each other. It was funny sometimes too. The things they did to each other. How far they would go.

Other times, not so much. Like now.

Ethan shivers. Telling himself he is just cold, that it isn't because he is freaked out. There is nothing to be scared of, is there? He's had enough now.

'Christopher? Louis? Come on, this isn't funny anymore. I give up! Come out!' Ethan shouts, deciding he is done with the game. He wants to go home.

The light is fading fast now. And his stomach is starting to rumble loudly as he thinks of the plain cheese sandwich that he'd eaten at lunchtime at school today. Lunch seems like a distant memory. It is almost dinner time. Bangers and mash. His favourite. That's what his mum told him this morning would be waiting for him when he got home. About to turn and do just that, he hears a noise which makes him stop dead.

The snap of a branch.

He listens.

And hears it again, a faint murmur, almost inaudible, but he heard it. It is coming from just up ahead of him. From behind the huge log stack standing at least eight feet high and almost just as wide. Of course! That's the perfect place to hide.

Ethan smirks then. It is payback.

His walk turns into a run as he jumps around the stack and shrieks loudly for maximum effect.

'Got you, you pair of shit-heads!'

Only he'd been mistaken. Terribly, terribly mistaken. The noise he'd heard hadn't come from Christopher or Louis at all.

'What the...?'

Ethan falters. His words spilling out of him incoherently as his brain fights hard to catch up. Stunned for a second, unable to register what his eyes are seeing.

A woman.

The clothes that she is wearing are dirty and smeared with something dark and sticky looking, the colour a deep red.

Blood, he realises. She is covered in blood.

She stares at him.

Her eyes full of fear. Pure terror beaming from them as she flinches at his sudden presence and she pushes herself up against the logs, her arms wrapped around her knees. In a bid to protect herself. As if she'd been expecting to see someone else. Her eyes search his then, as if she is assessing whether he might harm her.

Ethan can't take his eyes off her. The sight of her both horrific and mesmerising at the same time. He notes how the woman's skin is almost translucent. A sickly white tinged with shades of blue and purple in patches, mottled from the cold. Bruises?

She is shaking. Her body trembles violently. He isn't sure if she is cold or if it is because she is scared. Scared of him? He has to reassure her that he won't hurt her.

To tell her that he didn't mean to shriek and make her jump.

Ethan is beaten to it.

The young woman speaks first.

The words shaking as they leave her mouth, laced with urgency and panic.

'Help me. Please? Before he finds me!'

1

The cake is ruined.

Thick clouds of black smoke billowing out from the oven door had alerted Tessa to that.

Coughing and spluttering, Tessa grabs a tea towel and pulls her latest blackened creation out from the oven, trying not to burn herself in the process as she launches the roasting hot cake tin onto the metal draining board, next to the sink.

'Well done, Tessa! Another foolproof recipe that you've managed to completely balls up!' Tessa mutters to herself, disheartened now, as she picks up the entire thing and throws it in the bin, before opening the kitchen window so she can eliminate some of the smoke and the lingering smell of burning before Amelia gets home. Because it is embarrassing enough, isn't it? How she can't even follow a simple basic cake recipe without her girlfriend ribbing her for her failed efforts.

Only she'd been so engrossed in trying to make the cake perfect that the whole afternoon must have slipped away from her, because before she even opens the first window latch, she hears the sound of the front door slamming and Amelia throwing her keys down on the hallway table. The same routine as always when she is back after a busy day at work.

'Mmm! Something smells... interesting!' Amelia walks into the room and wafts her hand in front of her face dramatically as she puts on a fake, exaggerated cough.

'Interesting is one word to describe it. If you must know, it was supposed to be a birthday cake!' Tessa declares. 'And please don't worry, you don't have to do the whole spiel of eating it and pretending that it's good to spare my feelings. It's so awful that I threw it straight in the bin. You're safe! For now.' Tessa tries to hide the wobble in her tone. But Amelia hears it. She can read Tessa like a book. She knows that she is upset.

'Hey, come here. I'm only kidding!' Amelia smiles again, pulling Tessa up to her feet before wrapping her arms around her. 'It's just a cake. Who cares? I don't. It's the thought that counts. And that was a really lovely gesture.'

'I just wanted to surprise you. I wanted to do something nice for you for a change. Because you always do nice things for me,' Tessa explains. 'And it will happen, one day, you'll come home and find a home-made feast waiting for you. I promise you that!'

'Woah, that almost sounds like a threat!' Amelia grins before kissing Tessa on the mouth. 'But seriously, the last thing I care about is a feast. Or a silly cake. No offence but birthday cakes can be pretty overrated after the first few mouthfuls anyway!' Amelia says, before adding sincerely, 'All I care about coming home to is you. Every single day.'

'You mean that?'

'I mean that!' Amelia says. 'Though it would be nice to not have to search through the clouds of black smoke to find you! And speaking of smoke, your clothes stink of it. That can't be good for you, breathing all that in. If I were you, I'd take them off immediately...' She grins.

'Oh you would, would you? Well, thank God you're here and you're so good at looking after me. What would I ever do without you?' Tessa giggles, taking the hint as Amelia takes her hand and leads her into the bedroom.

All thoughts of that stupid burnt cake quickly forgotten.

2

'Kayla!' Sherrie gawps, open-mouthed in disbelief as she stares at the state of her daughter's bedroom, just as Kayla pulls a huge basket down from the dressing table and tips the contents out all over the floor, sending lotions, potions, perfumes and make-up rolling across the once beautifully cream-coloured carpet.

'What on earth? Look, love, I know you're upset, but you're wrecking the place!' Though why Sherrie is so shocked, she can't fathom. She is used to this by now. She can well believe the chaos and mess that Kayla has created. It had become a running joke between them all over the years. How Kayla may have inherited many of Sherrie's better qualities, but cleanliness had not been one of them.

The girl is an outright slob.

You must take after your father! Sherrie often quipped. *I'm forever picking up after him too. He leaves a trail of debris and mess wherever he goes. Drives me nuts!*

Tonight though, Sherrie isn't even exaggerating at how bad Kayla's room looks. It is beyond recognition; Sherrie can barely see the carpet now that Kayla seems set on completely trashing the place as she searches for her missing passport.

'I can't find it, Mum. I've searched everywhere...' Kayla shrieks, her voice laced with panic and frustration.

Sherrie can see that her daughter is on the verge of tears, but tearing the house apart isn't going to solve anything. It certainly isn't going to make her daughter's missing passport just suddenly reappear.

'Even if it's here, Kayla, you're probably burying it under all this stuff. It looks as though a bomb has gone off in here! You can't just leave that all there, Kayla. You might have more chance at finding it if you clear some of the junk away. Come on, love. Pick it all back up,' Sherrie says as she eyes the mattress that has been dragged from the bed and is currently propped up against the bedframe, before her gaze rests on the freshly washed bedding that she'd spent the afternoon ironing, which is now abandoned in a heap in the middle of the floor, surrounded by mounds of clothing. Dirty washing mixed with clean. Sherrie's biggest bugbear of them all.

'Kayla! I've only just washed and ironed that bedding! This is getting silly now, love. I know you're upset but this isn't going to help,' Sherrie says firmly, marching into the room and dragging the mattress back up onto the frame before she shakes the duvet out and begins re-making the bed.

Sherrie learned the hard way that sometimes it is just quicker this way. To take the initiative and just do things herself. Not only because this way is less painful, having fewer arguments with Kayla, but it also means that the job will get done properly too.

Because Sherrie likes everything in its place, and a place for everything. That is her motto. It drives Richard mad. That, and the way that Sherrie constantly fusses over Kayla and does everything for the girl. Mollycoddling, he calls it.

How's she ever going to learn if you always do everything for her? he would argue. *You can't keep wrapping her up in cotton wool. She's not a baby anymore.*

But Richard is wrong about that, because no matter her age Kayla will always be Sherrie's baby. Besides, Sherrie likes it. The fussing and the 'mollycoddling'. It gives her a sense of purpose. A feeling of being needed.

Men don't understand that.

How as a mother you can never just switch it off: all those years of providing, protecting and teaching your child. It doesn't matter how old they are, those attributes are always there.

And Richard can't talk. He isn't much better when it comes to looking after himself, though of course he'd never admit that. And Sherrie has certainly never seen him complaining when it is him that she is running around for or cleaning up after. Besides, it is different with Kayla. Sherrie is just leading by example, isn't she? Truly believing that if she did this often enough, if she fussed and tidied and cleaned up after Kayla, that one day, Kayla might learn to crave the cleanliness over the dirt and chaos too. Just like Sherrie once had.

'It's gone, Mum! I've looked everywhere! What am I going to do?' Kayla wails, her body slumping down onto a mound of clothes as if she wants the floor to swallow her whole.

And it is only then that Sherrie realises that Kayla is crying. Sitting there with tears streaming down her face, her shoulders shaking with each heartfelt sob. Crumbling under the weight of the situation she has found herself in.

'Oh, darling!'

Sherrie knew that this was coming because it has been brewing all day. She'd tried her very best to appease her daughter. Hoping to keep her melt down at bay by not acknowledging it. Or she would have got stressed out too. Instead, she'd busied herself cooking Kayla's favourite dinner. Spaghetti Bolognese and garlic bread loaded with extra cheese, just the way Kayla liked it, though Kayla had barely touched it. And Sherrie and Richard had been forced to search for the passport too.

Kayla's melt down tonight had been inevitable really, when

it still hadn't turned up after two days of searching high and low for it. Between the three of them, they had all but ripped the house apart. Kayla a little more literally by the looks of it, Sherrie realises now. They'd searched every drawer, every cupboard, every filing cabinet. And so far, it had been to no avail. It is starting to feel as if Kayla's passport has simply vanished into thin air.

Are you sure you didn't leave it at one of your friends' houses the last time you went to the cinema? Because I'm almost sure you took it with you. The other week, remember? That film you needed ID for. The creepy one about the woman who lives in the cabin in the woods... Or was it the one about the zombies?

But Kayla insisted that she'd brought it home with her and put it back in the filing cabinet just like Sherrie had asked her to. Both times. So that she could keep it safe with all their important documents that Sherrie neatly labelled and stored away in their own designated folders. The passports and birth certificates. Along with every other document that came into this house, every bill and bank statement.

Only they'd all searched the filing cabinet and there had been no sign of it at all.

Sherrie doesn't want to upset Kayla further, but the truth is that they are running out of time. The school trip is tomorrow morning and the coach is leaving at 6 a.m. Sherrie is gutted for her daughter because she knows how much Kayla has been looking forward to the prospect of going to France with her friends for the week. She is so excited to go on her first real holiday abroad, and without her parents too. So much so, she'd spoken of nothing else for weeks, driving Sherrie and Richard around the bend.

But it is looking more and more likely that Kayla won't be going, and judging by the desperate state of the bedroom and how distraught her daughter looks, the reality that she might not be going is clearly starting to dawn on Kayla now too.

'If I don't find it by tomorrow, they won't let me go. Everyone else will be there apart from me. I'll miss it all. It's not fair, Mum! What am I going to do?' Kayla pleads with her. Her pretty blue eyes now puffy and swollen from where she's been crying. That is all it takes. A crying daughter. That pleading puppy-eyed look.

Sherrie is on her knees now. Crouching down and hugging her sobbing daughter to her, because seeing Kayla in so much pain is breaking Sherrie's heart in two. Even though Kayla always claimed lately that she was too old and too cool to hug her mum these days, for once, tonight, Kayla lets her. In fact, this time she hugs Sherrie back, folding herself in on her mother, crying loudly as big wracking sobs shake her entire body. Believing that somehow Sherrie can fix this. That Sherrie will do what she always does and somehow make this all better. And there is nothing in the world that Sherrie wants more than to make her daughter feel better.

But even she can't magic a missing passport out of thin air.

'Oh, darling. I know how upset you are. But these things happen unfortunately. And I'm sure it will turn up... eventually,' Sherrie says. 'Though I think you need to face it that it might not happen in time for the school trip tomorrow. But listen, I've spoken to your dad, and we thought that if we don't find it, how about we go down to the coast for a few days next week? The three of us. We can rent one of those fancy beach huts down on the seafront. The ones on the stilts overlooking the sand. And we could go for a walk along the pier and get pizza and donuts. We can have anything you want.'

Sherrie tries to let Kayla down gently as she hints that, this time, she might not be able to fix it. No matter how much she wants to. But she could do the next best thing, which is try and cheer Kayla up any way that she can. Even though Sherrie knows that no matter what she does or says, the next few days will be insufferable. And no doubt, if they did go away Kayla would sulk around the beach hut the whole time, wishing more than anything that she had gone on the school trip instead of to the beach with her parents. But Sherrie is willing to do it. To at least try and put a smile back on Kayla's face. She is a sucker like that.

She'll do anything, if it means that her Kayla will be happy again.

'Your dad can take a few days off work. And I'm sure that the school won't mind you having a few days out, given the circumstances. And how about when your friends get back from France, you invite them here? Abbey and Kayleigh, and even Libby if you want? Though I know you two are forever falling out. You can have a sleepover here. What do you say?'

'But I want to go to France, Mum... with my mates. We had it all planned. We're sharing a room!' Kayla says, her chest heaving with every sob as the reality finally sinks in that if her mum is suggesting other arrangements then this really is bad.

'I know you do, sweetheart. And I want that for you too. I really do. We're not giving up just yet. We'll keep looking. How about we get this mess tidied up a bit, hey? We might come across it still whilst we're clearing all this lot up! You never know,' Sherrie says, trying to sound optimistic, even though she's already resigned herself to the fact that there is no way that Kayla will be going now.

Not when they have spent the whole day looking for it.

To her surprise Kayla nods and does as she is asked. Getting up from the floor, she begins picking up the clothes that are strewn all around her. Checking the pockets and shaking each item as she goes. Still holding on to the smallest grain of hope that they will find it.

'If we still don't find it, then you can get into bed and get yourself an early night, just in case. And me and your dad will keep on looking. We'll go back through the whole of the downstairs tonight, I promise you. Whatever happens, you'll have a lovely holiday somewhere. How does that sound!?'

'Okay, Mum. Thank you.'

And Sherrie's heart swells at that. How her daughter takes everything in her stride. How she doesn't stay down for long. She is strong. Just like Sherrie, in so many ways. Except for the untidiness.

Though Sherrie loves her so much that she could just about forgive her that.

3

Tessa throws the last of the ingredients into the basket and scans the list she made earlier before she'd left the house. Checking that she has everything she needs. Because the chances are that she's forgotten something vital.

Flour, caster sugar, eggs. Check.

Chocolate sprinkles! That's what she still needs. She smiles to herself, as if chocolate sprinkles are going to be this masterpiece of a cake's saving grace.

Though secretly Tessa hopes that they might be. She needs all the help that she can get after yesterday's disastrous attempt. Still, today is a new day and she is back on a mission to make sure that Amelia has the best birthday cake that she's ever seen or tasted. And what will make this cake even more miraculous, other than her not burning it to a cinder, is that Tessa bakes and decorates it with her own two fair hands.

Though just a few minutes ago, Tessa had made her way down the cake aisle and considered buying one of the perfectly decorated ready-made celebration cakes and passing it off as her own. They'd all sounded so delicious. Triple chocolate layers, carrot cake, red velvet. Of course, Amelia would never have fallen for that, because they'd all looked too perfect for Tessa to have baked. And Amelia would have guessed, even if Tessa had scraped at the icing with a fork to make it more rugged and home-made looking. Pressing down with her body weight on one side of the cake to make it look a bit lopsided and less symmetrical. Which she had secretly considered doing. Amelia would have known the second that she tasted it, and Tessa just didn't have it in her to lie.

Nope, yesterday had been the trial run, and today she is full of optimism that finally she will get it right. Even if it means that she can't take her eyes off it for a second, if she has to physically sit in front of the oven and watch it as it cooks through the glass, she will. This cake is going to turn out so good that Amelia is going to think it was shop bought and that Tessa is pulling a fast one and trying to pass it off as her own.

She grins to herself now as she weaves her way through the steady stream of people walking towards her in the baking aisle. All pushing shopping trollies and carrying baskets. She hadn't anticipated the lunchtime rush when she'd left home late this morning. She usually made a point of avoiding the busier times of day because it normally felt too much for her. To be around this many people all at once. All the noise and the chaos. The fact that she is here, and she is coping, is testament to how far she has come the past few years. Because normally she would have fled by now, back to the sanctuary of home. Or she would have made weak, pathetic excuses why she couldn't come here at all.

Amelia had been the one to do that. She had given Tessa the strength and the confidence again to help her overcome her fears, just by having someone to believe in her and care for her no matter what. Which was one of the reasons why Tessa had wanted to do something nice for her today too, to show her how much she loved and appreciated her.

To show her how grateful she is.

'There you are!' Tessa murmurs to herself, spotting the pot of chocolate sprinkles on the bottom shelf before placing them in her basket. Mission accomplished. She can get home now and make a start.

In her eagerness to get out of there, Tessa steps back without looking and collides into the trolley behind her. Sending it skidding across the floor, away from a woman who had been poised next to it, ready to place down the huge pile of cooking ingredients laden in her arms.

'Oh, I am so sorry!' Tessa apologises. Grabbing the trolley and pulling it back for the woman. 'Here, please, let me help you.' Without waiting for an answer, she places her own basket down on the floor and helps to take the items from the struggling woman's hold before she drops them.

'Thank you!' the woman says, gratefully, as Tessa sets them down in her trolley. 'Honestly, between you and me, I think it would be a lot cheaper and a lot less faff if we just bought the ready-made in the next aisle. It would save on all the washing-up afterwards too. And I mean, would anyone really even notice?'

Tessa can't help but laugh at that.

'Trust me, I've already considered that, but with my cooking they'd notice! Though this will be the second cake I've made in two days, so if this one goes wrong too, I'll be doing exactly that!' Tessa smiles, picking up her basket again, before saying goodbye to the woman and making her way to the tills.

The queues are long now, twisting back into the aisles and forcing Tessa to stand patiently in line behind people dressed smartly in their suits and uniforms, who've all come in to grab a meal-deal for lunch.

Not being one for small talk, Tessa keeps her head down and focuses on reciting the recipe to herself over and over again as she mentally checks off every item in her basket. Tessa takes out her purse, fumbling around inside amongst the loose change for the right amount of money.

'Thanks again!' Tessa turns, seeing the woman that she'd bumped into earlier, calling out to her as she passes. 'And good luck with the cake!'

'Thanks, I'll need it!' Tessa waves, secretly miffed that she has clearly picked the longest queue going, if the woman is already done before her.

'Sorry, love. That's £8.65,' the cashier says, again. Sounding almost apologetic that she is disrupting Tessa's thoughts.

Tessa had been about to pass it over, holding the loose change in her hand, but as she'd held it out her eyes caught the gaze of the man who had been walking directly behind the woman she'd been speaking to.

He had turned around and looked her way. The vaguest flicker of interest at who the woman had just been talking to radiating out from his steely eyes.

Eyes that were now locked on hers.

Eyes she has seen before.

And it is as if for a few moments time suddenly stands still.

The noise goes first. The loud shrill of the supermarket suddenly quietens into nothing. Then a distorted, faint ringing sounds inside her ears, as if Tessa's head is submerged beneath violent waves of deep, gushing water. The floor feels as if it has started to sway now, too, as if it is moving. Or perhaps that is her? Unsteady on her feet because she feels as if she has just been punched. As if the air has been sucked right out from her lungs.

The money falling from her shaking hands as she grabs on to the countertop in a bid to steady herself.

'Are you alright, love? Do you need a hand? Do you want me to get someone?' The cashier's voice is laced with concern. And it is enough to pull Tessa back from her trance. From the dark thoughts that were quickly gathering inside of her head as

Tessa stood clutching the counter, panting for breath. Desperately trying to compose herself.

She looks again.

He is gone and for a second, she wonders if perhaps she imagined it.

Perhaps she imagined *him*?

Because it wouldn't be the first time, would it? that she'd thought she'd seen him.

Or someone that looked just like him.

Only this time it feels different. This time it really was him, wasn't it? Her eyes weren't playing tricks on her.

'No. I'm fine. I'm fine,' Tessa stutters unconvincingly, aware of the line of impatient looking faces behind her in the queue, all staring her way. Willing her to hurry up and pay so that they can take their turn. She is making a spectacle of herself, holding everyone up. She needs to move. To pay. To grab her shopping and get out of here.

Only she can't think straight. She can't think at all.

Focus!

Dropping to the floor, Tessa scrapes up the money from where it lands at her feet, before handing the exact amount of change to the awaiting cashier. Then shoving her purse back into her bag and muttering her thanks, she hurries towards the exit. Because she has to double-check. She must make sure that this time it really is him.

'Excuse me, love, you forgot your shopping,' the cashier shouts after her.

Tessa turns back, feeling her cheeks burn bright red as people behind her look at her, irritated, as she steps back and grabs the carrier bag from where she left it at the till in her haste to get away.

Seconds later, she is standing in the carpark, scanning the people and the cars in search of him.

Grateful, now, for the blast of cool breeze as it sweeps over her as she looks past the hordes of people loading bags full of shopping into their boots, cars reversing in and out of spaces. A child somewhere nearby screeching loudly, the sound making her jump with fright.

He has gone.

She was too slow. She lost him.

Resigned to giving up and going home, Tessa makes her way to her own car parked at the back of the carpark. As she starts the engine, she tells herself that she was wrong about him anyway.

Of course, she was. She was seeing things that weren't there. Yes, he had looked similar, but it couldn't have been him, because really, what were the chances?

She needs to go home and concentrate on the cake. Tessa blearily eyes the four-wheel drive just a few spaces down from her moving off, and does a second take.

It is him.

Sitting in the driver's seat.

Only from here she can't get a very clear look at him. And she tries, even when he drives straight past her.

But it is too quick, too fleeting.

Did he see her too? Is that why he is driving so fast?

Tessa pulls out of the space.

Before she knows what she is doing, she has put her foot down and is following him.

4

'I thought we could have a Mexican feast for dinner tonight. What do you say, Kayla? Chilli con carne, tacos and I'll make some home-made guacamole again; you liked it last time! With the extra chillies,' Sherrie says as she glances out the window and sees Richard pulling up on the driveway and getting out of the car. Making his way around to the boot, he picks up the bags full of groceries that Sherrie had instructed him to get from the list she'd given him.

Knowing full well that Mexican food is Kayla's favourite, and if this didn't cheer her up, nothing would.

'Yeah, whatever! I'm not really hungry though,' Kayla says, not looking up from where she is sitting on the sofa. Sherrie had felt so sorry for Kayla, that she let her take the day off school, only instead of making Kayla feel better, it had done the opposite and Kayla hadn't moved all morning. It is breaking Sherrie's heart to see her moping around the place looking so miserable.

'Well, you have to eat something, Kayla.' Sherrie opens the front door and beams at Richard as he makes his way up the driveway. 'You'll have some chilli, Richard. Won't you?'

'If that's what you're making, I won't say no,' Richard says, dutifully carting the bags through the tight gap between them as he makes his way inside the house, the keys still in his hand. 'Oh, there's a parcel down there on the doorstep, Sherrie!'

'Ooh, that will be Kayla's new dress!' Sherrie says, scooping it up and making her way back inside towards the lounge, to see if the new dress would get more of a reaction from her daughter than the mention of her infamous chilli.

'Spending more money?' Richard says, raising his brow disapprovingly.

'Oh, shh! It's a one-off for the party on Friday night. One of the girls at her shop is leaving, so they're having a little celebration for her. She wasn't going to go because she thought she would be in France,' Sherrie says, giving Richard a knowing look. 'But now she's here, she's decided she might as well go after all. And it's only a dress!

'Kayla, darling, there's a parcel here for you.'

'My dress!' Kayla exclaims excitedly. 'Can I go and try it on, Mum?' Already she is up off the sofa and stepping over the bags that Richard had placed down on the hallway floor, eager to get to her purchase. 'I might practise my make-up too. I'm trying out a new look.'

'A new look? What's wrong with your old one? You look good enough to me!' Sherrie says, unable to help herself but laugh as she remembers only too well the buzz of being a teenager all those years ago, and the endless hours she pored over outfits trying to decide what to wear, and what style to do her hair.

Make-up back then seemed a lot simpler too. Just a slick of mascara and some lip gloss and she was done. None of this contouring and highlighting stuff the girls did now, as they slathered fifty million different products on their skin. Still, getting ready had been half the fun.

'Go on, then! Your dad will help me put this lot away. Won't you, Richard?' Sherrie says, just happy to see her daughter smiling again, before staring down at the bags strewn out on her once-clean floor. 'I'm going to give this floor another mop through too,' she says, before catching her husband shooting Kayla a conspiring look. Rolling his eyes up at Sherrie's suggestion.

'Well, you just don't know how many germy pairs of hands have been touching those carrier bags. I'd rather be safe than sorry!' Sherrie justifies as Kayla laughs and then leaves the room, Richard staring after her.

'I knew that would put a smile back on her face,' Sherrie says victoriously.

'Look, I know she's upset about the France trip, Sherrie, but you can't keep throwing money and mini-breaks at her,' Richard says, carefully, because he knows full well that any kind of criticism regarding Sherrie's parenting would not be taken lightly and more than likely start a row. But Sherrie isn't biting today. In her element at the thought of cooking up one of her speciality feasts for Kayla, once she has finished putting the shopping away and cleaning the floors, she simply shrugs her shoulders.

'Spoiling her? Don't be silly, Richard. She's our daughter that's what we are supposed to do.'

'You can't keep doing it, Sherrie!' Richard says again more sternly.

And Sherrie goes quiet at that. They both know that he is no longer talking about spoiling her or about her buying her the dress.

'She's not stupid, Sherrie. If you don't be careful, you'll end up pushing her away from you for good.'

5

Tessa switches the car's engine off and sinks down low in her seat as the car pulls up on the driveway outside one of the houses ahead. She is far enough away that he won't notice her from here, lurking at the end of their street. As she watches him, he gets out of his car and unloads the shopping bags from the boot.

Oblivious that he led her right to his home.

So this is where he lives! she thinks as she eyes him warily, watching as he carries the bags down the driveway and into the house. Before coming back out for more just a few minutes later. Tessa sees him lock the car before he walks towards the house.

His house.

She sees her then. The attractive, middle-aged woman standing in the doorway, smiling straight at him as she talks animatedly.

Is he married now, she wonders? *Is this his wife?*

Her heart pounds inside her chest and she feels sick suddenly. Unable to tear herself away from the sight of the woman's hair, because it's the same vibrant shade of flaming red as Tessa's own. He clearly has a type, she thinks bitterly.

She wants to see more. To see how they interact with one another, to watch them talking just the two of them. Because there's something about observing that level of intimacy between two people. Of seeing how they act when they are purely themselves. Comfortable and at ease, oblivious that anyone is watching. Only she loses sight of them both as they slip back inside their picture-perfect looking home.

Closing the door behind them.

Shutting her out.

Tessa is stunned. She can't quite get her head around it. That he could be capable of having a normal, happy relationship. That someone could know him, really know him and actually love him back. Nor can she believe that he lives right here. In a street just a few miles from her own. Though from the outside looking in, their lives are worlds apart.

Hackney can be like that, a mishmash of old and new. From the dingy, overcrowded housing estates, with the two-bedroom pokey new-builds that back up onto the River Lea, which she and Amelia rent. To plush streets like this. The contrast couldn't even compare. With its rows of big, fancy-looking detached houses, with huge sash windows and perfectly landscaped gardens.

How was any of it fair? And perhaps that's what hurts her the most as she sits here feeling a tightness in her chest. The realisation that he has been here this whole time. Hiding here in plain sight. In this perfect life of his.

That he has all of this, and she was left with nothing.

She'd spent most of her life picking up the pieces after he had destroyed everything. Trying to stop her head from sinking down under the crashing waves of her life. Struggling to salvage what she could from the wreckage that he had caused. It pained her that instead of living, she'd been forced to simply just survive. Always feeling as if she wasn't normal. As if her life was in limbo. As if one day, he would find her again.

And the irony is that she has found him.

She should feel triumphant, victorious even that the tables have turned and for once she is one step ahead of him. Instead, she can feel the tears as they fill her eyes at the injustice of it all. This isn't how he was supposed to be living when she'd imagined what his life might look like over the years.

And she had imagined it a thousand different ways, a thousand different times. Sometimes it had felt as if that was all she had thought about.

Him.

How his life would be bleak and dark and rancid, just like him. Because that was what he deserved, wasn't it? A hollow, empty existence, not this perfect, idyllic life of his.

Though she had fallen for that once herself too, hadn't she? Believing that he was a good person. Convincing herself that she could trust him. And look where that had got her.

None of it had been real, all of it had just been an illusion. An act he put on. He hid it well. So well that Tessa could guarantee that nobody who knew him now would know about his secrets. None of his neighbours or friends, not even his wife would know the evil that lurked beneath his skin.

Especially not his wife. He wouldn't be living here if she did.

She watches, now, as there's movement again at his front door. Tessa holds her breath as a dark shadowy figure emerges.

It's him.

He's back outside, his eyes sweeping the grass. She watches as he picks up the couple of pieces of litter that the wind must have blown onto his otherwise perfect lawn and throws it in the recycling bin. Standing there then, his eyes scanning the street, as if he's king of his castle. Tessa can see him clearly now as he casts his gaze across the road to a neighbour coming out of one of the houses opposite and exchanges a few polite words. Tipping his head back with laughter at whatever amusing thing the younger woman says. Tessa's gut twists into tight knots. Pretending to all his well-to-do neighbours that he isn't the monster that Tessa knew him once to be.

She is right. He has everyone fooled but her. Only she can see him for who he really is. Because she knows him. The real him. And he still looks the same. He's aged now, of course; sixteen years will do that to a man. She's aged too. But then, Tessa has had more time on her side; she'd barely been more than a child herself back then. Eighteen. Young and dumb and innocent. Until he took that from her too.

He wears glasses now with thick-rimmed black frames. His once jet-black hair now peppered with flecks of white and grey. He has a beard now and a moustache too.

But it is still him festering under there, beneath his disguise.

He isn't fooling her.

He turns then to go back inside the house, and as he does, he must feel the pull of her gaze, the way her eyes are burning into him. The pure hatred that radiates from her. Because he turns his head and stares right at her.

Time stands still and, in a heartbeat, she is catapulted right back there again. Her whole body paralysed with fear. The earlier bravado she'd felt when she'd followed him, gone now, replaced with a feeling of icy trepidation.

Does he see her?

Does he recognise her too, after all this time?

Her anxiety is building, quickly gathering momentum. But she can't move. Even if she wanted to, which she does. Of course, she does. She needs to get away. To start the engine and put her foot to the floor. Or she could get out of the car and run. Only she can't do either of those things because her legs have turned so weak that she fears they won't be able to hold her if she stands.

Lock the door, she tells herself quickly.

As if that will be enough to stop him.

As if that will be enough to protect her from him.

But she needs to at least try to keep him out. To keep him away from her. She reaches for the button, the movement feels shaky and disjointed, as if her limbs are no longer attached to her body, yet somehow she manages to press the button down hard.

Click.

She's locked herself in. And now she's stuck in here, she realises. And he's out there.

On the other side of the door.

And it's the thought of the door that sends her mind plummeting.

The door is locked. The door is locked.

She can't get out.

BREATHE!

It's too late. Her chest constricts tightly, her breathing shallow. She feels it, the onslaught of a panic attack. She hasn't had one of those for years. And she can't afford to have one now.

Not here. Not now! Not with him standing right in front of her.

BREATHE.

You're safe. You're safe. She whispers the mantra that one of her therapists had taught her, though she doesn't really believe it. As if she really possessed that kind of power, to talk her mind out of the dark places it wants to drag her back to.

Because it's all lies, isn't it?

You're safe now.

Empty words from people who couldn't even comprehend the horrors that she'd been through. They couldn't even imagine. Safe is just an illusion. She learned that the hard way. The truth is that none of them were ever really that: safe. Not really.

But she feels so scared and so desperate now that she wills herself to believe it.

She needs to believe it.

I am safe. I am safe.

Only when she looks again, she knows that she is far from safe. He is walking towards her, his eyes fixed on her. An expression on his face as if he can't quite believe that it's her. He's not sure.

Somehow, despite her slow reflexes and the violent shaking of her hands, she manages to turn the key and pull at the gear-stick before accelerating out of the street as fast as she can. All the while staring into her rear-view mirror to make sure that he's not following her. Her eyes flickering from the road to the mirror again until his silhouette shrinks to nothing before he disappears completely.

I found him, she thinks.

But now, he has found her too.

6

Placing the mop down next to the cleaning caddy that is sitting in the middle of the kitchen floor, Sherrie glances around her immaculately clean kitchen and beams to herself happily as the late afternoon light hits the porcelain tiles making them gleam. The floor is so clean now that Sherrie would lay money on the fact that she could probably eat her dinner off it.

Not that she would ever do that, of course.

Richard sometimes refers to her as a control freak, not that she minds because even Sherrie can admit that she is. There is just something about a clean and tidy house that makes her feel so content and satisfied. That somehow, over the years, she has become addicted to it. An obsession, according to Richard, a form of OCD.

She is compulsive, she thinks. Physically unable to relax until she has polished and scrubbed and buffed every single surface of every single room in the house. She needs to do it daily too, to stick to the strict routine that has become so regimented to her. Richard thinks she is mad for spending time constantly cleaning, but Sherrie believes that it has become almost a therapy to her, of sorts, bringing order and control to her life.

Sherrie needs that feeling of being in control.

She needs that feeling of worth afterwards, too, when she stands back once everything is done and admires her handiwork. She always feels so much calmer then and put together. A clean home is a happy home, as far as Sherrie is concerned. And that's exactly what her family deserves.

She knows that some people cast their aspersions at her over the years, 'for not having a proper job', and especially now Kayla is at the age she is, but the truth is this is very much Sherrie's proper job. She takes her role as wife and mother very seriously, and she works bloody hard at it too. Taking pride in everything she does. Always striving to be the very best at everything she turns her hand to. Cooking the tastiest meals. Sewing clothes if they got snagged or damaged, or if a hem needed taking up. And the house is always cleaned spotlessly.

Being a mother and a wife is everything to Sherrie and what's more she is good at it. She is a natural.

'Mum, can I show you my new outfit?'

Spinning around as Kayla's voice pulls her back from her daydream, Sherrie's mouth falls open as she does a double-take at the sight of the beautiful young woman who stands in the kitchen doorway.

'Oh, Kayla!' Sherrie exclaims, taking in the sight of her daughter's heavily painted face, her hair piled high on top of her head. Kayla looks at least five years older than her years. How did they come to this? Her little baby, all grown up. She must have blinked somehow, and in that millisecond Kayla's entire childhood had simply passed her by.

God, she isn't ready for it.

'What? Don't you like it? Be honest...' Kayla begs, and she sees the crestfallen look wash over Sherrie's face.

'It's not that I don't like it, Kayla,' Sherrie begins, knowing that what she is honestly thinking right now is the last thing that Kayla wants to hear as she eyes the minuscule bit of material wrapped around her, which is supposed to pass as a dress.

'You just look so much older,' Sherrie says finally. There is no denying that. 'You do look very pretty,' she continues, not wanting to put a dampener on Kayla's excitement. Even though pretty wasn't the word that she'd meant at all. What she meant was that Kayla looked sexy. And as far as Sherrie is concerned, sexy isn't a look that any fifteen-year-old should be striving for, especially when said fifteen-year-old is her own daughter.

'Do you think that it might be a bit – short?' Sherrie says gently. She is starting to regret telling Kayla that she could buy anything she wanted to wear for her friend's party on Friday night, to make up for her disappointment at not being able to go to France with her friends. And her plan seemed to be working; Kayla did seem happier now. Though, by the look of what she is wearing, Sherrie's good intentions and generosity may well have backfired on her.

'Turn around and let me see it from the back,' Sherrie says, buying more time, so that she can try to think of the right words to tell Kayla that she can't wear that outfit out of the house. She looks too provocative in it. It is far too old for her. Far too revealing.

Kayla does as she asks, twirling around unsteadily on her ridiculously high heels oblivious to her mother's discomfort, so that her mum can admire the dress from behind. Almost losing her balance in the process, she grabs hold of the doorframe to steady herself.

Sherrie bites her lip, no longer trusting which words might slip from her mouth, because the back of the outfit is even worse than she had imagined. The hem of the skirt barely covering Kayla's bottom.

'It's er... nice, Kayla. But there's just not a lot of it. Maybe you could you wear a pair of tights under it?' Sherrie says, trying her hardest to be kind and tactful because Kayla can be so sensitive at times. Another trait she inherited from her father, no doubt, because Sherrie has far thicker skin than the two of them put together.

'What do you think, Richard? Kayla's thinking of wearing this to the party tomorrow night,' Sherrie says, raising her eyes at Richard as he walks into the kitchen with the newspaper in his hand, hoping that he'd take the hint and back her up at trying to persuade their daughter to go out in something else.

'It's a little bit short, isn't it? Do you think she should put some tights on, because it's a bit nippy out there, isn't it?' Sherrie braces herself, waiting for Richard to do his usual and mutter something unhelpful, like, 'You look lovely, dear'. Like he normally did in these situations in his bid to stay neutral. To always seem like the good guy, leaving Sherrie to be the one putting her foot down.

'What party?' Richard asks.

'The party tomorrow night. I just told you. The one she was invited to from the girls at her weekend job. Do you ever listen?'

'Oh, right. Er, yeah, it looks really lovely, Kayla,' Richard says, vaguely, and Sherrie can see by the flustered look on his face that he hadn't been paying attention at all. His head is elsewhere, and he completely misses the subtle glares that she is shooting him. He'd barely even glanced at what Kayla was wearing.

'Do you not think it's just a little bit too short?' Sherrie says then, her eyes wider, as if she is staring right into him. Willing him to take the hint and say something to support her. To back her up. Only he stands there gormlessly, distracted about something as Sherrie continues. 'The heels are very high, Kayla. Can you even walk in them?'

'I'll only put them on when I get to Emma's, Mum. It's only us girls from the shop. They'll all be dressed like this. It's called fashion,' Kayla says, her eyes pleading with her mother to say something nice about her outfit, even though Sherrie has made it very clear that she doesn't like it.

'Fine,' Sherrie says eventually, giving in then. Because she doesn't have the heart to tell Kayla that she can't go out of the house dressed as she is. Not when she'd been so upset the past few days. Not when Richard can't even be bothered to back her up.

'I'll drive you!' Richard says suddenly, which is something.

'See, I knew you had your reservations about it!' Sherrie says. At least she knows that Kayla will get there and back safely.

'Your dad will drive you, and I'll pick you up. You'll have to wear a coat too. You'll catch your death out there.'

'Mum.' Kayla rolls her eyes. 'I'm fifteen. I don't need to be told to wear a coat. I'm not a baby.'

'I know you're not. And I know you just think I'm an old fusspot, but I just want to make sure you get there and home in one piece, safely. Because a pretty-looking girl like yourself could get the wrong kind of attention going out dressed like that.'

'Fine! Whatever.' Kayla finally agrees, knowing that if she didn't agree to letting her dad take her, and to wearing a coat, her mother would never stop harping on about it.

'Can you not give me at least some support?' Sherrie spits, furious with Richard, as soon as Kayla had left the room. 'Did you see how short that dress was? You could have at least backed me up.'

'What?' Richard says, shaking his head as if he hadn't even been listening. As if he is only just now back in the room.

'The dress, Richard, I wanted you to back me up. Why's it always got to be me that's the bad guy around here? It's always me that tells her no.'

'The only reason you're falling over yourself to make it up to her and not be the "bad guy" this time, Sherrie, is because you feel guilty about her not going to France. Because you hid her passport!' Richard smarts, tapping his forehead knowingly.

'Don't!' Richard holds his hand up just as Sherrie is about to interrupt him. 'You can't have it both ways, Sherrie. She's home, isn't she? Why do you need to make such a big deal about her dress? There's always something with you, Sherrie. She's right you know. She's fifteen. She's not a little kid anymore. So for Christ's sake, just let her go and have some fun for once.' Richard marches from the kitchen, his point well and truly made.

Alone again, Sherrie stands in the middle of the kitchen and places her hand on her chest as she tries to steady the pounding of her heart, still none the wiser at what caused Richard's sudden outburst, because he rarely ever raises his voice to her like that.

7

'I'm sorry, I'm sorry, I'm sorry!' Tessa exclaims as she bursts through the front door and sees Amelia sitting on the sofa, watching TV all on her own. Their cat, Spud, curled up at her feet.

She'd planned to get home hours ago, wanting to have everything ready before Amelia had arrived home.

It had become a tradition that whenever it was one of their birthdays, the other one would decorate the house. Silly little gestures really, like pinning a couple of silver foil birthday banners to the doors and scattering a few balloons around the room, but it meant a lot to both of them that there was some kind of fuss. That someone cared enough to make an effort.

Then they would spend the evening snuggled up, just the two of them, with their favourite takeaway and a movie. Only this year, Tessa had been set on making Amelia a birthday cake too. She wanted to have it all ready for her for when she got home today, to make up for yesterday's burnt fiasco. But instead of all of that, she'd been sidetracked by *him*. And Amelia had come home to an empty house.

'I got held up at the supermarket,' Tessa explains weakly.

And even though it isn't strictly a lie, it isn't the entire truth either and Amelia, being Amelia, instantly picks up on it. 'Buy much?' she says, her gaze going from Tessa's empty hands to the blank space at her feet, as she raises her eyes with an expression of curiosity as to where the shopping bags are.

'Shit! I left the bags in the car,' Tessa says, squeezing her eyes shut. She'd forgotten all about them. The bags of ingredients that have sat there all afternoon in the boot of her car. For a cake that now she no longer has the time nor inclination to bake. She wishes she'd just bought a ready-made cake after all. Because not only has she already ruined Amelia's surprise by coming home late, she doesn't have any cake for her now at all.

'And then I popped in on Aunt Jacqui on the way home, to see how she was doing. You know how she likes to talk. I'm so sorry, I just didn't realise the time...'

'Oh, yes! Aunt Jacqui can talk for England!' Amelia quips, throwing her a small smile. 'She texted me this morning to wish me a happy birthday. I said we'd have her over to dinner one evening next week.'

'Great!' Tessa nods. She can see that Amelia is trying to hide her disappointment at coming home to an empty house, with no signs of a promised birthday cake and a girlfriend who looks as if she hasn't made any kind of effort for her. But Amelia does what she always does, and downplays it, which only makes Tessa feel worse. Amelia has every right to feel disappointed. She at least deserves an honest explanation.

Only where would Tessa even begin?

How can she confess to Amelia where she has been, and how her day was highjacked by *him*? That instead of being here for her when she'd got home from work, she'd been so blinded by fear that she couldn't even remember her journey back home through Hackney's congested streets. How she'd almost made it back here, only she hadn't been able to stop the burning bile as it had shot up her throat, and she'd been forced to pull over in the local community centre's carpark, leaning out from the driver's seat and emptying the contents of her stomach all over the ground. A group of rowdy teenagers carrying skateboards had watched on, laughing and jeering at her in disgust. She'd even caught one of the little shits aiming the camera on his phone at her.

Tessa hadn't been able to start her car after that, not until the tears that blurred her vision had finally subsided and her hands had stopped violently shaking. Which had somehow turned into hours, sitting in that grotty carpark, trying to get her head straight.

It had floored her that all it had taken, after all this time, was just one look. Somehow, he managed to annihilate her to nothing once more. It felt as if no time had passed since then, as if still she wasn't free from him. And if she confessed all of that now, tonight, she would only end up ruining Amelia's birthday. Amelia would only worry about her, she'd make everything about Tessa, because Amelia is caring like that, it's what Amelia does. Puts everyone ahead of herself. Especially Tessa.

Hasn't she ruined enough of her day already? Tessa doesn't want that. Tonight, she wants to make it up to her. To make it all about Amelia. Just as it should be.

'Right, birthday girl. Forget about the cake! We both know that I'd have probably only killed us both with another attempt at baking one anyway! I'll grab the bags in a minute, but first I'm going to order us a Chinese and pour you a very large glass of wine. And you, my love, are going to sit right there and do absolutely nothing all evening.' Tessa smiles. Trying her hardest to salvage what she can of Amelia's birthday evening. 'Come on, feet up. I'm going to wait on you hand and foot.'

'Oh, are you now? That I very much like the sound of!' Amelia giggles, instantly perking up at the suggestion. Doing as she is told, she sits back and watches as Tessa runs around the flat, making sure everything is just so. Pulling the curtains and lighting candles, before ordering their food from an app on her phone. Returning to Amelia just minutes later with a large glass of wine just as she promised.

'Here we go, madam. Dinner is on the way, and *this* is for you.' Tessa places the small, beautifully wrapped present in Amelia's hand and laughs as Amelia stares down at it in wonder, beaming like an excited child at Christmas.

'Ohh, what is it?' she screeches, already tearing off the paper.

'Well, I was going to say open it and see!' Tessa laughs, watching as Amelia opens the small box inside and gasps out loud at the sight of the shimmering necklace, a pendant of two beautiful diamond hearts, entwined together as one, hanging from its centre.

'Oh, Tess! it's beautiful. I absolutely love it. Thank you!' Amelia says with tears in her eyes. Taking it out of the box and wrapping it around her neck, immediately wanting to put it on. Just as Tessa had hoped.

'Here, let me,' Tessa says, placing her hands around Amelia's neck and doing up the delicate clasp before leaning in for a kiss.

'I'm sorry that I wasn't here when you got home tonight and that the cake was a complete disaster and that I forgot about the balloons. It's just been one of those days, you know.'

'Oh Tess, I'm sorry!' Amelia nods, instantly understanding, as she gives Tessa's hand a reassuring squeeze. 'Is that why you wanted to go and see Aunt Jacqui? So you could talk?'

Tessa nods her head now, unable to bring herself to physically speak the lie.

She hadn't gone to Aunt Jacqui's at all and she feels truly awful for not being completely honest with Amelia, for playing on today being just another one of her 'bad days' that she still sometimes has on the rare occasion. Today hadn't been that at all. It had been so much worse.

'Are you okay now?'

Tessa nods, which is the truth. She is feeling okay now. Now that she is back home, and safe.

When the food arrives shortly afterwards, Tessa forces each mouthful down, trying her best to act normal and not let on that her appetite has gone. Or show that the sickly feeling that swirled in her stomach earlier is still lingering with every bite that she takes.

She is glad when the meal is finally over and she can turn the lights out and plunge the room into darkness, Amelia snuggling into her, resting her head on Tessa's lap as the film starts. Tessa is glad, too, that Amelia seems distracted now, because it is easier to pretend, to be alone with her thoughts, sitting here, her eyes fixed on the flickering lights that glare out from the TV screen. Her head back there with him.

Tessa has lost count of the times she thought about him over the years. How she'd wondered where he was now. Whether or not he was dead or alive.

She'd wished him dead almost every day of her life.

She'd stopped telling people that though, how much she thought about him, after her last counsellor had suggested that she might have developed a fixation on him. She hadn't actually said the words out loud, but she'd implied that if Tessa wasn't careful, that if she didn't shift her focus, he would win. Because Tessa was still allowing him to occupy the space inside her head.

Tessa had pushed her thoughts of him down after that. Pretending that she was better, that she was finally free from him, but really she'd just learned how to conceal her true thoughts better. To hide the hate that she felt for him. Her wishes that he had suffered too.

But they had always been there, swirling like a thick fog behind her eyes, the dark, morbid thoughts of him.

Maybe he had won in the end after all.

Living there in that perfect house, all this time, in his perfect little life. She imagines him right now, sitting in that house. Watching his own TV. A hot meal on the table. Normality. He doesn't deserve that. The more she thinks about it, the more she is engulfed with fury at the injustice of it all.

Is it any wonder why she has been so fixated on him?

At how he got away with it, while she scraped through, barely surviving.

He completely destroyed her life. He deserves that fate too.

8

'I got you a hot chocolate, Kayla,' Sherrie says, placing the drink down on the bedside cabinet, before sitting down on the edge of her daughter's bed. Kayla has cocooned herself beneath her duvet, burying her face away so that Sherrie can't see her crying.

But Sherrie knows that she is upset.

'Kayla, darling? Whatever's the matter?' Sherrie places her hand on the mound that is her daughter before giving her back a soothing rub. 'I didn't mean to sound harsh earlier. It was just a bit of shock, seeing you dressed like that. My little girl looking so grown up. Because we forget sometimes just how grown up you are now. I still can't believe that you'll be sixteen soon.

'Where in the world does the time go? It only seems like yesterday when you were oh-so-tiny, that you were twirling about in that frilly pink tutu dress that your father bought you. Do you remember it? You'd been obsessed with it.'

Sherrie shifts on the bed to make herself more comfortable. She can feel Kayla relax slightly. The way her back rises and falls with each slow, deep breath she takes. She has stopped crying, for now at least, and is listening. It is a start.

'Your dad bought it for you, and you loved it so much we couldn't get you out of the bloody thing. You wore it to the park once when it was raining, pairing it with your red wellington boots. And you looked absolutely ridiculous but you didn't care. While the other kids were all stomping about in puddles, you were twirling about like a fairy. In a world of your own. And one night, you even insisted on wearing it to bed instead of your pyjamas! You had a right old tantrum too, until me and your father had no choice but to finally give in and let you have your way.'

'What happened to it?' Kayla mumbles from underneath the covers.

Sherrie smiles at that. Kayla still remembers it.

'You wore it so much that the fabric frayed and ripped, and eventually you outgrew it. Which is just as well because I think your father had mentioned having you surgically removed from it!' Sherrie smiles at the memory. 'You were like a dainty looking china doll with your curly red hair and those big blue eyes of yours.'

Kayla emerges from the covers. Her blue eyes, red and puffy now from where she'd been crying. Sherrie passes her drink over.

'And look at you now. A young woman. Me and your dad just want to make sure that you are safe. There are a lot of bad people out there in the world, Kayla. People who would see an innocent, beautiful girl like yourself and take advantage of you. We just worry about you that's all.'

'But you don't need to worry. You don't need to treat me like a baby,' Kayla starts. 'It's too much, Mum! You never let me go anywhere. You always make excuses.'

'That's not true—' Sherrie starts to defend herself, but Kayla cuts her off. Her voice louder now, her tone full of outrage.

'I heard what Dad said. I was standing on the stairs, listening. He said you are only being nice to me because you feel guilty about hiding my passport!' Kayla repeats her father word for word. A confused expression on her face as she eyes her mother. As if she'd heard the words but couldn't bring herself to believe they were true. 'Why would you do that? You knew how much I wanted to go on that trip. You knew how much I was looking forward to it.'

Kayla is crying again. Beside herself at the thought that her mother could do something so cruel to her.

'Kayla? What on Earth? Of course I didn't hide your passport! You must have misheard him. Your dad didn't say that,' Sherrie says, holding Kayla's arm and pleading with her to believe her. 'He said that I feel guilty for *not finding* your passport. And I do, Kayla. Really, I do. I have searched this house with a fine-tooth comb. You know I have. You saw me.' Her lie is gaining traction. Because she could never let on to Kayla it is the truth. That the real reason she didn't go away with the school to France is because Sherrie's anxiety wouldn't have been able to take it.

She would have been on tenterhooks until the minute that she returned home.

'Your dad is right, I am trying to cheer you up. I hate seeing you so upset, you know that I'd do anything for you... but hiding your passport? Kayla, why would I ever do that to you?'

'I know! I'm sorry. I was just so upset. I thought that's what I heard him say!'

'Oh darling! Come here.' Sherrie hugs her daughter tightly to her. Glad that she has managed to persuade Kayla to believe her.

'Wear the dress, because you look absolutely stunning in it,' Sherrie says finally. Determined to do what she can now to make Kayla trust her again. 'It just makes me feel old, having such a beautiful young woman as my daughter. Because no matter what age you are, you'll always be my baby. You know that, don't you?' Sherrie winks at Kayla. 'Now drink up your hot chocolate before it gets cold.'

9

Her mother is lying to her. That is Kayla's only thought as she creeps along the landing and stands outside her mother's bedroom. Her hand hovering on the door handle as she checks that the coast is clear.

She can hear the hum of the dishwasher floating up from the kitchen below, now that dinner is over, and her mother has finished clearing up. The sound of her mum's favourite true crime shows starting on the telly.

She'll be sitting on the sofa now, a blanket draped over her lap and a hot mug of tea in her hand, content for the evening. Her dad will be sitting in the armchair opposite, no interest in her mother's programme, too engrossed in one of his many books.

Why on Earth would I ever do that to you? That's what her mother had said to her earlier when she'd sat on her bed beside her. Planting the tiniest seeds inside Kayla's head. The tiniest hint of desperation in her mother's tone as she pleaded with Kayla to believe her. That was all it had taken, as she had begun to wonder that too.

Why would her mum hide her passport? What would she possibly have to gain?

She'd thought about nothing else all through dinner. Nodding and smiling in all the right places as she'd sat at the table with her parents, but aware all the while that something was off between them. They were acting. Pretending that everything was fine when it clearly was not.

Her mum had been fine about the trip, hadn't she? Paying for it in full months in advance, as soon as Kayla had placed the permission slip in her hand and begged her to let her go. She'd agreed straight away, without so much as a hint of concern or reservation at Kayla being so far away from her, taking Kayla by surprise initially, because she'd been expecting the usual fussing and fretting her mother did at the thought of Kayla being away.

She'd been ready for all the usual excuses about why she wouldn't be able to go.

Oh, sorry, darling, that's the week we're going to Devon, remember? We booked it ages ago, she'd said the last time, when the school had organised a history trip to Germany.

Another time when her friend had asked if she could go to Ireland with her and her family for a long weekend, Sherrie had told her that they couldn't afford it. That they had too much to pay out for, that she could go next time. Only next time never came; there always seemed to be some excuse. Deep down Kayla knew why. Her mum had always been fiercely overprotective of her. Constantly warning her about all the bad things that could happen to her out there. Drumming into her that the world was full of bad people, evil people. People who would think nothing of hurting an innocent, beautiful girl like Kayla.

That's why she liked to keep Kayla close to her. So that she could make sure that she was safe.

So that she could protect her.

And for a long while it had worked.

Growing up, Kayla had happily lived underneath her mother's watchful shadow. So brainwashed by the stories that her mother had instilled into her, about the dangers that lurked all around her, that she refused to go to the park with her friends or stay over at their houses by choice. Her mother had always made a bit of joke about it to other people, referring to Kayla as shy and clingy, explaining why she refused to stay away from home, away from her for too long.

Kayla had started to wonder about that lately too. How she wasn't actually shy and clingy at all. Hadn't it been her mother's doing that she'd been made to live such a sheltered life? Because she was confident and curious, and she wanted to see the world. She wasn't shy at all. And the older she became the more her fear of the world had begun to waver.

Yes, there were bad people out there, Kayla only had to watch the news to see that was true. But she didn't need to live in fear of everything and everyone around her to the point where she wasn't living at all.

Not everyone is bad. She isn't.

She desperately wants to have a life. A normal, full life. Making memories with her friends. She wants to go to the cinema, have sleepovers and go to parties. Have a boyfriend. Kayla stupidly thought that her mum was finally starting to accept that too, that she was growing up. That she'll be sixteen soon; she'll be able to do what she wants to then. But now Kayla can't shake the feeling that her mother planned this all along. That secretly she never wanted her to go at all, but instead of telling Kayla that, instead of making up yet another weak excuse that Kayla would no doubt see straight through, her mother used another tactic completely. She'd taken her passport and hidden it from her.

Her dad is right, Kayla thinks as she pulls the door handle down as quietly as she can and slips inside her mother's room. She'd heard the force of her father's accusation, the fury behind it. Sherrie took her passport and hid it somewhere. That's why she is feeling guilty and plying Kayla with treats and promises of beach holidays and new dresses.

Kayla scans the room wondering where to start. It is the only room in the house that she hasn't searched. She hadn't needed to. Her mother insisted that she'd do it herself, that she'd pulled it apart. Though staring at the immaculately clean and tidy room, Kayla very much doubts that. Kayla didn't expect anything else if she is honest. Her mother always said that she couldn't sleep in mess and dirt. That the slightest sign of any jobs that needed doing would keep her awake with insomnia all night. Kayla wondered if that had more to do with the room's busy-looking décor.

Granny-fied. That's what Kayla had said when she'd first set eyes on this room after her mother had finished decorating it again, for the umpteenth time. Not keen on the garish, sickly peach wallpaper and the bed and windows adorned with bold, floral fabrics. Her dad had even agreed with her. Making a joke about it looking like it had come right from the pages of a magazine.

One of those pamphlets for the local old people's home.

They had both chuckled at that. Only her mother hadn't laughed. In fact, she'd taken no notice of him at all. But then, her father's opinion didn't really count for much when it came to the interior of the house. That was always her mother's domain. Her dad never really seemed bothered that her mum always took over, that she always had the last word. He seemed happy to leave Sherrie to it.

It keeps her busy! he would often say.

And Kayla always secretly wondered if her dad preferred it that way. Her mother busy. Busy doting on her and the house, so that he avoided her nagging at him.

Besides, it wasn't as if her dad would be the one having to sleep in this room.

He'd been banished to the small box room at the opposite

end of the landing, on account of his chronic snoring. So long ago that Kayla couldn't remember a time when they'd ever shared a bed together.

She makes her way across the room, towards the wardrobe. Gently eases the doors open, before sweeping her hand across the shelf on the bottom, and then doing the same with the top of the wardrobe too. She begins checking in the chest of drawers. Carefully lifting each neatly folded item of clothing and feeling her way through the fabric to make sure that nothing is hidden inside, before placing them back down exactly the way she found them, otherwise her mum would know that she'd been in here, snooping around.

Kayla turns and eyes where to look next. Underneath the bed?

Tiptoeing across the floor she crouches down, pressing her face to the carpet as she peers in the space beneath the bed. It is spotless. There is nothing under there at all.

She wonders if it is pointless, searching up here at all, because she knows that her mother wouldn't keep any paper-work up here. It is all kept downstairs in the alcove cupboard next to the stairs that her mother refers to as her 'office'.

Which was exactly where Kayla remembered putting her passport, the last time she'd seen it. How she slid it into the folder marked 'important documents' to stop her mother nagging at her to make sure she put it back. Someone must have moved it: it couldn't have simply disappeared into thin air.

Creeping across the floor, there is only one place left to look. The bedside table.

Slowly Kayla inches the drawer open and starts to remove her mother's books and numerous jars of face and eye creams, before placing them down gently on her mother's bed until the drawer sits empty. It isn't there.

Kayla feels silly now, and stupid. For ever suspecting her mother of being capable of doing something so cruel. Or course her mother wouldn't have done that to her. She loves her. She only wants the best for her. For her to be happy!

Not wanting her mother to catch her in here, and to know that Kayla doubted her, Kayla hurries, placing her mother's face cream jars back inside and pushing them to the back. Doing a double-take as she does so, when she spots the faint outline of the rectangular shape that protrudes through the floral scented drawer liner.

Something is under there, right at the very back. Hidden away. Kayla peels at the paper. Telling herself that it can't be. Because she'd resigned herself, hadn't she? That her mother wouldn't do that to her.

Only as she peels back the paper, and sees the passport hidden there, something breaks in two inside of her. Her mother did it. She took her passport and hid it from her. Worse than that, she'd pretended to help her find it; she'd stood back and watched as Kayla had been distraught, dragging the entire house apart. Even earlier today, when Kayla had outright asked her if she'd taken it, her mother had sat there and lied right to her face.

Why?

Kayla should cry. She should weep with sadness that her mother would do something so cruel to her. Only all she feels is anger as it bubbles deep in the pit of her stomach. Is it really any surprise? That's what made it even sadder, that somehow Kayla had expected this. She'd known it deep down. Because this is what her mother did. She's done it her entire life. Hiding behind the guise of good intentions and wanting to keep Kayla safe. To keep her near. To keep anything bad from happening to her. But in doing so, hurting her in other ways. She isn't protecting her; she is treating her like a baby. She is stopping her from being her own woman. From living her own life.

Well, no more.

From now on, Kayla is going to do as she pleases.

Starting with the party tomorrow night.

Hadn't the girls mentioned about going to a nightclub afterwards?

Even her mother had said how grown up she looked. Older than her years. Old enough to sneak her way into a nightclub, maybe.

It is worth a try.

If her mother didn't know, then there was nothing she could do to stop her.

10

It had taken Tessa half the morning to convince Amelia that she really was okay to be left on her own. Having spent the entire night tossing and turning in bed, wide awake, her thoughts back on him. She'd lied and called in sick to work. It was only a call centre, a room full of anonymous voices manning the phones. Cold-calling people, which meant mainly having the phone slammed down on her before she'd even read out the heavily rehearsed sales pitch. It wasn't like her colleagues were going to miss her either. They barely noticed she was there as it was.

Though calling in sick may have backfired on her, she realised as again she caught Amelia lingering in the lounge like a bad smell. Pretending that she was checking something on her phone, when Tessa knew that secretly she was peering at her over the top of the screen and trying to gauge how Tessa was feeling before she decided if she should stay home and look after her.

She was worried about her.

That was Tessa's own fault she realised for admitting that she'd had a bad day yesterday. For telling her she'd been to see her aunt Jacqui. For seeming so distracted for the rest of the evening, even though she'd tried so hard to stay present. To pretend that nothing was up.

Amelia always knew.

Or at least, she thought she did. The truth was, she didn't know the half of it.

'Seriously, Amelia. I'm fine. Go to work!' Tessa had insisted, 'Sitting here all day, babysitting me, is complete madness. I just need some sleep, that's all.'

'I wouldn't be babysitting, silly! Besides it wouldn't hurt to have a day at home together, would it? We could both just chill out here and watch a film, or maybe get out for a bit? Go for a walk? Spend some proper time together.' Amelia had started, only Tessa quickly shut her down.

'Honestly, Amelia, I'm exhausted. I barely slept a wink all night. I'll be the worst company ever.'

No matter how good Amelia's intentions were, the last thing she wanted today was Amelia watching over her. She needed space so that she could try and get her head straight.

'I'll only end up zonking out on the sofa and you'll be bored out of your mind. It will be a waste of a day off.'

'I don't mind if you sleep. I can catch up on one of my programmes.' Amelia had persevered.

'No, Amelia. Please!' Tessa snapped, before seeing the hurt look on Amelia's face.

'I'm sorry, I'm just so tired. I promise you, I'm fine. I'll be fine. Go to work.'

'Okay, fine,' Amelia said, shooting Tessa a small, reluctant smile. Because she knew she wasn't going to win this one. 'But if I'm going to work, then I want you to try and get some proper rest! Don't just sit here dozing on the sofa. Go to bed and get some sleep. Promise me you'll try?'

Tessa smiled too.

'Deal!' she said, because she knew that agreeing to her terms would be the only way to get Amelia to actually leave the house.

'And you're only a phone call away. If I need anything, I'll call you!'

Tessa had devoured the peace and quiet of the place for a few moments once Amelia had finally gone. She'd even debated going back to bed and getting a few hours' sleep just as she'd promised. Considering it for about all of two seconds, because deep down, she knew that there would be no point. Sleep wouldn't come. She'd be too wired, too caught up with the thoughts of him that had wormed their way back inside her head. All rationality must have once again left her – before she knew it, she was back in her car. Pulling up in the road adjacent to his street.

Because it didn't hurt to check, did it? To make sure that it really had been him that she'd seen.

And now here she sits.

She is careful this time, parking at a safe enough distance so that she can see his house, but far enough away that he couldn't see her here.

Watching him.

If it really is him.

Because she is questioning everything now.

What she thought she saw, how she really felt. Was it really him, or had her eyes been playing tricks on her?

It had looked enough like him that it had set something off inside her. The same crippling fear that had taken her years to overcome, that raging paranoia.

They are back with a vengeance.

She'd lain awake all night paralysed by those feelings.

Unable to stop thinking about him again. How familiar he had seemed, still, after all these years as she had sat just feet away, watching him with his wife. Playing the role of a loving, dutiful husband.

Lies. All lies.

She feels a flush of shame sweep over her now as she allows

her mind to wander to what could have been. It could have been her, couldn't it? Living there in that house with him. Her husband. Her family. Hadn't she wanted that once?

A life with that monster.

How deluded she had been!

Sometimes, that was the hardest part of all of this for her. Admitting that some of it had been her fault. That she had brought it on herself. That she'd once had feelings for him. It didn't matter how many times over the years her counsellors had told her that she wasn't to blame. That she couldn't control the actions of others. The fact remained: she had let him in.

And in doing so, he had ruined her entire life. She'd never told Amelia that: that she had loved him once. She had wanted to, of course she had. Right from the very start she'd wanted to tell Amelia everything. All of it. The truth.

Because what she had with Amelia was good and pure and everything so completely opposite to what she'd thought she'd had with him. Only Tessa hadn't known where to begin with it all. The longer she put it off, the harder it was to admit the things that were almost incomprehensible even to her, and she had been the one who had lived through it.

Part of her wasn't sure if Amelia would understand.

Amelia only knew the hate that lingered now. The marks that man had left behind in his wake. Scars of him.

She didn't know about the him before.

Before his mask had slipped and he'd revealed exactly what he really was.

It pains Tessa to admit that they have secrets now, her and Amelia, festering between them, an invisible void that will only keep growing. Which is why Tessa knows that she has to do this, to come here today and find out if it really is him. Because she needs answers.

She needs justice, finally.

11

Wrapping her dressing gown tightly around her body, Sherrie pads her way out to the landing, and leans on the banister. Listening intently as Richard and Kayla's raised, angry voices float up the stairs to where she is standing.

That must have been what had woken her, though Sherrie can't make out the exact words from here, just the riled up, fractured tones they are spoken in. She thinks about jumping in the shower and washing her hair, leaving them both to hash out whatever it is between themselves. Only the sound of what she assumes is a china cup being slammed against the breakfast bar stops her in her tracks. She rolls her eyes up, guessing that Richard's temper has got the better of him.

What has got into him lately? He seemed off with her yesterday too. If he wasn't careful, he'd end up breaking something else.

Making her way downstairs, Sherrie braces herself to be the one who is forced in the middle of whatever their spat is about. And usually, it goes without saying, Sherrie would always pick Kayla's side. No matter if she agreed with her or not.

Only Sherrie is still riled by Richard's words from yesterday. How his words had almost sounded like a threat. Letting her know that he knew full well what she'd done and, if he had to, he'd use it against her and tell Kayla that she had taken her passport.

Thanks to him, Kayla was already acting suspicious enough.

Either way Sherrie would have to back her husband up or risk him going against her.

Richard was right about something though. Kayla was growing up, she wasn't a little kid anymore. And Sherrie misses that. She is still unable to get that image from yesterday, of the young woman standing in her kitchen, out of her head. Kayla had looked so beautiful, yet so grown up.

Sherrie isn't ready for it. And she wonders if that's what had tipped Richard over too. The thought of Kayla growing up and eventually leaving home.

It had been a reminder to them both, that soon Kayla would be doing whatever she wanted to do, and going wherever she wanted to go. And they would both have no say in the matter. She'd be choosing what kind of career she'd like to have, and visiting universities she'd like to attend. Sherrie couldn't bear to think about that.

Kayla living away from home. Away from her.

There would be boyfriends to contend with. Sherrie and Richard would no longer be the centre of her world. And even though Richard didn't ever really voice his feelings, and even though he isn't as close to Kayla as Sherrie, he must feel exactly like she does; he must have had the same feeling given his reaction. Maybe that's why he behaved the way he did. Lashing out at her.

'Morning!' Sherrie exclaims, walking into the kitchen and eyeing her husband and daughter, standing at opposite sides of the breakfast bar as if they are in the middle of a showdown.

'Whatever is the matter, Kayla?' Sherrie asks, instantly able to tell by her daughter's red, puffy skin that she's been crying again.

'Nothing,' Kayla says without bothering to raise her head; instead, keeping her eyes down. Her lips pursed tightly together as if she is trying to force her words back inside of them. As if to stop herself from saying something she'll regret.

'Is everything alright?' Sherrie looks at Richard, noting how his complexion is growing puce. A red, mottled rash twisting its way up his neck towards his hairline, like it always does whenever he feels stressed.

'It's fine,' Richard insists, though Sherrie doesn't believe that for a minute.

The pair of them have fallen silent now, and to be honest, Sherrie wasn't expecting that. To feel so excluded, as if she'd walked in on a private conversation, as they both purposely shut her out.

'I heard raised voices...' Sherrie says, treading carefully, wondering if they'd been talking about her, if Richard had told Kayla the truth about her passport. Though if he had, they were both doing a great job of not letting on now.

Kayla wouldn't have been able to keep that to herself. She would have lashed out.

She would say something. It can't be that.

'I was just telling Kayla that I'd be driving her to school this week,' Richard replies, his voice quieter now, more controlled. Sherrie sees the look that flashes at her in his eyes. He'd made this decision, and she was to help him enforce it. It was Sherrie's turn to back him up.

'And I was just telling Dad that there's no need for him to drive me. I'll get the bus,' Kayla shoots back defiantly.

'I told you that I'm leaving at the same time as you, so it makes sense! Seeing as we are both going that way anyway.

Besides, it will save you the bus fare! Or rather, it will save me the bus fare, seeing as I'm the one who's paying it. And aren't you always wanting to help save the environment? Car-sharing. It all helps.' Richard tries to keep his voice light, but there is no denying the finality to his words. He's made his mind up; he isn't backing down on this.

He eyes Sherrie, almost as if challenging her.

'What do you think?'

Sherrie shrugs, knowing what he is goading her to say. She has no choice but to agree with him. Only Kayla beats her to it.

'You know what Mum thinks. She'd have you wrap me in bubble wrap and stick me in the boot, if it meant I was "safe". Though safe from what, I don't know. She needs to lay off all her true crime shows. It's making her paranoid. I suppose you're going to pick me up on the way home too?' Kayla says finally, grabbing her bag. 'Whatever! I'll be out by the car!'

Kayla stomps off outside. Not bothering to wait for an answer.

'Are you?' Sherrie says, staring at her husband and wondering what this is all about. 'Are you picking her up from school as well?'

Because isn't it normally Sherrie who is accused of the melodramatics when it comes to Kayla? Suddenly Richard is acting like the overprotective one.

'I happen to be coming back that way when the school finishes, so yes! I'll pick her up. Why not?' Richard says, though he is no longer looking at her. Instead he is busying himself grabbing his lunch and his keys from the kitchen side. As if he can't get out of the house quickly enough.

And Sherrie knows why. Because if he stays, if he looks her in the eye, Sherrie will see right through him. Richard is transparent like that.

'What's going on?'

'Nothing is going on, Sherrie,' Richard says tightly, making his way towards the front door. 'I'm allowed to take my daughter to and from school, aren't I? Or do you have a problem with that too?'

Sherrie winces as the front door slams loudly, Richard's defensive tone still ringing inside her ears.

12

Alert now, Tessa sees movement at the front of the house.

She sees the shock of flame-red hair and at first assumes that it's his wife as the figure makes her way up the driveway, before waiting patiently next to the car.

But this woman is a younger-looking version of the woman she saw yesterday. A teenage girl, dressed in a school uniform, with a rucksack hanging loosely from her shoulder.

He is outside now too. Dressed smartly in a shirt and trousers, his hand clutching a tatty brown satchel. As he makes his way towards the car. The same tatty old bag brimming full of books and test papers he'd carried around with him when he'd been a teacher at her school all those years ago.

Is he still teaching?

This girl isn't a student of his though.

Tessa watches as he reaches her, extending his arm, his hand placed gently on her shoulder as he leans in and says something to her. It's such a small gesture but Tessa can feel it, the paternal intimacy between them both. The expression on his face one of love, and although Tessa doesn't know what he is saying from this distance away, she assumes he's offering the younger girl some kind of comfort or apology.

Yet the soured look remains on the young girl's face and she shrugs him away.

There's tension here. Cracks forming before Tessa's very eyes as she watches as the girl shoots him a scornful look, before making a point of sticking her earphones in, and sliding in to the back of the car.

Not in the front with him.

They look as though they've had an argument. It's as if she can't stand the thought of being anywhere near him. He shakes his head despairingly like a father worn out from trying to appease his sulky teenager daughter.

It hits her then with its full ferocity.

The realisation that *he* has a child.

That this mini-clone of the red-headed woman from yesterday is his daughter.

This monster has a daughter.

There is a whooshing sound inside her ears, and the skin around Tessa's knuckles stretches to a pale white as she tightens her grip on the steering wheel as shock and anger swirl together furiously inside of her.

Tessa wonders if his daughter is going to the same school as him, or if he is dropping her off on the way. There is irony in that.

How he appears on the outside to be such a thoughtful, caring father, making sure that his daughter makes her way in the world safely. He of all people would be acutely aware of the dangers out there. Of the evil predators that roam amongst them, under the guise of everyday, normal people.

People just like him.

Exactly like him.

Tessa sinks down low in her seat and holds her breath as he pulls out of the driveway. Silently praying to herself that he doesn't glance in this direction as he passes. That he doesn't recognise her car, doesn't notice that she is sitting here again. Watching.

The car roars past, and when she sits back up again, she is filled with relief as his brake lights fade to nothing in the distance.

He's gone.

He didn't see her.

Though Tessa is good at hiding; she's had enough practice at it. Staying small and quiet for most of her life, never purposely drawing any attention to herself.

Because somewhere in the back of her mind, she was always terrified that somehow, one day, he would find her again. When the reality is that he had moved on. He had probably never given her another thought. And she had given him all of hers. Every waking minute of every day, for years she'd thought about nothing else but him. He even crept his way into her nightmares, haunting her dreams every night and staying with her long after she woke.

He had been like an obsession to her.

She sits with that for a while, thinking about how much of her life she has wasted because of him. How much he has ruined, how much he has taken from her.

She is different now though, isn't she?

She feels better, stronger. Happier. And a lot of it had been since she'd met Amelia. Would she end up losing all of that too, if she sat and did nothing knowing that he was right here? That he had got away with it all.

She can't just go home now and pretend that she hasn't seen him. She can't just do nothing, because she has been doing that for years and look at where that has got her.

There is a shift then, a tilt as something snaps deep inside her.

For the first time in years, she realises that in this moment, in this very second, she doesn't feel scared of him finding her.

Because she found him first.

She is the prey hunting the predator.

Seeking out her vengeance for everything that he did to her, for everything he took from her.

She will get her revenge, she resolves as her anxiety melts away, replaced with something far more powerful.

Rage.

13

Tessa stares at the windows of the house, wondering if his wife is still there, inside. Tessa could tell her. She could walk over there right now and knock on her door and tell his poor, unsuspecting wife everything.

How would she feel to find out the truth of who she's really been married to for all these years? How would she like to hear about all the evil, twisted secrets that her husband kept from her? That he kept from the world.

Though what were the chances that his wife would believe her? That she would take the word of a complete stranger, turning up unannounced on her doorstep, accusing her husband of unimaginable things, over the man that she spent so much of her life with? A man she probably believed that she knew better than anyone.

Maybe Tessa should just do it, anyway. Regardless of the outcome. Plant a seed of doubt in the woman's head, in the hope that she'll at least confront him. Even if he denies it, which of course he will, Tessa can then live in the hope that somewhere, deep down in the woman's gut, she will feel it.

Women's intuition is an incredible power. She will know,

won't she, that he isn't telling the truth? That Tessa isn't lying. That it is him. But would that really be enough for her though? Tessa wonders. To see his marriage blown wide open, to finally expose all of his secrets. To sit back then and watch with satisfaction as his perfect life burned down all around him.

Because it doesn't feel like nearly enough suffering, but it is a start, she reasons. It is something.

And she needs to do *something*.

Her fingers hook around the door handle as she wills herself the courage to do it, to get out and knock at the woman's door. To tell her everything. Only a tiny niggle of doubt has already set in, worming its way inside of her. What if she is wrong and it isn't him? Because she's been wrong before, hasn't she? Other times that she'd thought she'd seen him. When she'd convinced herself that this time she was certain.

It looked like him though, didn't it?

Tessa sinks back into the driver's seat, deflated, unsure what her next move should be now, because she didn't think that far ahead.

She'd thought about confronting him. About waiting for him to get home and then calling the police. But she can't afford to get it wrong again. What she needs is cast iron, solid proof that it is really him this time. She can't do anything until she's got that.

The door opens, and a woman emerges from the house.

Tessa drinks her in. Intrigued to see what sort of a woman had finally settled down with him, in her sensible woollen coat and her flat pointed shoes. She's not what Tessa would have expected for him, she thinks as she watches with interest at the interaction between the woman and the postman. As they exchange pleasantries. The woman's smile is warm. Her eyes crinkle at the edges as her lips turn up, and while she's not especially beautiful, Tessa can imagine that she had been years ago.

The woman gets in her car and drives away as the postman

continues his way towards the front door. Tessa watches as he pushes a small pile of envelopes in through the letterbox before walking away, leaving the edges poking out. The post didn't make it all the way in.

An idea forms in her head. The house sits empty. There is no one home.

She could check who the post was addressed to. She could find out what he calls himself, now. He changed his name after that time – she'd looked him up before, but he had disappeared.

If she had a name, she could see what she could gather about him on the internet.

It is worth a shot and right now it was her only one. Tessa takes her chance. Moving quickly towards the house, scanning the street as she goes, to make sure that no one is watching her. She reaches the front door, gently prising out the post from the letterbox before flicking through it, eyeing each envelope. *Mr and Mrs Richard Goldman*. Is that the name he is going by now? That's how he managed to get away with it for all these years, living here, so smugly, so brazenly under a fake identity. Fooling everyone around him. Even his own wife and daughter.

Until now.

Because he's not fooling Tessa.

His real name is Nick Reading and all she has to do is prove it.

14

The letters aren't enough. Not if she wants Amelia and the police to believe that it is him. They don't prove anything. All she has is a name, and it isn't his. Tessa needs more.

She stares at the door, her hand reaching out and pulling down the handle. Though it meets its resistance, of course. It's locked. She hadn't expected anything else.

She eyes the back gate. She's made it this far, and there's no one here to stop her from creeping around the back of the house and just having a look.

A look wouldn't hurt anyone.

Tessa does exactly that. Slipping through the gate, she makes her way around to the back door, trying the handle there too. Which is also locked. But here, out of sight, she can be more brazen, as she peers through the windows and tries to get a good look at what his house is like inside. Curious now at how he lives. She tries the windows. Half-heartedly wedging her fingers between the gaps of the PVC and pulling at them, assuming they will all be locked too.

Except, one of the windows moves as she yanks it. As if

someone had pulled it to, but they had forgotten to properly lock it from the inside. Before she even knows what possesses her, she's clambering through it. The open window a sign of a personal invitation. Hoisting herself up the wall and climbing inside, she's full of urgency at getting inside before she's seen. Full of curiosity too at what she might find. Because she knows that she'll find something in here. She has to. She's crawling now, making her way across the kitchen worktop before she lowers herself so she's standing on the floor. She's in. She's standing in the middle of the kitchen.

Her heart is pounding as it hits her that she's actually standing inside *his* house. It's nothing like she'd envisaged.

The heady smell of bleach mixed with overpowering floral air-freshers lingers in the air, filling her nose. The place looks so clean and tidy it could be a show home. Unlike her own house, there are no signs of dirty dishes stacked in the sink, or teabag stains on the worktops. Every room in the house is exactly the same, she realises as she begins making her way through them. Taking everything in as she searches for clues for anything that might tell her more about who he is now.

Or at least who he is pretending to be.

Opening a door in the hallway, Tessa eyes the rows of neatly arranged shoes on a rack. A pile of coats hanging from hooks on the wall. Even the cupboards are tidy!

And it irks her, because this isn't what she had imagined for him. Living in a well-kept, lovely house like this. He doesn't deserve this.

Making her way upstairs, Tessa examines the collage of photographs that span the wall like a shrine to their daughter. There are hardly any photos of him she notices; it is mainly the mother and the girl. The two of them smiling out from every image. The daughter looks younger in most of the images. A goofy, freckle-faced child beaming back at the camera. All the typical milestone pictures that parents insist on taking when their children are small and more compliant.

The sunny beach holidays. The extravagant birthday parties. Obligatory yearly school uniform photographs. There were only a couple of recent ones of her now, older, but Tessa guesses that the girl had grown out of posing for hundreds of photos at her parents' request.

Next she looks at a photo of his wife. A close-up of her, her creamy pale complexion. Her hair flaming red just like her daughter's. Tessa wonders about her. What kind of a woman she must be, that she could be content with someone like him. To love this man enough to build a life with him, to bear a child together.

Does she have any kind of suspicions at who he really is? Tessa doubts it. Tessa can't imagine anyone ever loving someone like him willingly, if they knew the truth about him. Unless of course he has changed. Maybe he is different with her.

Tessa highly doubts that, too.

No one could change that much.

From pure evil to a loving, caring husband and father? It doesn't work like that. He is still in there, hiding somewhere behind the guise of this new man. He'd got good at it, she guesses. He has lived this lie for so long now, that even he has started to believe it. And now Tessa is here to undo it.

Reaching the first bedroom, she peers inside at the bright peach walls and the busy floral printed bedspread with its matching curtains. Too sensible and grown up to belong to that of a teenage girl. Their room, she wonders? eyeing the neatly made bed that is so crisp and smooth it looks as if it hasn't been slept in at all.

A vision hits her now, invading her head.

Tessa in bed with him. Their limbs entwined in each other's.

His skin on hers.

Bile burns at the back of her throat at the mere thought that she'd craved that once. That she had trusted him. When she had barely been little more than a child herself back then. She had been so innocent and so naive, and he had taken advantage of that. She hadn't known any better.

She won't be sick. She cannot be sick.

She closes her eyes in a bid to shut him out. She needs to get on with what she came here to do.

Opening the drawers, she begins lifting each garment up, gently, carefully so as not to show that anything has been disturbed. So that he won't know that she's been here. Though there's nothing of any interest in here. It's just clothes. All women's clothes. There's nothing that belongs to him. This isn't his room. He doesn't sleep in here.

Making her way along the landing to the next room, Tessa stands in the doorway and looks at the chair in the corner of the bedroom, a man's sweater neatly hung over the back of it. A chunky, black watch on the bedside table. Bottles of aftershave lined up on the shelf above the TV.

This is more like it.

And she's on autopilot when she does it. When her hands reach out for the jumper that sits on the top of the chair. Holding it to her nose as she breathes it in.

Breathes him in.

Bracing herself for that familiar musky smell of his to overpower her once more. That same spiced aftershave that she'd smelt on her own skin long after she'd been with him.

Only there is nothing.

His smell is absent, replaced now with the potent scent of lavender fabric softener. Tessa throws the jumper back down from where she'd picked it up, before she starts to search through his wardrobe and drawers. It is all just clothes.

There are no photographs in here, there's no paperwork or documents. There is nothing that so much as hints at who he really is. Just like the rest of the house, the room is tidy. Clean. To the point of sterile.

There is no sign of life. No sign of any real personality.

She thought of her and Amelia's home then, how cluttered it feels in comparison. How lived in and loved it is. Adorned with bold, brightly painted artwork, hanging proudly from the walls. Stacks of their favourite books, tatty, well-thumbed, covering every tabletop, every shelf. Piled high at one end of their bath. There is a frayed colourful blanket draped over their sofa that Amelia had cherished since her childhood. A neatly stitched patchwork of square cuts of material all from her late grandad's shirts. She grinned then at the thought of Amelia's nauseating twee printed cushions that she insisted on having on both the sofa and the bed. Tessa often took the mick out of the silly slogans on them. Exclaiming often that while she could just about live with an embroidered 'home sweet home' she firmly drew the line at 'live, laugh, love'. Amelia had laughed at that.

And it had become a thing. That on every special occasion Amelia would gift Tessa another printed cushion to add to their growing collection, seeing as she loved them so much.

They didn't have much, but what they did have meant something.

Unlike here.

Here, it feels as if it is all just for show. It feels desolate. A house without a beating heart to make it a home. Making her way to the last room, Tessa lets out a gasp as she pushes the door open, before she starts to laugh. Finally, some personality. Though from the state of the bombsite of a bedroom, this personality belongs to that of their teenage daughter. The room looks as if it had been ransacked. Such a contrast to the rest of the house. Clothing strewn all over the floor and bulging out of half-closed drawers. A plate smeared with the remnants of food peeks out from where it's been roughly shoved under the edge of the bed. And every surface, every shelf, every bit of furniture is covered with clutter. Jewellery, make-up, lotions and potions.

This room smells sickly sweet. A mix of cheap perfumes and body sprays fills her nose as she tiptoes her way around all the chaos and mess. This must drive the mother crazy, having a child as messy as this. Tessa makes her way around the room picking up numerous trinkets and knick-knacks from the girl's shelves and cupboards, examining them closely, as if they will somehow reveal a piece of her.

A piece of them all.

But it's all just standard stuff that a million other typical teenage girls' bedrooms would be full of. What girl really knows herself at this age anyway?

Tessa didn't.

Though of course back then, when she was this girl's age, she'd thought she knew it all. Who she was. Where her life was going. Until he came along and ruined it all.

Tessa wonders what she is like, his daughter, a child born of him, as she sits down on the bed and smoothes her palm across the silky soft sheets, before placing a hand on the girl's pillow, trying to imagine her lying here at night. Her eyes closed, her hair splayed out across her pillow. As she sleeps soundly.

A tiny part of her envies her that.

Because even now, years later, Tessa doesn't sleep much at all. Not without the help of sleeping tablets. Night times are still the worst for her, the endless hours of being plagued with insomnia. Wide awake as anxiety consumes her every thought.

Thoughts of him.

Because he had got away; the police had never found him.

It was as if he'd simply vanished into thin air.

Except he hadn't at all. He had been right here. Right in this very house where she now sat. In his teenage daughter's bedroom.

A shiver rippled through her then, at the girl coming home and finding her here. This stranger sitting in her bedroom.

What the hell is she doing? Didn't this make her just as bad? This was the definition of madness, creeping around inside someone else's house. Rifling through this young girl's personal belongings. She shouldn't have come here. She shouldn't be here now. What if he came back and found her here? What if they called the police? What if she couldn't prove it was him?

Panic consumes her now.

Stupid girl!

She should have listened to Amelia and stayed at home and got some sleep.

That's what she'd do. She'd go home right now and get into bed before Amelia came back from work. Standing up, Tessa catches sight of the shiny glimmer of something hidden amongst the carpet pile. She reaches down and picks it up. It's a small heart-shaped locket on a thin gold chain. The casing is old and tatty and covered in tiny dinks. And Tessa wonders if it's been down there long. Tucked between the bed and the bedside table. Out of sight and long forgotten.

Making her way over towards the window so that she can see it in a better light, Tessa jams her nails into the tightly shut clasp, prising it open. Inside, the photographs are worn and faded. The photograph on the left is easier to make out. It's more recent. Just a few years ago, Tessa guesses from the look of the girl's face and the way that her hair is styled. Her arm is draped around her mother and they are both smiling. The other side of the locket it's the mother holding her newborn baby.

His wife, holding *their* baby.

That could have been her, Tessa thinks sadly.

The grief for what might have once been so overwhelming suddenly, that for a second she is forced to hold her breath as the heaviness in her heart consumes her. Almost collapsing back onto the bed, placing a hand on the wall to steady herself as she blocks it out.

Unable to let her mind take her back there. To that.

She can't. She mustn't.

It's only then that she hears another voice in the house and realises that she's no longer alone.

'Richard? Kayla? Is that you?'

His wife is back.

15

From the minute she opens the front door, Sherrie knows that she isn't alone in the house.

'Richard?' she calls out, standing deadly still in the hallway, the carrier bag she was holding gripped tightly to her side so that it won't make a sound as she listens out for his reply.

Only he doesn't answer. Sherrie hadn't expected him to, his car hadn't been on the driveway. She knew that it wouldn't be him.

'Kayla, darling?' Sherrie shouts once more, hopeful, as she awaits an answer.

Though what were the chances? Why would she come back here in the middle of the day? When she would be at school?

'Is that you, love?' Sherrie says, frozen with fear now as she's met by only silence.

She hears another creak. This time it's louder. More prominent. The sound of footsteps making their way across one of the bedroom carpets. She knows with certainty now, that's she's not imagining it.

Someone is inside the house.

She wonders if she might be in danger. If whoever is up

there is capable of doing her harm. She should leave. She should go to the neighbours and get some help. She should call the police. Only as the house sits in silence once more, Sherrie realises that whoever is up there has heard her too. They are trying to stay quiet, remain unnoticed. They would know that the only way out is to get past her.

They are stuck here now.

As the creaking noise comes again, Sherrie works it out. Exactly which room it's coming from, by the sound of the dodgy floorboard by the radiator in Kayla's bedroom. Someone is in her daughter's bedroom.

Sherrie is incensed. Overcome with anger as she grabs at the golfing umbrella that is cradled in the holder next to the front door.

'I know someone is up here! I've called the police!' Sherrie lies. Gripping the umbrella tightly and making her way up the stairs. Wanting whoever is up here to know that she's not scared of them.

She makes her way cautiously along the landing, her heart hammering loudly inside her chest. The sharp pointed end of the umbrella facing outwards, ready to strike if anyone jumps out at her.

She stands outside Kayla's bedroom door, her hand hovering over the handle as she gathers the last of her courage and pushes the bedroom door wide open.

'Kayla?' Sherrie stares expectantly around the room. Only it is empty. There is no one in here.

Relieved, Sherrie lets out a short, sharp breath.

Had she been hearing things? Had she freaked herself out and had simply imagined that someone was in here? A cold rush of air sweeps across the room towards her. The curtains dancing, swaying in and out of the room in time with the breeze from the open bedroom window.

The bedroom window is wide open.

Kayla would never have opened it. Sherrie is sure of that. Another thing that drove Sherrie crazy. On top of the mess and the clutter and the chaos, was how stuffy the room always seems, the stagnant air lingering in here, because Kayla point-blank refuses to open the window so much as an inch, convinced that enormous spiders would crawl from the brick-work outside and find their way in here.

So someone has been in here. In her daughter's room.

Just the thought of it makes Sherrie feel sick. Someone violated her home, invaded her privacy. How dare they break into her house and rummage around amongst her daughter's things?

Storming across the room to the window, Sherrie leans out, staring down to where they would have landed in a bid to catch them, because they couldn't have got very far.

But there is no sign of anyone out there.

There are signs that she just missed them though, given the state of her once perfectly tended flowerbed beneath the window, now completely trampled. Her beautiful plants and shrubs squashed flat under the weight of whoever had just landed on top of them.

Sherrie searches her neighbours' gardens now too, before she runs her gaze along the alleyway along the back of their houses. But whoever it was had obviously run fast, determined not to be seen.

Sherrie stares around the room searching for any obvious damage or signs that anything might be missing. Kayla's valuable items are still in the room. Her iPad is sitting on her dressing table, where she'd left it. Her jewellery displayed neatly in the jewellery box. The TV still inside the bracket on the wall.

Whoever was in here hadn't taken anything with them.

So, if they didn't break in to steal anything, why did they break in?

16

Tessa plummets. Dropping from the window, she hears a loud popping sound. Her foot bearing her whole weight as she lands awkwardly on top of it. Sharp spikey branches of the plants and shrubs claw at her skin, having already broken her fall.

The window above her is wide open. She pulls herself upright, wincing at what she suspects is a sprain, and eyes the gate at the back of the garden. It's her only chance of escape; she daren't go back the way she came in. She needs to go. She needs to get away from here before she is seen. Hobbling quickly then, unsteady on her feet until she reaches the gate.

Glancing at the window she'd just jumped out of, one last time, she's expecting to see a pair of eyes on her.

But there's nothing. No one. Not yet.

Limping, she runs down the alleyway that twists its way along the back of the row of houses, wincing in agony with every step as silent tears stream down her face.

She doesn't stop until she reaches her car.

Tessa clambers in, panting wildly as she locks the door behind her and sinks down into the driver's seat. Screwing the sleeve of her jumper up and shoving it into her mouth, to stifle the screech of panic that she can feel working its way up the back of her throat. What had she been thinking? Breaking into his house. Jumping out of an upstairs window.

She'd almost been caught.

Was she out of her mind?

She must be.

What if he'd been the one to find her there? What if he'd hurt her?

She of all people knows how dangerous he is. How anything could have happened to her. It was stupid of her, reckless. Her hands tremble as she puts her key in the ignition. About to go home. Only the shrill sound of her mobile phone radiates right through her.

It's Amelia.

And looking at her phone now, which she'd left in the car, she has six missed calls. All of them from Amelia. She'd be worried about her. Wondering where she is, wondering what she was doing, when she was supposed to be at home resting. Tessa cancels the call, before switching off her phone. She feels bad, but what would she say?

She didn't want to lie to Amelia, but she couldn't exactly tell her the truth either, that she was here, at his house. Only this time she'd actually broken in. This time she'd searched through his things, trying to find proof of who he is. Or at least proof of who he is pretending to be. How could she tell her that she had just jumped from the upstairs bedroom window when his wife had come home and caught her there? That she'd possibly sprained her ankle in the process when she landed.

Amelia would think that she was going crazy, and rightly so, after everything that she'd been through. But she'd assume that the way that Tessa is behaving right now, means that she isn't well again.

Tessa will have to wait it out, because she can't go home, not yet. Not like this.

She is running out of options though.

She needs to think of another way to get Richard Goldman to reveal who he really is.

17

'I'm going to call the police,' Sherrie says, when Richard finally answers the phone and she tells him that she'd come home to find someone had been inside their house.

'No,' Richard says a little too quickly.

But not quickly enough so that Sherrie hadn't heard it. The hastiness in his voice. The urgency there.

He'd heard it too. She hears him take a deep breath, contained, before he continues.

'There's no point involving the police, Sherrie. What are you going to tell them? That you think someone broke in? But you didn't see anyone and from what you've said, they didn't take anything either. All you know for certain is that the windows were left open. You really want them traipsing through the house? Going through all our things?'

'Richard, someone was here. In our daughter's bedroom. Rummaging around in her belongings. Don't you care? Doesn't that worry you? That some old pervert could have broken in and been rooting around in your daughter's underwear drawer?' Sherrie says, her voice high-pitched, still shaken. 'What if it was

Kayla who had been the one to come home and find someone hiding here. What if they'd hurt her?'

'And what if you've got it all wrong? What if Kayla did open her window this morning? Have you asked her?'

'No. I sent her a text in case she's in one of her lessons but she hasn't answered,' Sherrie says. 'I take it she's still upset about whatever it was you were arguing about this morning.' She waits for Richard to enlighten her on what had actually been said between the two of them. Only Richard isn't forthcoming.

Sherrie is about to tell Richard about the flowerbed, about how the plants were all trampled and flattened as if someone had landed on them. Only deep down she knows he is right. An open window and a few worst-for-wear-looking shrubs is all that Sherrie has. What would the police do if she called them anyway? Sherrie didn't want them here anymore than Richard did, snooping around their home, making a mess of the place. What would be the point of it? They would be just as clueless as they were.

'We'll just have to make sure that everything is more secure from now on. Check that all the windows and doors are locked when we are out,' Richard says assertively, before adding, 'And I don't think that Kayla should go to this party tonight either.'

Sherrie falters. Richard is taking this more seriously than he is letting on.

'You can't stop her from going to the party, Richard. She's almost sixteen! She won't listen.'

'Well, you need to make her listen,' Richard snaps.

Sherrie bristles, unable to shake the feeling that there is so much more to this. He has been acting strangely since yesterday, his mind seemingly elsewhere, in a world of his own. Insisting that he drive Kayla to and from school. And now this.

'Richard? Whatever has got into you?' Sherrie demands. 'Is something going on that I should know about?'

'Nothing is going on,' Richard replies. 'I think that just for tonight, she should stay home. We're being cautious, that's all.'

Sherrie doesn't believe him. Even though she can't see his expression, she knows him well enough to know by his voice when the lie pours out of him at the other end of the phone.

'Listen, I'll swing by the school and pick her up when school finishes. I'll tell her myself. It's not a big deal, just a precaution. And it is, Sherrie. If anything, I'd thought you'd be happy that she'd be staying home!' Richard mocks before hanging up.

Sherrie's mind is in overdrive at how strained Richard sounded, how flustered he seemed. She hadn't imagined that, had she? Instead of getting angry about the thought of someone breaking into their home, Richard had sounded genuinely worried.

Did he not think that they were safe?

Did he not think that Kayla was safe?

Sherrie is on edge now. Needing to keep busy and the only thing that helps her do that is to clean. Staring around her daughter's disgusting mess of a room, she figures it would be the perfect opportunity for her to make a start. She knows that Kayla won't be happy about her being in here, of course. Going through all her things. And the truth is that really bothers Sherrie. How Kayla suddenly started being so secretive and not wanting Sherrie touching any of her stuff. How she always insists that she needs her privacy and Sherrie should knock before she came in.

'It's my room, and it's my mess.' Kayla had argued any time the subject of her room was brought up. 'If you don't come in, you won't need to look at it.'

Sherrie had played along in the end. Sick of all the arguments. Making sure that she was more careful each time she snooped through her daughter's pockets after Kayla had been out with friends. Always ensuring that she'd logged back out of her social media accounts too, after she'd read through her messages. It was only for her own good though. Sherrie only ever had good intentions. It wasn't Kayla she was checking up on. It was everyone else that Sherrie didn't trust. She was just looking out for her daughter, making sure that she was happy and safe.

That's what mums did, wasn't it? They protected their children, at all costs.

Picking up all clothes that had been discarded like rags on the floor, Sherrie begins folding them in neat piles and placing them in the wardrobe and drawers. Going through all the pockets as she goes, before looking through all Kayla's bags too. An old school bag she no longer uses, a small little clutch bag that Kayla sometimes used when she went out. Her hands sifting around amongst all the junk and clutter. Not looking for anything in particular, because Kayla is a good girl. She doesn't have any secrets as far as Sherrie could tell.

It just feels, sometimes, that Sherrie is closer to her this way, because Kayla had started to shut her out. That was the saddest part of watching her grow up. How she had slowly moved away from her. Preferring to share things with her friends, rather than share them with her. Sherrie only ever wanted to be part of it. The smallest part of it. She was happy to take the crumbs, but these days, Kayla wouldn't even give her that.

'What are you doing?' Richard's voice carries across the bedroom, from where he stands in the doorway, making Sherrie jolt with fright. She'd lost track of time. She'd been holding the fresh duvet cover over Kayla's bed, shaking it out for the final time before throwing it evenly over the bed.

'Nothing, I just thought I'd give her room the once-over,'

Sherrie says, staring past Richard, expecting Kayla to make an appearance behind him.

Ready with her excuses.

Because she'd know instantly that Sherrie was snooping.

'Where is she?' she says, expectantly. Bracing herself for her daughter's dismay as she sees the state of her now pristine room.

'One of her friends at school said she'd already left. That she'd walked home with a friend. I was hoping that she would be here by now,' Richard replies.

Sherrie sees a flash of something cross his face. Panic in his eyes before he looks away. Quick to play down his concern.

'It's not like Kayla just to go off without letting one of us know where she was going,' Sherrie says.

And it isn't.

Sherrie always insists that she knows where Kayla is at all times.

'Have you tried her phone?'

'It's switched off.'

'Switched off?'

'Hmm, But I'll keep trying. Maybe I'll go back out. I probably drove straight past her.'

Sherrie nods her head, and Richard leaves the room.

The dress! Sherrie thinks to herself, rolling her eyes, as she realises that she's just tidied Kayla's entire room; she put away all her clothes but her new dress and ridiculously high shoes were nowhere to be seen, figuring that it had something to do with the row that Richard had had with Kayla this morning.

Recalling how teary Kayla had looked.

She's taken her outfit so that she could go straight out after school and not come home.

She is going to the bloody party.

She thinks about calling Richard and letting him know that she's worked it out. That Kayla is rebelling.

But as Sherrie steps back she becomes distracted, recognising the loud creak of the floorboard.

It's the same noise she heard earlier today, the one that had alerted Sherrie that someone was in here. That someone was in her house. In her daughter's room. Sherrie had been meaning to mention to Richard to fix the dodgy floorboard, when she'd noticed it a few weeks ago, but she'd forgotten all about it.

Bloody thing! she thinks, wondering why it didn't drive Kayla nuts, because she must have stepped on the thing every single time that she got out of her bed. It is right there. Right where she put her foot down. Only Kayla had never mentioned the fact that she had a loose floorboard. Not once.

Sherrie is curious now, pulling the carpet back and lifting the underlay. Assessing the loose board, the nails missing from it. One edge jutting slightly higher than the ones beside it. Pushing her fingers down into the narrow gap that line its edges, Sherrie prises the board free. Before staring down into the chunky timber joints that frame the dark gap in the floor's space.

Sherrie reaches inside to the contents that someone has shoved down there, purposely to keep out of sight.

A notebook.

Wiping her palm over the surface to clean the dust away. Sherrie realises that it's not a notepad at all. It's a diary.

And Kayla's name is written in bold letters across the front of it.

18

Sherrie shouldn't have read it.

That is her first thought as she tries to stop the trembling of her hands. And now this. Still reeling from reading all her daughter's intimate, private thoughts laid bare between the pages of her diary. It was human nature to look though. And how could she not? Especially when her daughter appeared so intent on keeping it hidden. Going as far as to stash the diary beneath the floorboards so that no one else would find it.

What had she been so desperate to hide?

Sherrie knew now.

Having read it from cover to cover, despite the foreboding that swept over her that she might not like what she read there between those pages. Most of it had been what she'd expected to find. Ramblings about school and friends and a few harmless comments here and there about boys. It had been the more recent pages that Sherrie hadn't liked. The venom that poured out in the words that Kayla had written about her, entwined with the ink.

For always trying to control her life. For smothering her.

Kayla had written that she felt as if sometimes she couldn't breathe.

That broke Sherrie's heart.

Sherrie only ever wanted to keep her safe.

Angry words scrawled so viciously across those pages as she detailed how her mother was a liar, how Sherrie had found her passport and hidden it from her. Sherrie hadn't needed to go to her bedroom drawer to check: the passport was here. It had been tucked inside the back of the diary. Hidden from her.

She thinks about the last time she'd sat in here, with Kayla. And the way that her daughter had asked her outright if she had taken her passport. Sherrie had lied. She regretted that now. Because Kayla had known. Bloody Richard and his big mouth.

Kayla had overheard him; she'd known Sherrie had taken it before she'd even asked her and when Sherrie had lied to her, she'd gone in search of it. That's what she had written in her diary.

Kayla had documented other things too. Like the time she hadn't been able to go to Ireland with a friend for the weekend. Or to Germany with the school.

She wrote how her mother was overprotective. That she was too controlling. Kayla had written how she couldn't wait to be finally free of her. And that had hurt Sherrie more than anything else she'd written in there. That had hurt her so much that she'd thought her heart would stop beating, right then and there on her daughter's grubby bedroom carpet.

Sherrie had spent her whole life doing everything for Kayla.

She'd lived for the girl.

Wanting only to make sure that she was safe and happy. Wanting only for her to know how much she was loved.

And this was how she'd misconstrued it. She thought her mother was overbearing. That she wanted to be free from her.

Still, Sherrie had read on.

Kayla had detailed how her father had told her that he

would be taking her to school that week and picking her up. How they'd argued about it. Sherrie had paused at the next line. Her finger poised on the sentence as if she was trying to work it out. Richard had asked Kayla if she'd seen anyone hanging around, outside the house. Or at her school. If she felt as if anyone had been watching her.

Why would Richard ask her that?

When today, when Sherrie had called him and told him that someone had broken into their house, he had so convincingly played it down. Trying to talk Sherrie in to believing that she'd left a window open, and that nothing appeared to have been taken or touched. Planting a seed in her head that she might have made a mistake.

What is he hiding from her?

Thinking about it now, he has been acting strange the past few days.

Sherrie doesn't trust him. That's what this all really boils down to.

Because she's lived through this once before.

Back then.

All his lies. All his secrets.

19

Pink fluffy slippers.

That's the thought that swims through Kayla's mind as she crosses the road and steps up the kerb, wincing at the pain that radiates through her feet, which are currently crammed into the ridiculously high pointed heels she is wearing. *How did other girls wear them? Were their feet secretly deformed?*

Her pink fluffy slippers. That's what she needs. Them, and the warmth of her bed. She is bloody freezing right now. Tugging down the minuscule material of her short skirt, she feels self-conscious as her mother's pearls of wisdom resound in her head.

Take a coat, or you'll catch your death.

Yeah, because not taking a coat is the cause of loads of deaths according to all the headstones at the cemetery, Mother! she'd quipped. Annoyed that her mum couldn't just let her be.

She was almost sixteen. Too old to be nagged and mollycoddled by her. Tonight she'd purposely gone out straight from school, making a point of not telling either of her parents where she was going, or who she was with. That would teach her mother for taking her passport and hiding it from her, so that she couldn't go to France.

It was unforgivable as far as Kayla was concerned and she had had enough. She'd voiced as much to her father this morning, and he'd done his usual trick of not wanting to escalate the situation. Making his usual excuses for her mother. Saying that she only ever wanted the best for her.

Which wasn't true. Because if her mother really wanted the best for her, she'd let her live her life the way that she wants. She'd stop being so controlling. Always panicking that something might happen.

So Kayla had shoved her new outfit into her school bag this morning and taken it with her to her workmate's house. She'd known all along that they'd only been planning pre-drinks at Emma's house. Before they all went to Roxy's nightclub. Only Kayla didn't have any intention of going there too.

Because she knew her parents wouldn't let her. She wasn't old enough to get in, or old enough to drink. But even her mother had told her how much older she looked in this outfit, and it appeared that the bouncers had agreed with that too. They hadn't even checked for ID, letting her slip in with the others, unnoticed.

The night hadn't been anything like Kayla had hoped; in fact, she'd spent the entire evening feeling overwhelmed. The alcohol going to her head, and every time she tried to move, or dance, or talk to her friends she found herself fighting off the unwitting attention from hordes of older men. So she'd left them all and decided to go home after all. But in her hurry, she'd left her coat in the club's cloakroom, which, as the cold night air picked up, whipping wildly around her, she instantly regretted.

Maybe, her mother had a point after all.

Stupid girl!

She should have been more patient and stayed in line at the taxi rank, because fifteen minutes wasn't really that long to wait for a cab. She'd probably have been home by now. Home, in the warm and the dry. But she had felt so sick. Standing outside the club, swaying unsteadily on her feet. It had been the stench from the grotty-looking burger van outside the club that had finally tipped her over. The overpowering smell of fatty beef burgers combined with the copious cheap shots she'd downed, threatening imminently to reappear.

She couldn't throw up there. In front of the club, dressed as she was, in front of all those people. Her house was only ten minutes away if she walked fast enough.

Only she'd slowed down now because her feet were killing her.

It wasn't much further now. Her house is only in the next street.

Another few minutes and her keys would be twisting inside the lock of the front door. Her feet would be out of these shoes and sinking into the warmth of the soft hallway carpet, and she'd be tiptoeing her way quietly upstairs to her bedroom so that she didn't wake her mum and start World War 3 for making her worry all night.

Good. Let her worry.

'Christ's sake!' she mutters as she stops for what feels the umpteenth time, as her four-inch spiky heel wedges itself down into yet another jagged crack of the pavement. She wobbles unsteadily on her feet before finally wrenching herself free.

Wincing as she feels the blister on her heel burst, the watery blood oozing from it into the expensive lined fabric of the shoes. She should take them off. She could walk the rest of the way home barefooted. It would be quicker too.

She leans down to do just that when she hears a noise behind her, close, making her stop dead still. A faint snap of twigs just to the edge of the grass bank. She turns and scans the street behind her. Eyeing the few houses that line the green.

Hadn't she heard a noise a few times now? The sound of footfall behind her. The crunch of gravel. The crackle of leaves.

Is she imagining it?

Someone following her. Someone hiding in the shadows, watching her.

Stop it. You're drunk and hearing things.

She tries her hardest to convince herself, but part of her feels the imminent danger as she keeps her eyes fixed on the sparse light that the street lamps throw out, the luminosity shimmering along the wet road up ahead. The warm hue of yellow reflecting back up at her as she seeks out the shadows. But there is no sign of life and instead of relief the abandoned street brings her no sense of comfort either.

She takes her phone from her pocket about to turn it back on, so that she can call her mother if she needs to.

If anything happened to her, here. Now. At this time of the morning, while she is out here all alone, what would she do? What could she do? She could shout for help. Loudly. In the hope that her cries would wake someone up from their sleep. That someone would hear her and come to her aid. But would they move quickly enough to help her? She doubts it.

Or she could run, making her way to the nearest front door where she could pound her fists against it. So that whoever is following would get scared of getting caught when they saw the lights inside come on.

It all sounds so easy in her head, so simple. The thought of her make-believe getaway. From the make-believe bad thing that might happen to her out here. Drunk, and oh-so paranoid.

Only as it turns out minutes later, she hadn't been so drunk and paranoid after all. And her getaway isn't that easy either.

The first thing she feels is a strong hand reaching around and clamping her tightly around her mouth as she opens it to scream, to shout out. To call for help.

Only the sound comes out strangled and muted, and is

instantly slammed back down into her throat along with the night's air.

Another arm wraps tightly around her; a body presses up against her.

She is suffocating. Sucking down the last remaining air into her lungs. Desperate now, convinced that her lungs may burst.

A sharp scrape of something scratching her skin.

The pierce of a needle?

Her body feels weak, and the faint glow of the street lamps is starting to fade.

And even as she glances further up the street, she sees a car there. The boot of the car wide open and she is dragged towards it. She tells herself that this can't be happening.

Because things like this didn't happen in real life.

They happen to other people.

Other people, not to her.

20

Creeping in through the front door, Tessa locks it quietly behind her and slips the chain over the latch. Twisting the key inside the lock too, for good measure. Before she leans up against it and takes a long, slow breath.

It has happened again, hasn't it?

She'd blacked out.

Instead of going home like she knew she should have, she'd stayed there all day. Outside his house. Waiting. Watching. One minute she'd been sitting in the car, watching them both. Him and his wife, rushing around, frantically. An air of panic around them as they'd both got in to separate cars and driven back and forth, to and from the house, late into the night.

They'd been looking for her, Tessa had realised. Their daughter, Kayla.

Because she hadn't yet come home.

Tessa had waited then too.

Aware of the charged energy around her, the feeling that something bad had happened. Or was about to.

Only she had sat there for so long that she must have fallen asleep. At least that's what she had first thought when she'd opened her eyes.

Except, as her focus adjusted and she glanced around she realised that she was no longer sitting in his road, in her car, watching his house. She was in a different part of London. Parked in an unfamiliar lay-by next to a disused warehouse down by the Thames.

The illuminated numbers on the dashboard's clock read 2 a.m.

She'd lost two hours and that terrified her. That she had no recollection of how she had got there or why.

How huge fragments of time and her memory could simply disappear like that.

Two a.m.? Shit! Amelia would be so worried about her. Tessa needed to get home.

She had reached out a shaky hand to turn the key in the ignition when an image flashed in her mind.

A young girl walking towards her car.

Tessa remembered thinking the girl must be so cold in just that tiny dress she wore. How she'd taken in the sight of those ridiculously sky-high heels that made her long skinny legs look bandy.

Like a baby deer trying to stay upright as it strutted across a sheet of ice.

Kayla.

Tessa had seen her, hadn't she? Just a few hours ago.

That had been her very last memory.

She'd been sitting in the car, watching her get closer and closer.

His daughter.

She'd thought about him then. How he would have held her in his arms after she'd been born. How he would have stared down at her with love.

Love that he hadn't ever had for her, not really.

Because he wasn't capable.

And she had felt so incensed. So furious that her insides bubbled with so much rage that she thought she might explode.

She wanted him to hurt him then, as much as she had been hurt.

She wanted to make him suffer. Make him pay.

Only that's where her memory ends. That's when she must have blacked out.

'Tessa?' Amelia's voice, cutting through the darkness from where she stands now, wrapped in her dressing gown in the lounge doorway, startles her.

'Shit! Amelia? I didn't think you'd still be up!' Tessa gasps, losing her balance, and grabbing on to the arm of the chair beside her, to steady herself before she sees Amelia.

Instantly seeing the strained look on her face that told Tessa she hasn't slept yet. She'd been waiting up for her.

'You scared the life out of me,' Tessa says, trying to compose herself and hide the guilty expression that she knows would be written all over her face, about where she'd been until this hour of the morning and, more importantly, what she'd been doing.

The irony isn't lost on her that she wants the same answers herself.

'I scared the life out of you? You didn't answer any of my calls, Tess! I've been worried about you. I got home hours ago. Thinking that you'd be in bed, resting. Like you said. I even called Jacqui.' Amelia paused. 'She said that she hadn't heard from you for days. You lied to me, Tessa! You said that you went to see her yesterday, but you didn't, did you? Where were you? And where have you been tonight?'

Amelia has a puzzled expression on her face, concern in her tone as she scans Tessa's clothes, taking in the sight of her bedraggled girlfriend. Covered in mud.

It is only now that Tessa sees it too. How dirty she is. She realises that the fabric of her jumper is torn too. Had that happened when she jumped from the window? Or later when she had no memory at all?

She isn't sure, but she knows from Amelia's expression that she must look a state.

'Clearly I'd been right to feel concerned! You're covered in mud, Tess. What happened to you? Are you okay?'

'I'm fine,' Tessa lies, trying to hold her nerve. She looks the exact opposite of whatever fine really looks like right now.

Remembering her foot now. How lucky that it is only a sprain. How she could have easily broken it the way that she landed earlier.

'Actually, I'm not fine at all. It's stupid really. My own fault. I was out running, and I fell... And I'm sorry I didn't hear your calls, my phone must have been on silent from when I had a nap earlier. And then because I didn't charge it, it died,' Tessa lies, silently praying that Amelia wouldn't call her number to purposely catch her out. 'I'm so sorry. The last thing I wanted to do was worry you,' Tessa says, knowing how weak her excuses sound, vague and unbelievable even to her own ears, let alone to Amelia's.

'You were out running?' Amelia says in a tone that tells Tessa she isn't falling for it as she glances up at the clock on the wall as if to prove a point. 'It's almost three a.m.!'

'I actually only went out to get some air...' Tessa begins weakly. Hobbling across the room, pretending that her foot is worse than it actually is. That it's so bad she can barely stand on it for a second longer. That the pain is so intense that she has no choice but to sink down on the floor.

She needs Amelia to believe her.

'After my sleep this afternoon. I must have just missed you,' Tessa says, hoping that Amelia hadn't come home too early today. That she hadn't noticed that Tessa was gone until she got home from work this evening. Because that bought her some time at least. 'I just felt like letting off a bit of steam. You know?

And I thought these would be okay,' Tessa says, easing her foot out from her plimsol as if to relieve the pressure a bit. 'That will teach me, won't it? It's no wonder I'm in agony.'

Not daring to look at Amelia, because Tessa knows that Amelia has already caught her out in her lie as they both stare down at her muddy Converse on the floor beside her.

Idiot!

Tessa would never wear plimsols for running. She isn't wearing any of her usual jogging gear either. Her thin frame is swamped in a huge oversized jumper, skinny denim jeggings on her legs. Still, she hopes that she sounds at least partly convincing. Amelia would know that Tessa was lying to her. She'd have known it from the second she'd opened her mouth. Amelia could read her like an open book.

'I fell, and stupidly twisted my ankle and then spent the rest of the evening sitting down at A&E. Along with half the population of Hackney.' Tessa glances at the clock, feigning surprise at the time.

'And you didn't think to phone me from the pay phone? They still have them these days, right?' Amelia says sarcastically.

'I should have. I'm sorry. I just didn't think. And I didn't mean to wake you,' Tessa says, deliberately wincing as she frees her foot from her shoe, in the hope of making the injury look believable and to gain some sympathy.

Apart from a mild swelling though, it didn't look too bad.

There is no bruising.

Amelia must think the same.

'What did the hospital say?'

'I didn't wait around to be seen,' Tessa says. 'There were so many people in front of me, and I'm so tired. I thought I'd come home and get some sleep and go back in the morning. If it's not any better.'

'You can't just leave it, Tess. If you can barely walk on it, then you need an X-ray. You should get it checked out properly!'

'No, honestly, it's fine,' Tessa says, feeling guilty for lying to Amelia. But what was she supposed to say? She couldn't exactly tell her the truth. Amelia wouldn't understand.

She can see that Amelia has already started to question her mindset, to realise how deep her terrors still run. As much as Amelia has supported her up until now, everyone has their breaking point. Everyone reaches a place eventually, when they just can't physically deal with anymore craziness in their lives. Tessa knows only too well, because she has lived that life too.

She'd been a completely different person when she'd met Amelia. Unrecognisable to who she is now.

She'd only met Amelia by chance. After plucking up courage to work in a call centre doing tele-sales, so that she could earn a living not having to deal with members of the public face-to-face.

Tessa had seen Amelia waiting patiently in the reception area, while Tessa's boss was tied up with someone else, and she'd offered to make her a coffee. They'd just started talking, and weirdly Tessa found that she hadn't been able to stop. When Amelia had left she'd given Tessa her number, and Tessa had taken it gratefully, because she'd needed a friend. Only their friendship evolved into a relationship, the connection between them was so instant, so real. Before they knew it, they were spending all their free time together. Bingeing on boxsets and going for long walks together in the local parks. They indulged in the odd trip to the cinema or the local pub.

Amelia had been the first person in a very long time to make Tessa feel like she was enough. So much so, that she had started to believe it too. Amelia had helped to build her confidence every day since. She had loved her unconditionally for the past two years. And because of that, because of her, Tessa had started to feel better again. To feel almost normal. Whatever the hell normal was.

So the last thing she wants to do is to mess all of that up. Tessa doesn't want to chance it. She doesn't want to risk trying to convince Amelia that, this time, she really has found him. Not yet.

Not until she has proof.

'Did you eat?' Amelia asks, not pushing it anymore, her voice softened, full of sympathy. 'I can make you a sandwich if you want?'

Tessa shakes her head. The last thing that she wants is for Amelia to fuss around her.

'You know what, I think I'm just going to take some pain killers and a sleeping pill and go to bed. Try and sleep some of this pain off.'

'Do you want me to give you a hand up the stairs?'

Tessa shakes her head, feeling teary now as she takes the stairs. Still faking the pain because she knows that Amelia's eyes are still on her. She feels bad about that. Amelia is so loving and caring, even though she must know deep down that Tessa is lying and keeping things from her. Sleep will do her good, she decides, as she sits down on her bed and swallows a couple of sleeping tablets, in the hope that they would allow her some proper rest. She'll feel better in the morning, when she wakes with a clearer head. Everything wouldn't feel as magnified.

Because she has been here before. Consumed by fear, taking too many risks, acting irrationally. Putting herself in dangerous situations.

But this time it is worth it.

Because Tessa is no longer at his mercy.

21

My eyes twitch as I strain to open them properly. I can't see a thing other than pitch blackness.

I try to focus, to search for that familiar slither of light that seeps in from beneath my bedroom doorway. Or to the dimly lit hue of the street lamp that flickers occasionally outside my bedroom window.

But there's nothing. Just black. And for a second, I wonder if there's been a power cut.

And then I register the dull throbbing pain behind my eyes. How my head feels groggy, and my body feels strange.

I lift my arm, but it feels heavy, as if it's been weighed down. And there's a different pain now too, at the crown of my skull. A slow, dull, constant stream of thudding, banging repeatedly inside my head as if my brain is trying to make its escape.

I move my fingers to the sore spot and instantly feel a dampness there. A warm and sticky patch against my fingertips. Wet. But thicker than water. And it's congealed in my hair.

I run my fingertips over the small, jagged cut.

I sit up and try to gather my bearings, but as I lift my head, I feel the heavy thud of something solid above me.

The impact sends me instantly back down to where I'd just been lying, and it's only then that I realise I'm not in my bed.

I'm not at home.

I'm inside the boot of a car.

I stretch my arms up as wide as they can go; my fingertips just about touch the walls either side of me. Panic swells inside me then at the narrowness of the confined space as I sweep my palms across the surfaces, searching a handle or a release button. For some way out.

Only there is nothing.

How did I get here?

A flash of memory enters my head. The tight grip of someone's hand around my face, my mouth. But that's all I can remember. Nothing else. It's as if my mind is missing vital pieces. Chunks of my memory are gone. But I know that someone has put me here intentionally. Someone who could only want to cause me real harm.

I need to get out.

Frantic now, I slide my hands quickly across every surface. Clawing with my nails until they bend and break as I search for a jagged ridge or a clasp or a lock. When I can't find anything, I hit out. Using as much force as I can muster, I smack my hands against the inside of the car. Elbowing them and stamping my feet. Hard and loud.

'HELP ME!' I scream. Repeatedly. Because I am desperate now.

I'm shouting so loudly that my throat feels coarse, burning dry. I scream until there is nothing left inside of me. Until I'm completely spent. The adrenaline that fuelled my earlier panic leaving me as quickly as it had come, replaced now with real debilitating fear.

I sink down to the boot's floor just as warm liquid pools out around me, and I wince with humiliation as the wetness seeps back into my clothes, turning quickly cold.

I've wet myself.

I start to cry.

And I wonder if I might die here, and that thought terrifies me.

'Please! Please help me,' I say again, quieter now as if reciting my very own silent prayer. Because it's too quiet. I know that no one can hear me. No one is listening.

I am completely and utterly alone.

22

Sherrie lights up another cigarette, unable to steady the trembling of her hands.

She and Richard had been out driving around the streets of London for hours, in search of their daughter. To no avail. She is wired now. Way past the point of needing sleep. Besides sleep wouldn't have come for her even if she tried. Not while Kayla still isn't home. She would have just lain awake all night, tossing and turning as a thousand thoughts and worries spun around wildly inside her head.

Sherrie scans the end of the street again. Holding her breath in anticipation that any minute now, Kayla would stroll around the corner and make her way up the street. Her bag swinging loosely over one shoulder. Head down, silly grin on her face as she gawped into that bloody iPhone of hers that was permanently glued to her hand. She'd roll her eyes up if she came home now and found Sherrie standing at the window, peering out through the net curtains at the darkened street.

Net curtains were out of fashion. Or according to Kayla, they'd never been in fashion.

Only grannies have nets up, Mum! Grannies that decorated

their houses way back in the seventies. Grannies who were partially sighted.

A small, tight smile escapes Sherrie's lips as she recalls the quickness of Kayla's sarcastic wit. A trait that she liked to think that Kayla had inherited from her. Besides, Sherrie likes the net curtains. She likes the privacy they give her. How they hang like a literal safety net that she could stand and hide behind. An invisible spectator watching the world go by.

And sometimes she did exactly that. Like this morning, chain-smoking cigarettes one after the other whilst cradling mug after mug of hot, sweet tea. Only the street is empty. Just rows of houses lined side by side, standing in darkness, the occupants inside still soundly asleep. Some appear awake, like her, early, a glimpse of warm yellow hues of light peeping out from beneath the curtains or blinds.

Her eyes go to the bright ball of light at the end of the street, fixes on it as the beam grows bigger as it makes its way towards her. Headlights. She bristles. Her chest constricting for a few seconds until it comes closer. Only relaxing when she sees that it is the familiar BMW of the house opposite hers: Mr Burns, as Sherrie nicknamed their neighbour, the miserable face reminding her of the character from *The Simpsons*. Home from his nightshift, parking up on the driveway.

Her eyes flicker back to the clock on the wall. Almost 7 a.m.

And 7 a.m. means that Kayla has been out all night.

Sherrie thinks about how anything could happen to a person in twelve hours. *Stop it, Sherrie. Stop thinking about it. Not yet. Not if you don't have to.* Because she'd fall apart completely.

Instead, she casts her eye back to the window, where she sees another movement. Old Hilda Ogden. At least that's what Sherrie liked to call the little old lady that lives at the other end of the street, with her scruffy-looking Yorkshire terrier in tow. Sherrie bit her lip. She personally couldn't stand the woman, and with good reason too. Hilda Ogden only came down this end of the street to let her dog shit all over the pavement or the grass. Up early, before the sun rose normally. Thinking that she'd be concealed by darkness, that she'd never have to bother to pick up her dog's mess.

The old lady caused quite a stir with the other residents of the street going by the influx of rants on the residents' WhatsApp group. The neighbours around here went nuts about it: the phantom dog-shitter. How they haven't worked out it is Old Hilda Ogden and her mangy-looking mutt is beyond Sherrie, because it isn't exactly rocket science. The old bat is out there most mornings. Hiding behind the guise of a sweet, helpless, little old lady.

That is the problem with guises.

People didn't often look beyond them. They took people at face value. Didn't question that there would be anything wrong there. But Sherrie knows better than that. She knows how cruel and disgusting people can be. How you couldn't trust anyone. Not really.

If she had wanted to, Sherrie could have told all her neighbours who the phantom dog-messer was, she could have put the lot of them out of their misery, but where's the fun in doing that? Because another thing Sherrie knows about people around here is that they love a drama. It gives them a sense of purpose, some common ground.

Except this morning, Sherrie is the least of Hilda's problems: now that Mr Burns has come home later than usual, he's seen her for himself. Catching her in the act of pulling her dog away from the fresh, steaming pile of dog poo just deposited on the edge of his driveway. The look on his face as he launches himself out of the driver's seat is priceless. His eyes dark, his mouth twisted in rage.

'This should be good!' Sherrie mutters to herself, secretly glad of the distraction now.

Glad of something to do, anything to keep her mind off Kayla for a few minutes longer.

It is a shame she can't hear their voices through the thick double-glazed windows, but she can see by the way Mr Burns stands over the old lady and points down at the floor then back to her, then to her dog, that he is fuming. Demanding that she pick up her dog's mess.

Only Hilda Ogden is giving back as good as she is getting it appears, going by the little old lady's contorted expression, as she too waves her arms around wildly. But she doesn't pick it up. Instead, she picks up her little scruffy dog, cradling it in her arms before stomping off.

And Sherrie didn't think that she'd ever seen Mr Burns look so angry as he did in that moment. Staring after the elderly woman, his fists locked at his sides as he shouts after her. But it's no use, Hilda doesn't give him the satisfaction of acknowledgement. She doesn't even turn her head.

She just keeps walking.

Sherrie smirks, impressed at how the woman stood her ground. How she refused to be intimidated by the man.

Maybe Sherrie hadn't given Old Hilda enough credit after all!

But Mr Burns isn't done yet. Sherrie watches as he marches back to his car, a thunderous look on his face, lost in his temper as he jumps back in his car.

For a few crazy moments Sherrie wonders if Mr Burns is going to go after Hilda.

That he'll shout and scream and force her to go back.

Or worse, maybe he is going to teach her a lesson, only his anger has got the better of him and he would end up running her over?

She watches with fascination as Mr Burns reaches down to the floor of his car and pulls out a magazine, before he walks back over to the poo and picks it up, disposing of it in his recycling bin. Before he finally goes into his house.

Sherrie snorts then, catching her unhinged thoughts. Unable to contain her laughter. Of course, he doesn't go after Hilda and run her down.

This isn't one of your sick and twisted true crime shows that you're addicted to, Sherrie!

No one's going to murder a little old lady over an argument about dog shit.

It's just normal early morning, in a normal street.

But there's nothing normal about today because Kayla still isn't home. She stares towards the end of the road again as another car makes its way up the road now. The headlights moving through the slowly brightening sky. Shining on her. Before the police car pulls up, directly outside her house.

She'd waited patiently until just before 7 a.m. to call. Richard had insisted on that. He'd told her to give Kayla the benefit of the doubt, as they'd both held on to the thin strand of hope that she might still turn up.

Only she hasn't.

Sherrie stares at the officer as he steps out of the vehicle and eyes her house.

'Richard!' Sherrie calls out to whatever part of the house her husband is currently lurking in. He can't handle her like this, in this frantic state. He can't bring her any comfort, so he's doing what he's always done, keeping out of her way.

'The police are here!'

The feeling of pure dread swirls in her stomach as a million scenarios start playing out in her head.

Sherrie breathes one last thick flume of smoke down into her lungs, because she needs something to steady her frayed nerves, but she inhales too quickly this time. The smoke fills her lungs. She starts to choke. Holding on to the windowsill she stubs the cigarette out and gasps for breath as the doorbell chimes loudly.

Bracing herself for whatever the officer has to say to her, she makes her way to the door. Her limbs feeling heavy, her chest tight.

But another part of her also feels numb.

She's waited her whole life for this, hasn't she?

For something bad to happen to her daughter. For someone to take her from her.

It is as if part of her had been expecting it.

As if she deserves it.

23

'Is that you, Amelia?' Tessa shouts, turning the shower off and shivering as droplets of water cascade down her skin, as she listens out for the noise she thought she'd just heard, whilst her head had been submerged underneath the steady stream of hot water.

'Don't tell me you've come back for your sandwich? Because that's twice in one week.' Tessa grins, about to add that she is supposed to be the scatty one. Only after last night's dramas she isn't sure Amelia will be in the mood for Tessa's playful sarcasm.

As it is, Tessa is met by silence.

Amelia didn't come home?

Did she imagine the noise?

That someone is here, inside the house with her?

BANG. BANG.

The pounding on the front door seconds later almost makes her jump out of her skin. Stepping out of the shower, she holds the towel against her body, whilst leaving puddles of water with each step she takes as she pads across the cold, tiled bathroom floor. She's in half a mind not to answer it; if it is that important whoever it is could come back later, couldn't they?

BANG. BANG.

The knocking comes again, loud and urgent. And as much as she wants to ignore it, she wonders if it might be something serious because they don't sound like they are going away any time soon.

Why are they banging like that?

Why didn't they just use the bell?

Or perhaps they had and she just hadn't heard it?

There is only one way to find out.

Making her way towards the bedroom so that she could at least throw her dressing gown on, rather than open the door practically naked to what might turn out to be a stranger, Tessa peers out through the top landing window to see if she can get a glimpse of who is down there.

Only whoever it is has tucked themselves away, concealed beneath the porch. She can just about make out the top of a man's head.

That's odd though, isn't it? The way he stood like that, his body pressed up against the door.

Banging so hard on the knocker repeatedly.

Though the banging has stopped now and the house plunges back into silence. Alarmed, Tessa feels a trickle of terror running through her as an awful thought crosses her mind. What if whoever is down there thinks that the house is empty? That no one is home and they are trying to break in?

The banging has stopped, but what if it they are trying to pick at the lock? She is here all alone. What could she do? She doesn't have any way of protecting herself. Rushing to the bedroom, Tessa grabs at her mobile phone from where she'd left it on the bed, her finger hovering over the number 9, ready to call the police if she needs to, all the while listening out for the sound of the door creaking open. Only the noise doesn't come.

Other than the sound of the tap dripping in the bathroom and the loud thudding of her heart, the house remains in silence.

Have they gone?

Peering out the window again, the man steps back, staring straight up at her now. His steely eyes locked on hers from behind the thick black-framed glasses.

Tessa brings her hand to her mouth in a failed attempt to stifle her scream.

No! no! It couldn't be.

It is him.

He has found her.

24

How did he know where she lived? It wasn't possible! She had checked, she'd made sure, staring into her rear-view mirror the whole way home the other night, certain that he hadn't tried to follow her.

But somehow he found her, because he is here now. He is standing on her doorstep, trying to get into her house, the front door the only thing stopping him from getting to her.

Her chest grows tight, her breath coming in short, sharp spurts. Desperate, she jabs at the screen of her phone with shaking hands as she calls the police, surprised when it is answered, to hear Amelia's voice at the other end. Tessa must have hit her number by mistake in her haste to call for help.

Amelia is talking, rambling. Guessing that Tessa is calling to apologise again for coming home so late last night. For not telling her where she had really been.

'Can't breathe,' Tessa mouths. Only the sound didn't leave her mouth as she tries to tell Amelia that she is in danger. Doubled over on the landing now.

'Amelia. He's here.' Tessa tries again. This time her voice comes out in a whispered squeak, barely even audible.

'Tessa?' Amelia says, realising instantly that something is wrong by the sound of urgency in Tessa's voice.

'He's here, Amelia. He's found me.' Screeching, finally managing to splutter the words out. Her voice feeling the full force of terror that this is really happening, that she doesn't have much time. 'He's right outside. I can see him.'

'Who's outside? At our house? Tessa, what is going on?' Amelia says, trying to make sense of Tessa's words, because she sounds as if she is verging on hysterics. She isn't making any sense.

'It's him, Amelia. It's him. He's found me.' Tessa's voice is louder as she shouts, desperate to make Amelia realise that this is very real. That she is in grave danger.

'I'm upstairs and he's trying to break in through the front door. He's trying to get inside. He's going to hurt me.'

'Okay, Tessa. Listen to me. I want you to go into the bathroom right now and I want you to lock the door. Drag the cabinet across too if you have to, okay?' Amelia says, trying to keep Tessa calm as she instructs her on what to do next. 'I'm going to call the police. And you are not to open that bathroom door until either me or the police get there. Okay?'

'Can you stay on the phone with me?' Tessa whimpers, pulling the towel back up as it slips from her body as she does as she is told, locking herself in the bathroom and dragging the small cabinet across the bathroom floor for good measure, barricading herself in.

'I can't. I've got to call the police. Just stay right where you are okay. I'm on my way.'

'Please, hurry!' Tessa pleads frantically, only Amelia has already hung up the phone. Slumping down to the floor, all Tessa can do is listen and pray that he can't get in. There is a faint noise of something scraping down by the front door, then a thump. Then nothing.

Is he already inside?

Is he creeping his way around her house?

Is he quietly making his way up the stairs? Towards her?

Tessa shoves her hands over her ears. Keeping her eyes squeezed tightly shut, as if somehow, that would keep him out. If she can't see him, then he can't get to her. She knows it doesn't work like that, but it is all she can do. Tessa can't go back there again.

She could never go back there to him.

25

Opening her eyes, Tessa is face down on the bathroom floor. Her cheek is pressed against the cold tiles. A trail of dribble pooling near her mouth. Had she blacked out again? She can hear a voice. Calling out her name. The noise is faint, as if it's coming from a distance. Before the bathroom door begins to slam repeatedly against the bathroom cabinet. Someone is trying to get inside. They are trying to get to her.

Him.

She remembers now. Terrified once more as she shuffles quickly backwards across the floor.

Pressing herself up against the far wall.

Her hands placed tightly over her ears again, as she closes her eyes.

Still trying her hardest to block him out.

Slam. Slam.

'Leave me alone. Please, leave me alone.' She is crying again. Repeating the same words over and over, her knees pulled in tightly around her. She's struggling to breathe.

Her rib cage has drawn in tightly around her lungs, crushing the last of the air from them.

Squeezing every last breath from within.

She is suffocating.

She is going to die.

The door keeps banging. Slamming harder, repeatedly against the wood. She keeps her eyes tightly shut, because she can't look. She can't bear to see his face again.

He is in the room. She senses his movement.

Wincing now at the footsteps coming towards her, a hand grasping her arm.

She is wild.

Lashing out at him ferociously with everything she has. Hitting and screaming and clawing at his face. Because she will not let him hurt her. Not again. Never again.

He is strong. Too strong. Grabbing at her. Holding her arms as she tries to fend him off.

'Tessa, it's me. You're safe.'

Amelia?

The sound of Amelia's voice pulls Tessa back into the room as her eyes fly open. Tears of relief forming.

Amelia is here. And there are more footsteps. Two more unfamiliar faces stare down at her. Police officers. One of them is holding her arms as Amelia crouches down on the floor in front of her, and Tessa is vaguely aware of her trying to cover her exposed nakedness with a towel.

'Tessa, I need you to focus, okay!' Amelia says sternly, and all Tessa can do is raise her hand to show her that she acknowledges that she's there, because she can't talk.

She can't find her voice.

'You're safe. You're okay,' Amelia tells her as she places one hand behind her back and guides her up onto the bathroom stool. Away from the hold of the police officer. Before she crouches back down on her knees in front of her.

'I'm right here with you. Breathe! In through the nose, out

through the mouth. Slow deep breaths.' Her voice calm and soothing.

Tessa does as she says, clinging to Amelia's every word. Because she knows the strength they hold. That these are not meaningless words of comfort Amelia is saying. She has done this countless times before.

Talked Tessa down from where she had stood on that dangerous ledge inside of her head. Talked her back down to reality. To the present.

Away from the dark thoughts that spiral inside her mind.

'Are you okay?'

Finally, Tessa nods her head, and then stares at the trail of blood that trickles from Amelia's nose, the scratches on her face. Her hair in clumps as if it's been ripped from her ponytail.

'Oh my god! What happened?' Tessa asks, seeing Amelia's eyes alert now, full of concern and tears. 'Did he do this to you? Did he hurt you?'

'No, Tessa!' Amelia says, shaking her head sadly. 'It's not him, Tessa. You made a mistake. The man outside was here to take the meter reading. That's what he was doing.'

'You're wrong! I saw him with my own eyes. He's clever. He's trying to fool you, he's trying to fool you all. That's what he does. That's what he's always done.'

Amelia shakes her head.

'The meter in the box next to the front door. He wasn't trying to get in. He heard you screaming and he went to get one of the neighbours. And then the police turned up. He's talking to them as we speak. But I promise you, it isn't him, Tessa.'

'No, you're wrong. You're wrong.' Tessa shakes her head disbelievingly, convinced now that he is once again getting away with it. Again.

Getting up and making her way to the landing, Tessa feels braver now that the police are here. The towel wrapped tightly around her body, she looks out the window.

To the police officer, standing outside the front door surrounded by a few of the neighbours. He is there too.

Only now that she is looking properly, she can see that this man is shorter. He is broader in the shoulders too. And his dark framed glasses look more of a mottled blue colour. He has an ID hanging from a lanyard around his neck. A navy and sky-blue gas uniform on. Tessa shakes her head. She doesn't understand. Because it had been him, hadn't it?

She had seen him.

Only she couldn't have. That man isn't him.

And it dawns on her then, as she turns and sees Amelia pressing a tissue to her bleeding nose. If he isn't here, who did that to Amelia's face?

'Oh my god! Did I do that?' Tessa whimpers. A sinking feeling in her stomach because she already knows the answer even before Amelia speaks.

'It was an accident,' Amelia offers. 'You were having a panic attack. You didn't know what you were doing. You were confused. You blacked out.'

She'd blacked out again. And look at the damage she'd caused this time.

What else is she capable of doing?

What else has she erased from her memory?

She thinks of Kayla now. Her heels echoing off the pavement as she walked up the street and towards the car that Tessa had been sitting in.

Then *flash*. The memory is gone.

'Oh, Amelia. I'm so sorry...' she starts, wanting to confess about where she'd been last night, about what she'd done. She wants to tell Amelia everything.

Only Amelia stops her dead.

Putting her hand up to mute her. As if she is one step ahead of her, already anticipating Tessa's apology. She's been here before too. They both have.

Except Tessa has never lashed out and hurt her like this.

Tessa thinks about the first time that she'd ever had a panic attack in front of Amelia. How they'd only just started dating, and Tessa had felt beyond mortified afterwards at the state she'd got herself in and how she'd behaved. She'd been so convinced that she'd ruined everything, now that Amelia had seen the real her. She wouldn't be interested in a nutcase like Tessa. But Amelia had surprised her. Not only had she stayed and coaxed Tessa out of her state of panic, but she'd also done it with so much compassion and kindness that she had made Tessa physically weep. Afterwards, Amelia had told her about her younger brother, Josh. How he suffered the most horrendous panic attacks for most of his life.

'The first time it happened, we all thought Josh was having an actual heart attack. Because it looks like that from the outside. And I guess Josh felt it too. Because he clutched his chest and just fell to the ground. And I honestly thought he was dying, right there, on the grass at my feet.' Amelia had told her with tears in her eyes at the memory of the ordeal. 'I know how bad they can feel.'

Amelia hadn't just told her that story to make herself feel better. She had meant it. She understood what Tessa was going through because she'd lived through it herself. And she had been there for almost every panic attack of Tessa's since. Fortunately, these days there were much fewer. But this was the first time that Tessa had lashed out at Amelia. That terrified her. That she was so scared, so caught up in the moment, that she couldn't even see straight.

Zoning back in, Tessa can hear the police officer ask Amelia if she is okay, if she needs someone to look at her injuries. If she feels safe.

Safe?

Tessa feels sick because she knows exactly what the police officer is implying.

He is asking if Amelia thinks that Tessa is at risk of causing harm to herself or others.

Others, being... Amelia.

Who was currently standing in her bathroom, surrounded by police, her nose bleeding, her face all scratched. Tessa did that to her.

The police officer is just doing his job. She understands that, but it still hurts. How these strangers standing in her house now are trying to work out if she is stable, if she has done something like this before or if she is likely to do something like it again.

'Tessa wouldn't hurt a fly!' Amelia insists, flinching as she speaks as if she only just realises that she still has folded tissue paper pressed against her nose to stem the bleeding. 'She was diagnosed with PTSD some years ago. But she sometimes still has the occasional panic attacks. She gets caught up in them. But she hasn't had one for a while.' Amelia explains how Tessa has been so much better lately. 'She has medication for it. Paranoia Ideation is one of the symptoms. Which as the name suggests, makes her paranoid. She hallucinates sometimes too. She's been better lately though. Or at least she seemed better...'

And she really had been better, hadn't she? Tessa thinks. She hasn't had an attack for almost a year. She'd started to believe that she might not have one again, Amelia believed it too by the sounds of it.

'Something must have triggered her. I don't know, maybe the man outside looked familiar. Tessa's been through a lot in her past... But she is getting there,' Amelia says, without divulging any further details about anything that Tessa had been through in the past. Not if she doesn't have to. She knows how upsetting it would be, to bring it all back up. For them to all talk about it.

Tessa feels so grateful for that.

'She'll be fine now. I'll look after her,' Tessa hears Amelia say, and she must have sounded convincing because the police officer took her word at that. Thanking them for their help, before she showed them out.

'I'm so sorry. I don't know what happened,' Tessa cries, after the police finally leave and they are alone again.

Not brave enough to come clean and tell the truth just yet. To admit to Amelia what had triggered her attack this time. That she'd seen him again.

'I told you before, you do not need to say sorry to me. Ever. You've done nothing wrong. None of this is your fault.'

Tessa nods, unable to find her voice to speak. Because it is all that she can do to not break down and cry at that. Amelia doesn't know the half of it.

Today was very much Tessa's fault. She'd caused all of this, hadn't she?

For stupidly following him home. For breaking in to his house.

That's why she is acting paranoid again, isn't it? Because she allowed him to crawl back inside her head again. She allowed him to get to her, even now. And the irony of it all is that now, she wasn't even sure if it really was him.

She'd believed that the man on her doorstep had been him too, and she had been wrong about that. Had she been seeing things that weren't really there yesterday too?

Had it really been his daughter that she'd seen making her way up the street, in the dead of night, last night?

What had happened to Kayla? Because Tessa had no memory after that.

She is no longer sure that she can trust anything she saw. She isn't sure if she can trust herself.

26

When I open my eyes, the room is spinning so fast, so violently, that it's all I can do not to throw up.

BREATHE, I tell myself silently as I try to steady myself. Lifting my head to gather my bearings. Only I feel so disorientated, and there's a constant thudding pressure pulsating inside my skull and across the front of my face. The pain is excruciating.

The last thing I remember was a sharp prick on my skin. The stab of a needle? Whoever it is who is holding me here has drugged me.

I need to focus, to stay strong. I need to work out a way that I can survive this ordeal. I must survive it. I absolutely must.

I concentrate on the thin sliver of light that pours in from the tiny gap that runs beneath the door. It's not much but it's just enough so that I can make out my surroundings.

That's when I realise that I'm not in that small, tiny space anymore.

He's moved me.

I'm inside what looks like a bedroom. And I'm not sure if

I'm in a basement or the roof, because there are no windows in here.

Just a single door.

I stand, unsteady on my feet as the remnants of whatever it was that's been injected into me still lingers in my blood stream. I know even before I reach it, even before I yank at the handle and pull at the door, that he's locked me in.

It's useless. Pointless. No matter how hard I tug at it, it doesn't give.

Turning, I scan the room.

Staring at the grubby-looking mattress on the floor along the back wall. A blanket that is crumpled, pushed down by my feet, as if I'd slept fretfully. My head full of bad dreams. I have no recollection of the bad dreams now. I have no memory of anything really.

My head feels fuzzy.

I can't seem to focus for very long.

I'm not wearing my clothes, I realise as I look down and tug at the unfamiliar grey tracksuit. The baggy material swamping my small frame.

He undressed me.

He's removed my soiled clothes from my body.

And what frightens me more than anything is that I don't have any recollection of him doing it.

I have no recollection of him at all.

I look around the room for clues of where I am, of what he wants. But there is nothing. The rest of the room is bare, void of toys or furniture and any other personal possessions. I turn back to the mattress and it's only then I notice the tray that's been placed on the floor at the end of the makeshift bed.

I must have missed that somehow in my blurry haze. Two slices of toast and the glass of water.

I don't think twice, instinctively I sink to my knees, drinking down the water first in big, greedy gulps. Letting it pour down my chin and clothes in my haste, before I cram a large piece of dry toast into my mouth. Ripping the huge mouthfuls of bread and crust between my teeth. Swallowing them down before I'd barely chewed them. I can't remember how long it's been since I last ate, and have no idea when I will eat again.

When I'm finished, I slump back down onto the mattress and that's when I see the bucket. Sitting in the opposite corner of the room. What it symbolises fills me with so much terror that my stomach violently lurches and it's all I can do to stop myself from physically being sick.

He's not going to let me out of here. Not even to use the toilet. Not for anything. I lean my head back against the wall and cry silently to myself as I try to concoct a plan.

I'm his prisoner.

I'm completely at his mercy.

All I can do is try and stay alive.

To eat and rest and keep telling myself that I am strong. That I will get through this. That I will get out of here. I won't let him break my mind. When the times comes, I'm going to get myself out of here.

27

Tessa stares at her reflection in the mirror.

There's something very wrong with it and it takes her a few minutes to work out what, because the image is so distorted and grainy that she can barely make it out.

It's not her, she realises.

The woman looking back at her is not her.

It's the girl. His daughter.

Kayla.

Why is she here? Does she need help?

Pressing her palm up against the mirrored glass, Tessa whispers as she reaches out her hand, willing the girl to let her help her.

'I can get you out of there. I can get you away from him.'

Only Kayla doesn't take it.

She is talking though, her mouth is moving, she is saying something.

But there's no sound.

It's as if she's been silenced. Silenced by him.

'I can help you,' Tessa says, pressing her face up against the cool mirrored surface as she mouths the words loudly, so that

Kayla can hear her. But as she does so, she feels the vicelike grip of two claw-like hands grabbing at her shoulders. Dragging her inside.

It's him.

The monster.

He had been pretending to be the girl to lure her back here. To him.

He's dragging her inside now, into the contorted prism of mirrors that surrounds her like a curved prison wall.

Locking her inside. There's no way out.

Tessa searches frantically for a door, for a way out, but she's surrounded only by images of herself. Screaming, terrified images of her trying to get away from him. And there are thousands of them. Staring back at her. Taunting her.

The girl is back. This time she is close. So close that Tessa can see the gold locket as it dangles from the dainty chain around her neck. The way it sparkles so elegantly as the light hits it.

'Come with me?' Tessa tries again, but Kayla shakes her head. She doesn't believe that Tessa is here to help her. She doesn't believe that she's in danger. She thinks that she's safe. But she doesn't really know him. She doesn't know what he is really capable of.

She won't come.

'You must!'

Tessa grabs at her then, forcefully, her fingers looping around the chain she's wearing as she tries to yank her, to pull her back through the mirrored glass. Only the glass is solid now. The portal to get back has gone. Tessa hits out, pounding loudly with her fists. Because that is the only way that they are going to get out of there.

Away from him.

Thud. Thud.

The mirror finally cracks. Splintering into a thousand fragmented pieces, cutting at her skin. She feels the trail of warm blood as it trickles down her hands. And suddenly she is falling backwards. Back through the mirror. Kayla's necklace snapping in her hands.

Breaking free from her.

Kayla is still back there.

Tessa can't reach her.

She's gone.

She looks down at her hands and sees the locket. The chain wrapped around her blood-soaked fingers.

The almighty scream wakes her, pulling Tessa from her bad dream.

She'd been stuck there. Trapped inside of it, thanks to the sleeping pills she'd taken. She has woken Amelia too.

Amelia has jolted forward in the bed. She's sitting up now, pressing the bedside lamp on. The bright light floods the room.

'Tessa?' Amelia asks, staring at Tessa as Tessa stands dead still at the edge of the room. Hovering by the wardrobe.

'What's happened? Are you okay?' Amelia asks, eyeing the vacant look on Tessa's face. The film of perspiration that covers her skin glistening, illuminated by the glow of the bedroom lamp.

'What am I doing?' Tessa says, awake, her face twisting in confusion as she stares down at the jeans she's holding in her hands. Her jeans. Her fingers tucked deep into the pockets.

'It's just another nightmare, baby! You were sleepwalking that's all. Come back to bed.'

Tessa nods her head. Feeling stupid as she does what Amelia tells her. Climbing back into the bed and allowing Amelia to place her arms around her. To pull her in for a hug and give her some much-needed comfort.

'It's okay! I'm here. It's over now.'

'I'm sorry!'

'Don't be sorry. It was just a dream!'

'No. It wasn't. At least I don't think it was,' Tessa says, still disorientated. Not making any sense. 'It felt so much more real than that,' Tessa says, shaking her head, a terrified expression still fixed on her face, as if she is still back there. Still caught up in her nightmares. Still not really here, back in the room with Amelia. 'It felt so real. I couldn't get back out... I cut my hands... Why aren't I bleeding?'

Tessa stares at her hands now. Wondering where the deep gouges in her hands and wrists have gone. Why wasn't she still bleeding?

'I had it. The locket. The photos of them. It was covered in blood. In my blood.'

'Tess, darling. I think you're still asleep. You're not making any sense right now. What locket? There's no blood. You're safe, Tessa,' Amelia says, staring at Tessa with mild amusement as she tries to work out if she is coherent, or if she is still sleep-walking. Questioning whether she even realises that she is talking to her right now.

'It's not real. It was just a nightmare. Come on, try and go back to sleep. The tablets have probably made you a bit woozy that's all.'

'I had it, didn't I? The locket? I took it?' Tessa says, staring at the jeans that sit in the heap on the floor. 'That bit had been real, hadn't it?' Tessa is almost crying. Her brows furrowing in the middle, as if trying to work out a conundrum that only she has the correct answer to.

'Tessa, I don't know what locket you're talking about. Are you sure you didn't just dream it?' Amelia says with a small smile, trying to appease Tessa now. To calm her down and lighten the mood.

'Like the time you dreamt that Spud could talk. That was

trippy as Hell. Didn't you say all he did was follow us around the whole time demanding that we put food in his bowl and stroke him? Though to be fair, that sounds about right!' Amelia says with a grin.

Tessa knows that she's trying to make light of the situation. That she is trying to make Tessa feel better. But that is because she doesn't understand.

How could she when Tessa is keeping things from her?

'This wasn't just a dream, Amelia. There was a locket. It belonged to his daughter.'

'Whose daughter?' Amelia says, narrowing her eyes as she looks at Tessa strangely then.

'*His* daughter,' Tessa tries to explain.

Only immediately she senses the energy in the room change at the mere hint of talking about him.

She is wide awake now. No longer caught up in her bad dreams. But she can tell from Amelia's expression that she still isn't making much sense.

'Okay!?' Amelia says, her jaw tightening as she removes her arm from Tessa's shoulders. Not sure she understands what Tessa is telling her, but she is trying her hardest to listen, doing her upmost to give Tessa time to explain.

'You saw him, and his daughter in your dream? And a locket?' Amelia says, trying to piece the jumbled words together and make some sense of it all.

'No. Not in my dream. I saw them in real life,' Tessa says slowly, knowing how Amelia would take the news that Tessa had been hiding things from her. She'd been keeping the truth from her.

It is time for her to confess.

'I'm sorry. I should have told you. I should have said. But I didn't think that you'd believe me. I didn't think you'd listen, and I wanted proof. I've seen him, Amelia. He has a family now. He has a daughter.'

'Oh, Tessa! Are you really still doing this? Still fixating on him. Christ! We spoke about this. It wasn't him. The police confirmed that. None of this is about him. You know that, don't you? Deep down, you must know that. This is your anxiety making you believe things that aren't true, making you see things that aren't really there.'

'I'm not talking about the man who came to our house...' Tessa says, feeling her tears forming then. There's so much she has kept from Amelia. So much she hasn't said. Tessa had wanted to tell her the truth. Only she hadn't been sure that Amelia would ever understand. Not really.

Only now she's not sure she has any choice in the matter.

Withholding things from Amelia will only do more damage than good, she realises. She can feel it, Amelia is losing her patience with her. She's starting to think that Tessa is crazy. And maybe Tessa is acting crazy. But there is a reason for that. She needs to start being honest with her. She needs to tell Amelia the truth.

Because this is so much bigger than her. It is so much bigger than both of them.

'I went there.' Her voice is small then. 'To his house.'

Tessa sees the shock expression spread across Amelia's face, as she registers what she is telling her.

'You went where? To whose house? Tessa, what the fuck is going on?' Amelia shakes her head as if she can't comprehend what she is hearing, that now she's being told she doesn't want to hear it.

'I know it sounds crazy, trust me, I know it does. But I just wanted to get some proof. To show you, to show the police, that this time I haven't made a mistake. That it really is him.' Tessa shakes her head as if she can't believe it either. Even though she had seen him with her own two eyes. But it was him. She was certain of that now. She found him.

She found *him*.

'I followed him. The other day, on your birthday. That's why I was so late home. I followed him. I sat outside his house. I watched him with his family. And he looked so... normal. So ordinary. Unpacking the shopping from the back of the car, laughing and talking with his wife. Only I think he might have seen me. I wasn't sure, but I got out of there as quickly as I could. That's why I freaked out so much when I saw that other man was outside our front door, taking the meter reading. I thought it was him,' Tessa continued, knowing that being met with Amelia's silence wasn't a good sign, but she needs to make her understand.

She needs her to listen. Now more than ever before.

'I thought that he'd somehow followed me, or found out where I lived. I wasn't thinking straight. I wasn't thinking at all. That's why I reacted the way that I did. That's why I had that panic attack...'

'Because you followed someone home?' Amelia's eyes burn into her.

'Because I found him. It wasn't just a case of me following someone home, Amelia. It was him. I know you don't believe me, trust me I know how messed up it all sounds, but this time it really is him,' Tessa says, desperately trying to convince Amelia that this time she had seen him.

It is real.

'But what if it's not? What if you've got it wrong again?' Amelia lifts the covers and gets up from the bed. Pacing then. Striding back and forth across the room, and Tessa can see from the look on her face that this is so much worse than she initially thought.

'I can't believe you followed someone home!'

Tessa winces at the disappointment in her tone. That isn't even the worst bit. That isn't even a fraction of what she's done.

Tessa opens her mouth to tell her more, to confess that she broke into his house. That she sat outside until the early hours of the morning and how she'd seen the girl, his daughter. Walking along the road on her own in the dead of night. How she blacked out shortly afterwards and hasn't been able to shake the harrowing feeling that has weighed down on her since that something very bad has happened.

That she'd done something unspeakable. Only Amelia interrupts her before she can even begin.

'You realise that this is insane, don't you, Tessa? Doing these things. Acting like this. This isn't rational behaviour, Tessa. You're acting...' Amelia stops mid-sentence.

Feeling bad then. Because they both know that this isn't Tessa's fault.

Tessa knows that Amelia doesn't want to sound cruel. But it's too late. Her unspoken word hangs between them in the air. They both know what she was about to say. What she was about to accuse Tessa of being.

'What? Say it!' Tessa says. Feeling fresh tears fill her eyes as anger bubbles deep inside of her that Amelia is so quick to write her off and dismiss her. 'You think that I'm acting crazy, don't you? You still don't believe me. You think that this is all inside my head.' Tessa shakes her head, full of frustration. 'You won't even hear me out. You won't even consider for a second that this time, it might actually be different. That this time I might actually be telling you the truth.'

'I know you believe it, but that doesn't make it real...' Amelia starts.

'It is real. This time it's real. I have found him.'

Amelia shakes her head.

She can see by the stern look on Tessa's face that Tessa won't back down on this.

'Tessa, I'm not doing this. Not here, not right now.' Amelia no longer has the energy to fight. 'I'm not rowing with you, not when you're like this. It's pointless. You're not listening.'

'I'm the one not listening?' Tessa says, crying now. She

knew that it would come to this. Amelia would give up on her, that this would all be too much for her in the end.

'I'm trying to tell you, Amelia. That there is more to this than you know. There are things that I haven't told you. Things that I couldn't tell you. But I should have, and I'm so sorry for that. I should have been honest with you right from the start. I should have told you it all...'

'Do you know what, Tess. I really can't do this right now,' Amelia says, her tone hard as she holds her hand up to stop Tessa from saying anything else. Her hand trembling, not from fear, but fury. Because they were going round in circles. Repeating patterns and getting nowhere fast.

'Please, Amelia. Please just listen...'

'No! Enough, Tess!' Amelia shouts, grabbing a pillow from the bed. 'We'll talk later. Right now I can't even think straight. This isn't right, Tessa. I have no idea who you actually are. Because this... following people home? Sitting outside their homes and watching them...' Amelia points her finger at her. 'This isn't you.'

Amelia's words sting. But worse than that, Amelia is openly crying now too. There's something so scary about her raw display of emotion. So final, Tessa thinks. Because Amelia rarely cries at anything. She is always so in control. She always knows the answer to everything.

Except she doesn't have the answers for this.

She doesn't even know where to start.

And worse still, she doesn't even know the half of it.

What Tessa is capable of. Or what she's lied about.

When she storms from the room, Tessa doesn't go after her. They both need space. They both need time to calm down.

Laying back against the pillow then, Tessa starts to cry too; it's the first time in a long time that she's felt so alone. She is grateful when Spud jumps up on the bed and snuggles back in beside her. The warm fur of his body, pressing against hers.

'I'm sorry, Spuddy! I didn't mean to scare you,' Tessa whispers softly as she gently strokes him.

Had she imagined the locket? Had it just been part of her dream? She doesn't think so. And she can't shake the dream she's just had from her head.

It means something, she's sure of it.

The question is, what?

She'd been so sure yesterday, that he had come to her house.

That the man outside her front door had been him.

She has already mistaken one man's identity.

What if she is wrong about him too?

28

Sherrie doesn't want to be here, walking in to this large, stuffy conference room, filled with all these people, sandwiched between these two men as if they form a shield around her. Richard is walking closely behind her, the lead detective ahead of her as he guides the way. All of this means that Kayla is still missing.

Being here means that they still haven't found her.

And now Sherrie is expected to bare her soul to all these expectant strangers. The journalists and news reporters and TV presenters. Waiting for their little titbits of information so that they can broadcast her worst living nightmare onto every TV screen across the country. It will help them to find Kayla, the detective has promised her.

She must look terrible, she thinks, frightful, in fact. Because when she catches the sympathetic eye of one of the females who is sitting in the front row, she sees real pity there at her predicament. At the state Sherrie is in. Sherrie can't hold her eye, a journalist she guesses, with pen poised over her notebook. Her perfectly made-up face and not a single hair out of place. Teetering on the right side of professional with that slick of pink painted on her lips. A fitted, tight black dress that hugs her tiny frame. Sherrie envies the woman. Not just for her looks but also for her ignorance. For her detachment from it all, that this is just a job to her. But to Sherrie it's her whole life. Blown wide open for the whole world to see.

It's not just the woman who's looking. The whole room has turned to her and Richard, too, talking now in hushed whispers. Suddenly she's aware that she's wearing yesterday's clothes. In a few moments they'll be live on air and she is wearing the jeans and jumper that she'd scraped up from the bedroom floor that very morning. With almost the same amount of effort as she'd scraped her exhausted, sleep-deprived body from her bed.

She's conscious of how red and swollen her eyes must look, under the glare of harsh spotlights and cameras. How the skin around them is chafed and sore from where she's been constantly rubbing at them. Pointlessly wiping away her tears as she makes way for fresh ones.

And her hair. God, her hair. Had she even brushed it? She can't remember. Scraping her wild red locks to the side, self-consciously, someone puts their hand on her shoulder and guides her towards the empty seat at the table.

Facing the room. And the TV camera.

As Richard slides into the chair beside her, Sherrie feels grateful that he is sitting so close to her. She is not alone, which is a strange sensation when you are sitting in a packed room, staring out into a sea of faces. Every chair is taken, there are people standing up, lining the edges of the room. The noise is loud and constant. Whispers and murmurs buzzing with speculation. This is what they do. The journalists and police officers and family liaison officers and detectives. This is just part of their job. All poised ready with their notebooks and tape recorders.

These people who are all here for Kayla. Telling her the words that she so desperately needs to hear.

Tiptoeing around her, with well-rehearsed promises of doing everything they can to find Kayla.

To her it's all just white noise. Just sound penetrating her ears.

She can hear Richard's breathing. How slow and laboured each breath he takes is, as if he's trying to control it, to hide his nerves. He must be feeling this too. Of course he is. He hadn't wanted to do this either, to make such a public appeal. Because Richard, like her, is such a private person. Part of him still believes that Kayla would just turn up. That she isn't in any real danger, that she is just rebelling.

But the fact that he is here, sitting beside her, putting on this display as they beg for the safe return of their daughter shows that he must feel it too. The raw, excruciating pain that Sherrie can feel as it eats away at her.

But no one in this room, not even him, could possibly begin to imagine the pain that she is in. None of them could understand the fears that frantically whirl around inside of her.

She is the only mother here, in this room, who is missing a child.

She is the only one here fearing for her daughter's life.

Somebody pours her a glass of water, and Sherrie takes a sip.

Grateful for something to do with her shaking hands. Grateful to wash away the dryness that clings to the back of her throat. The staleness that has lingered from the numerous cups of coffee and from continual chain-smoking since she first realised that Kayla wasn't coming home.

Ten minutes max. That's all they need from her the detective had said when he'd told her the importance of what she is about to do. Ten minutes is all she needs to try and hold herself together, without sobbing. Without screaming. Without pacing the floor hysterically as her mind goes into overdrive about the million things that could have happened to her daughter since she went missing.

The detective stands up to address the room, and the voices quickly fade to quiet.

'It's been thirty-three hours since Kayla Goldman was last seen leaving Roxy's nightclub. We are currently pursuing several lines of enquiry in the investigation of her disappearance...'

Sherrie zones out. His voice is so formal, robotic, as if he is just reading from a script. The Kayla he is talking about belongs to someone else. Because this detective doesn't know her daughter. He doesn't know how Kayla likes to dance flamboyantly around the room on a Saturday night to *X-Factor*. How she would sing into her hairbrush as if she was right there, auditioning for a place in the show's next girl band.

Or how she has the quickest, darkest, most sarcastic sense of humour. Just like Sherrie's. How she could cut people in half with a well-timed jibe or leave them doubled over with laughter depending on her mood. That's why she is here, the detective had said: to make it more personal.

He wanted the 'audience' to connect with her, Kayla's distraught parents. Her mother particularly. He wanted them to feel Sherrie's aguish and her fear, to sympathise with her pain. They need to get people invested in the search for their missing daughter, he had told her. Sherrie is the best shot they have at getting Kayla back safely. The audience will pay more attention when Kayla's image is flashed up on their TV screens, if there's a family appealing for her safe return.

The audience.

His words had instantly filled Sherrie with rage.

This isn't a circus. This isn't a show.

This is her life.

This is her daughter's life.

The room is quiet, silent, and Sherrie realises that the detective has stopped talking and he's looking straight at her.

She's been so lost in her thoughts that she's missed her cue.

A room full of expectant faces stare at her as the red light of the camera blinks. Sherrie clears her throat, not sure that she trusts herself to speak. Not sure if she opens her mouth, any sound will come out. She swallows hard, forcing down the heavy lump that is lodged in the back of her throat.

And she forces herself to do this.

For Kayla's sake.

'There must be someone out there who knows something, or who saw something. Someone who knows where Kayla is. Please. We just want her home. We just want her back, safe, with us.'

Richard takes her hand then and gives her a reassuring squeeze.

And in that moment, it is all too much for her.

Sitting here, in this room, surrounded by all these people. Begging and pleading with some unknown, invisible monster to return their daughter to them.

'I just want Kayla back. Please!' Sherrie sobs as the tears take her again and violent sobs wrack her entire body. 'I want my baby back.'

Her loud frantic cries are drowned out by the barrage of questions that are thrown at her then, by the press, in their desperation to compete for tomorrow's front page headlines.

'What was the last thing you said to Kayla? How did Kayla seem the day she disappeared? Did Kayla have a boyfriend? Kayla is only fifteen, what was she doing in a nightclub? And drinking? Did she normally drink?'

Sherrie stares at the detective, unable to find her words. Incensed now that he failed to mention the small detail of how bloody awful and intrusive the public appeal would feel. How attacked she would feel.

'I didn't know she was at a nightclub...' She mouths finally through her sobs. 'She didn't tell me...'

Sherrie is crying. Feeling completely vulnerable as she breaks down in front of all these strangers that are sitting here watching her, judging her. Both here, in the room and at the other end of the camera, through their TV screens.

The detective stands up, shutting them down, calling the briefing to an end, apologising for no further questions. Sherrie feels Richard's arm as it hooks around her and he guides her up to her feet, before escorting her out of the room. Away from all the noise and the madness, away from the prying eyes of the TV camera and the rest of the watching world.

29

Tessa's eyes move to the headline that runs across the bottom of the screen. Taking in the bold letters stating that *Fifteen-year-old Kayla Goldman is missing,* the spoon drops from her grasp, landing with a splash in her bowl, as his face fills the screen.

Drops of milk and bits of cereal splatter over her clean clothes.

Her eyes don't move. They are fixed on his face.

Enlarged, up close, as he stares out at her from the TV.

Filling her screen.

The sight of him, staring back at her making the blood in her veins run ice cold.

Him. In her house. In her lounge.

Placing the bowl down on the coffee table, before she drops it, she wipes herself down. Her appetite has disappeared, replaced with a sickly feeling that swirls wildly in the pit of her stomach as the camera zooms in on him.

Part of her doesn't want to look away even if she could. Part of her needs to look at him. Part of her needs to know the truth. That this is really him, staring back at her. That Amelia is wrong about this being inside her head. She takes every detail of him in, her eyes transfixed then, by the familiarity of his face. By those same steely eyes. He is older. He has put on weight. He has changed.

She is certain this is him.

She has thought about this very moment more times than it was probably healthy, more times than she'd cared to admit to any other living person. To any other living soul, including Amelia. He consumed her. Her every thought, her every waking minute for years. She learned to hide that from the numerous counsellors she'd seen over the years after one of them had hinted that she had become obsessed with him.

As if they had any idea what they had been talking about. All those helpful strangers that had the impossible job of trying to help her and put her back together again after he had destroyed her. The people that had sifted through the ruins of what was left of her life.

Of course she was going to think about him, to wonder.

What he might be doing now. If he ever thought about her and the hurt he had caused. If he ever thought about the devastation he had left in his wake.

When she should have been focusing on getting better, getting stronger. On moving on. And she had started to, eventually. All those years later, when she had finally met Amelia and started living a real life again. She'd stopped obsessing, stopped thinking of him, stopped wondering.

And she'd found him anyway.

She feels sick. Because this time she knows that she is not hallucinating. She is not seeing things that aren't really there.

Not like all those other times.

She'd suffered acutely for years. Imagining he was following her when she was out in the street. Paranoid that he was hiding across the road from her house. Creeping behind nearby cars or bushes, watching her.

It had got so bad at one point that she'd even been terrified of being alone in her own bedroom. Forcing herself to check inside the wardrobes and under the bed each night, obsessively. A grown woman, behaving like a scared child with a vivid, overactive imagination, who wouldn't sleep until she knew that she wasn't locked away with monsters hiding underneath her bed.

That's how low it had brought her. To the very bottom.

She still does that sometimes now: check the house to make sure that she is really alone when Amelia isn't here. Though these days she is more subtle about it. Or at least she had been until the last few days. But maybe her fears and paranoia had never really left her completely. Maybe she just learned to quieten them so much that she had even ended up fooling herself.

Believing that she was better now, when really all it did was to fester inside of her. The fear. The hate.

But this isn't a case of her mind playing tricks on her this time. She sees him now. She recognises the woman sitting next to him too, the woman from all the photos that twisted their way up the walls inside of his house. His wife, an expression of pain is etched on her face, as the camera zooms in on her as she starts to talk.

Her mouth is moving but Tessa can't hear what she is saying. Because the ringing in her ears is so loud now, as the thud of her pulse pounds repeatedly through them. She is in shock, she realises.

Reaching for the remote control with trembling hand, she turns the volume up, so she can hear what his wife is saying.

'I just want Kayla back. Please. I want my baby back.'

She is crying now, sobbing inconsolably, and Tessa watches as he takes her hand in his. Squeezing it tentatively as if to offer some comfort. As if to remind her that she's not alone. That he is there. And Tessa can see it. Maybe she is the only one in the world that can. How the loving gesture seems so fake. How their hands sit limply between them. His expression remaining detached. A blank look in his eyes.

He is acting.

Playing the role of a dutiful father, a loving husband.

She knows him.

She has always known him.

She knows when he is lying.

30

'We need to talk,' Amelia resolves, tight-lipped as she walks into the lounge.

'I thought that you'd already left,' Tessa says, trying to hide the look of surprise she feels as she scrambles for the remote control, her fingers hitting frantically at the buttons. Only instead of switching it over she turns the volume up blaring loud.

The detective's voice fills the room.

Fifteen-year-old Kayla Goldman is missing.

Tessa presses pause. Flustered then.

'Yes, we do!' she says, deflecting, purposely diverting her gaze away from the screen. Hoping that talking looked like her real motive as to why she'd tried to turn the TV off, and eventually the volume down. Hoping that Amelia would be too distracted, too caught up in fixing this mess they were both in to notice the TV. That instead, she'd keep her eyes on her.

Though just the sight of Amelia's face, a thick layer of foundation painted over the jagged red scratches in a failed attempt to cover up the injuries that Tessa had inflicted on her, only fills her with more guilt.

Yesterday's panic attack had been her worst one yet.

'What were you watching?' Amelia asks. She isn't stupid. She knows Tessa. She knows when she's trying to hide something from her. And instantly she's suspicious. Her eyes going right to it. To the frame that is now paused on the television screen, where a woman is sobbing. The man, he is holding her up. A distraught look on his face. Amelia narrows her eyes as she realises that Tessa is watching the local news, a press conference. She reads the words at the bottom of the screen.

Fifteen-year-old Kayla Goldman is missing.

'Shit!' Amelia says, understanding.

Or at least thinking that she understands. Because cases like this have always set Tessa's anxiety off. They'd always brought her worst fears to the surface. She always becomes fixated with them. Watching and listening to every newspaper, every TV report, reading every bit of online information she can find. Obsessed with the case for days or weeks or months. Until the girl is found. Dead or alive.

That's what she thinks this is.

'This is why you've been so on edge the past few days? This is what has triggered you off, Tessa. You've been worrying about her? This missing girl on the news?' Amelia says, treading lightly because she knows how fragile Tessa is right now.

Tessa knows it too. How Amelia is of course right, how this is a pattern of hers. How she can sometimes work herself up so much it is as if she is possessed. As if she is no longer present inside her own head; as if something else has taken over.

And sometimes she'd stay that way for hours. Other times, the breakdowns could last for days at a time, and they were the worst. Those long, drawn-out panic attacks and hallucinations where Amelia would try and do her best to be patient, as Tessa slowly found her way back out of them again.

'She's only fifteen,' Tessa says quietly. Taking Amelia's lead and pretending that's exactly what this is. Another one of her obsessions. Another fixation that takes her back to the brink of her own nightmare.

'Look, I know stuff like this is going to bring it back up for you. But Tess, babe. You have to stop letting things like that affect you like this. It's too much. We can't just assume the worst every time something like this happens,' Amelia says cautiously as she reaches for the remote control, and presses play. Wanting to help Tessa by talking her through what is playing out on the screen. To show her that this is not what she thinks it might mean.

'Teenage girls go missing all the time. Missing doesn't always mean that she's in trouble, Tess. Maybe this girl is just hanging out with her mates, or a new boyfriend she hasn't told her parents about.'

A photo of the young girl's pretty face fills the screen then.

Her vibrant red hair. Her freckly nose.

'No one's saying that she's in any danger. They're just saying that she is missing. She might show up very soon. And all of this will be just one big misunderstanding. Not everything has to have a bad ending. Not everything has to lead back to him.'

She should tell her, she thinks.

She should just come out with it all and be honest. Finally.

Amelia deserves that much at least, the truth. Only Tessa can't speak. Her mouth is dry and her voice feels as if it's stuck, deep down, in her throat. Wedged there so that no sound can get out.

'Kayla went out on Friday night and hasn't come home. It's not like her. She's such a good girl,' the woman is saying through her tears. Her sobs drowning out the end of the sentence but Amelia catches it. Tessa sees the thoughtful look on her face, as if she can visibly see the cogs turning inside her head. The girl has been missing since Friday. And the TV camera is homing in on a street nearby, right here in Hackney. Just minutes away from where they live. These people are local. The girl hasn't been seen since Friday night.

'Friday night?' Amelia says as if something inside her mind has just clicked into place. She stares at the couple on the TV. Her eyes fixed on the man's face, searching for similarities.

Tessa knows that look because she's done it herself too.

Amelia knows what he looked like back then, because Tessa had showed her a photo of him when she'd first told her about who he was and what he had done to her.

Amelia had told her that she had memorised it. The image that the media had plastered over the internet and newspaper articles back then, that it would forever be engraved in her brain because of the damage he had caused Tessa.

For the physical and mental marks he'd permanently left on her.

Tessa waits until, finally, Amelia speaks.

'Oh my god! That's him, isn't it?'

'You can see it too?' Tessa nods her head, watching, as Amelia's expression changes then, to something that Tessa has never seen before, a look on Amelia's face that she doesn't recognise. She looks stricken. As the colour drains from her face.

'It's not just me, is it? Thank God! This isn't just inside my head?' She feels fresh tears fill her eyes as she breathes a sigh of relief.

Thank God! Thank God!

'I told you, didn't I! I told you it was him,' Tessa says, staring at Amelia, willing her to say something. Anything.

Only Amelia is in shock.

And Tessa knows exactly how that feels, because she has felt it too. Tessa rewinds the clip and plays it again. Pausing it when his face fills the screen. Forcing herself to look at him again too. To properly take him in. She has something to prove now.

He looks awkward, startled even. Like a deer caught in the

headlights, while all around him cameras flash. The room buzzing with the sound of police and journalists. Uncomfortable because he knows what he is. He knows what he's done. Now he's the one on the other side. No longer the perpetrator. He's the victim.

'Tessa!' Amelia says slowly. Her tone full of caution now. 'Please tell me that this isn't the man that you followed home? That this isn't the family you watched?'

Tessa falters as she realises she had read Amelia's reaction all wrong. That Amelia still doesn't see him at all.

Because she's not asking about him. She's asking about the man that Tessa followed home.

'You came home in the early hours of Saturday morning. You were covered in mud. You'd been there then, hadn't you? That night. Outside their house, watching them?' Amelia says, watching Tessa closely for her reaction.

'When you had that dream you said that he had a daughter. Kayla Goldman, this is her, isn't it? This is the family that you've been following. And now they are on the news? Now their daughter is missing?' Amelia looks shocked. Horrified at what she's just figured out.

This is why Tessa has been acting so strange.

There is so much more to this.

'How have I been so stupid? How did I not know that this is what you've been doing? You told me that you'd been out running and that you'd hurt your ankle, that you'd been to the hospital. But you were lying...' Amelia shakes her head as if trying to shake loose the tangled, web of thoughts from inside of it. 'You didn't limp when you got out of bed in search of that locket. After you had that bad dream. You didn't limp when the police were here either,' Amelia says now, recalling how Tessa had moved across the floor so easily that morning, still half asleep. How she'd made her way to the window that morning she'd thought that he'd come to their house, too.

She hadn't limped then either. Because Tessa was lying. She hadn't gone to the hospital Friday night. And she hadn't hurt her foot.

'I knew it. I knew you were lying to me, Tessa, but I didn't want to push you on it. I wanted you to tell me in your own time. Because of how you've been lately. I didn't want to add more pressure. Only you haven't told me the truth, have you, about any of this? And now you are keeping more secrets. You're shutting me out!'

'I'm sorry, Amelia, but it's not what you think...' Tessa starts, needing to make Amelia understand. Only everything Amelia just said is the truth. 'I only lied to you because I knew that you wouldn't believe me. If I told you that I found him. I knew that I needed proof. That's why I went back there. Because I needed to show you that this time, it really is him. And look! Don't you see it now? Don't you recognise him? It's him, Amelia. Look at him.'

Amelia glances at the TV, but her look is fleeting and quickly she shakes her head. Because they've been here before. They've done this so many times.

'No, Tessa. It's not him. That's not even his name. This man is called Richard Goldman. It's not Nick. It says it right there.'

'He's using a fake name. A fake identity. He's living a fake life. Look at him.'

'Tessa! We've been over this...' Amelia starts. Closing her eyes in despair.

And Tessa gets it. They have been over this too many times before. They are both used to the smallest similarity or familiarity setting Tessa off. The faintest notion of association to him. A similar hair colour. An expression on someone's face. And other times it wouldn't be anything familiar at all. It would be just a feeling that Tessa got.

Like that time someone had stood too close to her in a supermarket. Or another time when someone had stared at her – or had it been that they had 'purposely' not looked at her – when she'd turned and glanced at them in the street. How they'd diverted their gaze.

But this time it really is different.

Tessa is certain.

This time it really is him.

'I know you think that I've got caught up in it all again. In my anxiety and the panic attacks, and maybe I did a bit, with that man that came to the house. And I'm sorry for that, but going there and seeing him just triggered something inside me. It brought it all back. I am not hallucinating, Amelia. I am not sick. I am not seeing things and thinking things that aren't really there. I promise you that, Amelia. That really is him this time. You have to believe me.'

'Tessa, stop! That man is grieving his missing daughter. Look at his eyes, look at his face. He looks distraught and so does his wife. Not only that, it doesn't look anything like him!' Amelia says honestly.

'He's older now,' Tessa says, trying to convince Amelia. 'But look. If he was younger. Try and picture him without the beard and the glasses. They are all part of it. Part of his disguise.'

Amelia shakes her head.

In disbelief and something else, disappointment.

'So, you want me to imagine him looking completely different to what he actually looks now? You want me to imagine him looking like someone else altogether. Square peg, round hole. If the missing pieces of the puzzle don't fit, whack them with a hammer until they slot into place!? It doesn't work like that, Tessa!' Amelia says softly, as she stares at the man on the screen. 'Trust me, Tessa, there's nothing that would give me greater pleasure than to see that man found and punished for what he did to you. You know that... but this isn't him. And if it was, and I do mean IF that was him, do you really think he'd be stupid enough to go on national TV? Because that would be insane, wouldn't it? Putting himself out there for everyone to see. In front of the whole world.'

'Maybe he didn't have a choice. Maybe the police cornered him into talking on camera in a bid to find her. They might have put him on the spot. And what would he say then, what would be his reason to get out of it? Maybe he just went along with it, hoping that no one would recognise him now. But I recognise him. I know that's him,' Tessa says, trying to stand firm, only even she can hear the hesitation in her voice at how unlikely that would be. That after all this time, he would just show up staring back at her from the TV.

And he does look different now.

The facial hair and the glasses, the extra weight.

But people change, don't they? People age.

And it wasn't hard to change your name, was it?

But why would he live here, right back where it had all started?

Right here on her doorstep.

'I'm sure it's him...' Tessa falters, doubt slowly creeping in now. Because she is sure, isn't she? But then hadn't she also been sure that he had come to her house yesterday.

That the man outside her front door had been him, and that he had found her.

She has already mistaken one man's identity.

What if she is wrong about him too?

'I know how much you believe it, and I know how scared you are, Tessa. But you are wrong. It isn't him. That family is suffering, Tessa. They are missing a daughter.' Amelia gently shakes her head.

'Tessa, we can't keep pretending that this isn't happening. These sightings of him. They're happening too often. And worse, following someone home. Sitting outside his house and watching him. That's a whole other level. What do you think the police would think if they knew that you were there that night? Sitting outside his house. The night that his daughter went missing? Because they'll be searching for her, Tessa. They'll be trawling through cameras and CCTV. They'll be noting down licence plate numbers that were in the area at that time. It won't take much for them to lead right back here to you...'

'To me? What are you trying to say?' Tessa asks, confused now at how irate Amelia sounds. How on edge she seems. As if she doesn't even want to voice what she's thinking out loud, because once the question's out, they'll both have to deal with it.

Amelia will get her answer and she may not like what she hears.

'Tessa if you know something about that missing girl...' Amelia says, her voice so quiet it's as if she's too terrified to even voice the question.

Because now it's out there, there's no avoiding the answer.

She'll have to hear it.

'If you saw her... If you know anything at all... you have to tell me. You have to be honest with me.'

31

Something has woken me as I lie here frozen with terror in this cold, empty room.

Clank.

A noise.

I strain to listen. Someone is out there, I'm sure of it. Someone hovering on the other side of the door. For a few seconds I am filled with hope, with pure elation, that it might be my mum. Or the police. They have found me. They are going to bring me home.

'Please? I'm in here!' I cry out. Though I have no idea where here is. And I just hope that whoever is out there can hear me.

That they'll follow the sound of my voice. That they let me out of this room.

Another clank.

The sound of metal. A key turning inside a lock. I brace myself.

'I'm in here!' I repeat, but my voice cracks the second time, my mouth is so dry. My lips feel sore and split. I can't remember the last time I had a drink.

I've lost track of time.

Sitting in here for hours on end just staring at the walls.

And weirdly it is tiring. Doing nothing. Just waiting.

I can barely keep my eyes open.

But I need to try. Because they are here to save me now.

Only it suddenly occurs to me then, that they are not shouting back.

Whoever is out there. Why are they not shouting back? Letting me know that they are close, that this will soon be over?

It's him, I realise full of terror then. He's the one out there.

The one that put me here.

Pad. Pad.

Footsteps and then the creak of the door.

I push myself up against the wall, away from him as he enters the room.

His face covered with a black balaclava, just two steely eyes looking back at me through the round cut-out peepholes. He looks menacing, and I force myself to look, to stare back at him and show him that I'm not afraid of him.

But I am very much afraid.

I am terrified.

Rigid with terror as I silently pray that he hasn't come in here to hurt me. To do anything bad to me.

He crosses the room. And it's only then I realise that he is carrying a tray.

I eye the door.

Cracked open by just a few inches.

His hands clutch the tray of food.

Fear kicks in. Fuelled by my need to survive, my need to get away from him.

I take my chance and I run.

My feet winging across the worn carpet, my hand on the door.

The tray slaps loudly to the ground as he drops it, realising too late that he has been careless. That he has underestimated my want to get away from him.

I'm pulling the door open. I'm making my escape.

But then suddenly I am going backwards too. His hands are on me and I'm being dragged back inside the room.

My instinct is to fight with everything I have. Hadn't my mother taught me that? If I ever found myself in a bad situation I was to fight. To bite. To kick. Do whatever it took to get away. I will not allow this monster to hurt me, or worse rape or kill me.

I kick out. Bucking my leg out in the hope of temporarily maiming my abductor; only he manages to move behind me. I snap my head back repeatedly, in the hope that I can smack my skull against his face. So that I can crack his nose wide open.

He is so much stronger than me.

He slams me down.

And it's my nose that cracks open. As I land face down on the floor. My face breaking my fall, my nose exploding on impact.

CRACK.

It's broken. I can taste the warm, acrid blood as it trickles down into my mouth. The pain inside my head excruciating.

Then another pain.

A sharp scratch of a needle.

Followed by a rush of warmth inside me as my body goes completely numb.

When the darkness comes for me this time, I welcome it wholly.

32

Sherrie can't remember the last time she felt this drunk. She doesn't keep alcohol in the house as a rule these days. Because she doesn't like the pull of it, knowing it is there. Taunting her, tempting her. The hold it has over her. Still, after all these years.

She'd found the small bottle of brandy shoved in the back of the cupboard. Half-empty remnants of what had been left after she'd made last year's Christmas cake. Out of sight, and forgotten, until today, when she had drunk it down in one.

Willing the numbness to come for her.

The disconnect that she so desperately needed as she tried to blank it all out. The last time she'd been drunk had been just before Kayla. Back in the days when she used to pour alcohol on her problems as if it would somehow make them dissolve. And for a short time, mostly, they disappeared for a while. Until Sherrie inevitably sobered up; after that they all came roaring back.

If anything, her problems had felt worse then. More magnified. More depressing.

Drinking had been Sherrie's vice. She probably would have continued too, drinking herself into daily stupors. Stuck in that cycle until she died. If it hadn't been for Kayla. Having Kayla had literally saved Sherrie's life. Her beautiful daughter had given her a second chance. She had given her a reason to stop drinking. A reason to finally exist.

And Sherrie had taken it gladly. Living her life vicariously through her daughter. She hadn't needed anything or anyone else since. Only now Kayla was gone and Sherrie had needed a drink.

She had savoured it too, that first mouthful, that long forgotten familiar burn at the back of her throat. Desperately needed it, something to take the edge from her dark mood. The past couple of days had all been too much for her. Every time she closed her eyes she pictured Kayla crying, her face stricken, in pain.

It was breaking her.

Her heart physically ached for her daughter. And the brandy hadn't been nearly enough.

It hadn't numbed her, it hadn't given her the oblivion that she so badly craved. She had still been able to feel everything. Every inch of deep hollowness that swirled aimlessly inside of her. Every sharp jolt of agonising pain as she thought about her daughter not being here, at home with her, where she belonged. She needed more.

So she had driven herself to the nearest off-licence, buying herself a couple of bottles of wine. Wine would do it. That had always been her drink of choice.

And it is starting to work, her vision blurry, her head feeling fuzzy, but being drunk doesn't feel anything like how it used to feel. There is no euphoria. No feeling of triumph or relief. Drunk and miserable, forced to sit alone with her demons in her empty kitchen, Sherrie stares down at the photos spread out all over the table.

Hundreds of photographs. All documenting her daughter's entire childhood.

This is the Kayla she wants to see when she closes her eyes. Her happy, little girl smiling back at her.

Sherrie picks up the photograph of Kayla sitting in a sink full of bubbles in the kitchen. Her chubby cheeks glowing red. Too red for it to be just the temperature of the water. Sherrie remembers how Kayla had been teething then. Her first stubborn tooth breaking through her gums.

She'd screamed so much that Richard had joked that their child had a flip-top head. And Sherrie hadn't slept for almost a week as she'd comforted her. As she'd writhed around in constant wild pain. So much so, that Sherrie was certain that she could physically feel it too. The agony her daughter had endured as her teeth pierced through her gums. How raw and consuming it had been. Because that's what mothers did. They took on their children's pain.

And if there was any way Sherrie could have taken it away for her, even just for a second, a moment. She would have. No matter what it had cost her.

She picks up another photograph, and Kayla is older in this one. The writing scrawled on the back of the photo states simply 'Kayla – ten months old'. She is standing in this one, her plump little legs strong beneath her as she bravely takes her very first steps. And Sherrie remembers showing Kayla how to hold on to the handle of her trolley, full of coloured building blocks. And how Kayla had brushed her hand away, point-blank refusing her help as she moved on her own unaided.

And in this photo, Sherrie can really see it. The pure determination that shines out from Kayla's eyes to do it all by herself. That makes her smile. Even though she knows there is nothing really to smile about now. Maybe there won't be ever again.

Maybe these photos are all she will have left of her daughter.

Kayla was always so determined, so headstrong, even way back then. Even when she was so tiny.

She had hit every one of the milestones early according to the vast collection of baby books that Sherrie had lived by.

Her first crawl, her first steps, her first tooth. All reached weeks, sometimes months, in advance. Much earlier than your average child.

But then Kayla was far from average. And Sherrie liked to think that her daughter got her strength from her.

Always so fiercely independent. Always so determined to prove herself.

And that should give her hope, shouldn't it? Only somehow it just makes everything feel so much worse.

Sherrie pulls out the crumpled, yellow photograph from the middle of the pile. Every single one of these photos is precious to Sherrie. Always. But even more so now. But this one, this first photo of Kayla as a baby is the one that means the most. She flips it over and stares at the black rushed handwriting scribbled on the back: '15 November 2006'.

Sixteen years ago? How can that be? Because it feels like it was a lifetime ago, yet she remembers that day as if it had been yesterday.

Blinking away her tears she turns it back over and stares down at the image.

Kayla as a newborn baby, wrapped in a yellow blanket, just a few hours old. And she's lying draped across Sherrie's chest. Her big, blue eyes open and staring right up at Sherrie's face. Her expression full of wonderment. Completely coherent, as if she's completely aware of her surroundings. As if she's taking it all in.

And she's looking up at Sherrie with her eyes as if she's talking.

'I see you, Mummy! I see you.'

And that was exactly what it had felt like. In that one, single, breathtaking moment, Sherrie had felt as if she was finally being seen.

It felt like, right up until then she'd been holding her breath. Waiting for her life to really begin. With Kayla in her arms, it finally had.

Sherrie closes her eyes, willing herself to remember every single second of that moment. The click and flash of the camera. Richard had taken the photo.

But he was no longer her Richard by then.

She'd lost him. The Richard she'd known and loved before everything had gone so bad. Before she'd found out the truth about him. Before she'd found out what he'd done.

His betrayal.

That's when it had all started to become so tainted and rotten between them. That's when the decay and maggots had set in. It had been there ever since. Growing silently between them. Festering.

Sherrie shudders, just the thought of being anywhere near him physically after all of that had made her skin crawl. They'd slept in separate beds ever since.

For the whole of their marriage. There are no photos of him, not a single one.

Sherrie made sure of that.

Mentally and physically trying to shut him out. Even though she knew they'd never be free of each other. Not all the time Kayla bound them both together. The photos were all of her. Her and Kayla. Mother and daughter. Her precious baby. Her entire world.

Sherrie had never felt a love like it, before or since.

When that first photo had been taken, the sudden glare of the flash made Kayla wince and cry out loudly. And Sherrie had cupped the soft flesh of her palm over Kayla's eyes in protection and promised her sweet baby daughter that she'd never let any harm come to her.

That she'd never let anyone hurt her.

She had failed miserably on all accounts now though, hadn't she, because Kayla has gone.

Gathering up the photos in a pile, Sherrie reaches for the box. She's had enough of reminiscing. Her vision is blurred through her tears now, and her reflexes are slow. And she doesn't register that she's knocked her wine glass over until it's too late.

The dark red liquid pools out across the table, soaking all Sherrie's precious photographs in its wake.

'NO!' Sherrie screeches. Jumping to her feet, leaning across the table and scooping the worst affected ones up. Shaking them desperately, to shake the wine from them. As the faces blur, the corners of the paper curl in.

Already she knows that they are ruined.

Soaked and sticky. They clump together in her hand.

Sherrie picks up her favourite one from the pile and cries.

Staring down at the very first photo of her with Kayla.

The most precious one of them all.

Praying that there is some way she can salvage it. That she can take it to one of those specialists and that they can restore it. Because it's the only one of these that she's got.

No! It's not.

Relief floods through her then. She had had a copy made. For Kayla's locket that Sherrie had given to her on her fifteenth birthday. The locket that Sherrie had so painstakingly, lovingly chosen to put photos of the two of them inside. Wanting it to be special. Wanting Kayla to cherish it.

Only Kayla rarely wore the thing, she said it was too big, too clumpy. Too old-fashioned looking.

No one wears gold anymore, Mum! It's all about silver.

Even though Kayla didn't wear it, it pleased Sherrie somewhat that it sat pride of place on her bedside table. That Kayla must have looked at it some nights. It gave Sherrie hope that in time she'd grow to love it; she'd realise how special it was.

Sherrie didn't recall seeing it in her room though, when she'd gone through it, cleaning it from top to bottom. When she'd sorted through all Kayla's things. On the day of the break-in.

She hadn't seen it when the police had searched it either. In search of clues as to where Kayla may have gone.

Her stomach lurches then.

Recalling how relieved she'd felt that whoever had broken into their home hadn't touched anything.

She'd reassured the police of that too.

That there hadn't been any damage done, and nothing had been taken.

But what if it had?

Because whoever had been in her house had been in Kayla's room. They'd been searching through her things.

What if someone took her locket?

33

Kayla's room is ransacked. All Sherrie's previous efforts of sorting out the chaos has been completely undone.

Only this time, Sherrie doesn't care that the place is wrecked. She no longer cares about the state of the house at all. None of that is important right now. Deep in her gut, even before she'd started ripping the place apart, she'd already known that Kayla's locket would be missing.

She'd known it even as she pulled out all the drawers, the cupboards, the wardrobes. Emptying the contents into one massive, big heap in the middle of the floor, even before she began sifting through all of Kayla's things. Searching inside bags and pockets.

It isn't here.

Whoever broke in took it. She is sure of it.

Worse than that, Sherrie couldn't find the letters that she'd kept. The letters that no one else knew she had, not even Richard.

The letters that incriminated him.

She'd hidden them in the same bedroom drawer as the passport. Right at the back underneath the lining. Certain that they would be safe there. That no one would ever know she was in possession of them.

She'd only thought to check that they were still there now. While she'd thought of them.

They are gone. Sherrie can't find them. Kayla must have taken them too. She must have read them. She must have wondered what they had meant.

Just the thought of them falling into the wrong hands fills her with dread.

What a mess.

The pain in Sherrie's heart is back with a vengeance, magnified now that the wine she drank earlier has worn off. It feels stronger and more agonising than ever. It isn't fair. The photos are ruined and the locket is missing and, worst of all, her daughter is gone. Sherrie just wants her back. She wants to rewind the past few days and start again. To have her baby back, here with her, where she belongs.

Sherrie loses it.

She lashes out wildly, hitting out at the mattress on Kayla's bed. Punching the pillows with a ferocity she hadn't realised was in her. All the while screaming at the top of her lungs as her tears start to fall. What did she do to deserve this? How is any of this bloody fair? Finally, exhausted, she collapses into a heap on the floor.

The floorboard creaks beneath the weight of her. Reminding her of the diary that she had found and stuffed back down there. She hadn't wanted Kayla to know that she had found it. She hadn't wanted to add anything else to Kayla's already long list of gripes about her.

Only Kayla hadn't come home, had she?

And in amongst all the chaos, Sherrie had forgotten about it. Now, just the thought of anyone else finding it, of it ever getting in to the hands of the national press, fills Sherrie with dread. It would break her heart for people to think those things that Kayla had written about her held any real truth.

Sherrie claws at the carpet, unable to bear the thought of it.

How Kayla had documented how her father was questioning her about someone watching her. How her mother deliberately hid her passport from her. How it made them sound like awful parents, but that wasn't the case at all.

Perhaps the letter was there, tucked inside one of the pages. Perhaps Sherrie had missed it.

She pulls the wooden floorboard free and breathes a sigh of relief as she sees the diary is still there, but there are no letters inside.

It is a small mercy that she had been the only one to find the diary, at least. That no one else would ever need to know the awful words about her that were scrawled inside its pages.

They are good parents.

She is a good mother.

Sherrie wants it gone.

She wants the diary out of her house, for good.

Opening the door of the log burner, Sherrie's vision blurs as fresh tears fill her eyes.

Her hands shake with wild fury as she strikes the match. Watching the tiny flicker of the orange flames dance around as she holds it to the fire-lighter and it ignites. And she is mesmerised by its tenacity. How small but mighty the flame appears.

The real power it holds.

Sometimes Sherrie feels a bit like that too. How people often underestimate her. Even on her lowest of days, she still continues on, navigating her way through the bullshit. Surviving any way she can.

It's what she's always done.

And she will get through this too.

Holding Kayla's diary in her hands one last time, Sherrie throws it in to the fire and closes the door of the log burner.

This was all Richard's fault, she thinks as the rage she feels for him burns inside of her still. It grows stronger every year. Every time she thinks about what he did. It is his fault Sherrie can't trust anyone. He made her like this. Worried sick that something might happen to her daughter. Worried sick that someone would take her from them.

Sherrie tried to put it out of her head; she'd tried to pretend that it hadn't happened. But it had happened.

She couldn't forgive him.

And she had grown to loathe him over the years, aware of the distance that had crept in-between them and pushed them further and further apart. It was as if they were strangers, living together in the same house, but with completely separate lives. Maybe that was what marriage became eventually for most people.

Kayla was the glue, she kept them both bound so tightly together. Sherrie had thought that they'd hidden it well from her. The indifference that they felt for one another. How the love they'd once felt for each other had soured over the years, that these days they barely even tolerated each other. Kayla had felt it though.

She had seen it too. And what's more she had documented it all down in her diary. The arguments that she hadn't thought Kayla had heard. The times they'd got out of hand. The raised voices, the raised hands. Sherrie closes her eyes and feels shame wash over her that her daughter had been subjected to that. She had tried so hard to protect her from that the most. The physical fighting. The hits. The slaps. The punches. It is all written here, for anyone now to find and read.

She watches intently as the growing flames lick at the pages and the fire finally takes hold. The intense heat radiating out and warming her face, while inside the flames roar ferociously as the fire gathers its momentum. The outcome inevitable now. The fire is winning, annihilating all trace of the words inside, all those short angry paragraphs that Kayla had poured out. Sherrie eyes the blackened edges of the book as they curl in on themselves, getting smaller, the fire raging its way through it until it has burned away its entire existence.

As if the words on those pages had never existed.

The diary is gone.

Replaced with molten red, burning hot ashes.

34

He's here again. And he's angry with me for the last time when I tried to escape.

I can tell by the way his eyes burn into mine, telling me to heed a warning.

My earlier bravado is gone now. I can't hold his gaze. I know what he is capable of. I know that he will hurt me. This time, when he brings my food, he makes a point of shutting the door and locking it behind him, before he crosses the room and places the tray down next to my bed.

I scramble backwards, pushing myself up against the wall in a bid to stay as far away from him as possible.

'Who are you?' I ask, my eyes fixed on him. Trying to work it out. Do I know him? Because there's something about his stance that tells me that I do. Something familiar about him, even though I can't see his face.

'Why are you keeping me here? What do you want from me?' I manage to find my voice, but it's so small and the words tremble as they leave my mouth, because I am terrified of his answer.

He snatched me from the street, he stuck a needle in my

arm and drugged me, and now he's keeping me here, locked away in this makeshift prison.

Is he going to do things to me? Is he going to act out his own sick, depraved fantasies on me?

He doesn't answer me.

He just nods down to my food, instructing me to eat.

And I do. Because I don't want to rile him and give him any reason to hurt me.

He stands over me waiting for me to make a start.

My third meal of the day. Pasta.

It's like clockwork.

That's the pattern. That's the way I work out what time of the day it is. What day it is full stop.

Breakfast: porridge made with milk. Lunch: fried eggs on toast with a small scraping of butter and a glass of water. Dinner: congealed pasta in a thick, bland tomato sauce. All of it served on paper plates, along with one plastic spoon: he's taking no chances.

It's been three days.

And I think I've worked out how to stop myself from gagging from the smell of the bucket while I eat. I've held it in all day. Holding my bowels until I finish this last meal, no matter how hard my stomach cramps.

He waits patiently for me to finish every mouthful before he takes the tray away and leaves me to finally use the bucket.

And it's only when I hear the final turn of the key that I can go.

That I can empty the contents of my stomach.

Though when he returns to empty the soiled contents of the bucket, the smell somehow lingers in the room.

It's on me, engrained in my skin. The smell of my own piss and shit combined with my musty, rank body odour. The thought of it making me feel itchy and dirty and tainted. I long to wash myself. To bathe in clean water. To feel the steady jets of the shower head massage my skin.

But part of me hopes that he can smell it too. That I'll repel him and he'll leave me alone. That's what I'm praying when he places the clean bucket down in the corner of the room again. Then he stands there staring at me.

His eyes wander. His gaze sweeps over me, taking in the sight of me.

Please, God, No. I pray to myself silently. *Please don't hurt me.*

It's only when he leaves for the third time, locking me in for the night, that I sink back down on to the mattress, full of relief that he didn't do anything to me.

That, for now, he's leaving me be.

I'm ready to close my eyes.

To will myself to try to sleep, because sleep is the only thing that gives me respite from this nightmare I am living.

It's only then do I see what he left on the end of my bed.

A blank piece of paper and the orange crayon. I reach out to pick them up and holding them in my hands, checking that they're real.

He is giving me something to do. He knows that if he doesn't I will slowly go out of my mind.

I think of my mother. Holding an image of her in my head, because she is the one person who is keeping me going through all of this. I remind myself of her strength. Of her sheer determination to keep me safe.

Of her love for me.

Because she has always loved me so fiercely and I'm counting on her not to give up on me. Only with each passing hour the strong image I have in my head of her slowly diminishes. Replaced by the visual of a sad, broken woman.

She'll be lost without me. She will be fearing the worst.

That I am dead.

She doesn't know that being dead is not the worst thing that could happen to me.

Being here is. Being his prisoner.

I'm trapped, alone, in this decrepit room. Trapped inside the darkest places inside my own head. With no TV to keep me occupied. No books to read. Nothing to do or see. I'm just here in limbo, in this one room. Left only to my thoughts.

Slowly going mad.

Dear Mum, I'm okay.

I drag the crayon across the paper. Writing the same sentence over and over again.

LIES. All lies.

I'm okay. I'm okay. I'm okay.

I don't stop until the page is filled with rows of bright orange scrawl and there are tears running down my cheeks. My body is shaking as I fold the letter up and slide it underneath the tiny gap beneath the door.

Even though deep down, I know that he won't send it to her, that my mum will never get to read it. But it feels like hope. It feels like a connection with the outside world. I lie back down on the bed and close my eyes. Imagining him reading it. I'm sure he will.

Those cold beady eyes scanning my words.

Something niggles at me then, teetering just on the edge of my consciousness, and I'm not sure what it is.

His eyes. The balaclava.

He has covered his face.

He's worn it each time he's come into the room and that can only mean one of two things. That I know him? Do I know him? Is that why he's so desperate to hide his identity from me? Or is he just stopping me from seeing what he actually looks like, so that I can't describe him to the police. If and when I ever get out of here.

He's going to let me go, I realise.

Either way, that's why he's hiding his face from me, because he's going to let me go. Eventually.

That's my lifeline right there.

The tiny bit of hope that I hold on to.

One day, I will get out of here.

I will get away from him.

And hope is all I have right now.

Hope is what I am clinging on to for dear life.

35

'I thought that she was on the game. Dressed like that.' Jean Ikes purses her lips as if trying to dispel a bitter taste from her mouth. 'Walking the streets at that ungodly hour. Because you know, sometimes they come up as far as this way. Those girls that work down by the canal, under the bridge. They follow the money, don't they? That's what my Harry says. And she looked like she could give that lot a run for their money let me tell you. Her skirt barely covered her bottom. But then, that's the fashion these days it seems.'

Jean has the officer's full attention as she recites what she'd seen the night that Kayla Goldman had gone missing.

'Girls seem to put everything out there on display. There's no sense of dignity or decorum anymore. In my day we had a bit of class. We liked to maintain an air of mystery, you know. We wore our dresses tight enough to show that we were women, but loose enough to show that we were also ladies—'

'And can you talk me through exactly what it is that you think you saw in the early hours of Saturday morning, Mrs Ikes? From the beginning,' the police officer interrupts.

Causing Jean to bristle, recognising the impatience in the

younger man's tone. Almost as if he was deliberately hurrying her along. That's another problem with the younger generation, as far as she is concerned, a distinct lack of manners. This one looks like he is young enough to still be delivering her newspapers.

It doesn't cost anything to be polite and patient, but now isn't a time to educate him. She needs to stay focused. Because what she had seen in the early hours of Saturday morning may have been important. She doesn't want to leave anything out.

'Well, now. Let me see. From the beginning. Okay, I came downstairs to get a drink. I should really take one up with me, but I don't sleep that well most nights anyway you see. I suffer terribly with insomnia. And the pills the doctor prescribes don't even touch the sides. They just leave me feeling a bit confused and fuzzy. So sometimes I don't take them. But then I get it in the other ear... Because my Harry, he's a snorer you see. So, I often end up getting up several times during the night, just so that I don't end up murdering him.' Jean adds a nervous chuckle as she nods down at the police officer's poised pen on his notepad. Noticing that he has stopped writing. 'That's a joke by the way! Just in case I've incriminated myself for plotting my husband's demise if, Heaven forbid, it ever came true, and my Harry popped his clogs.'

She coughs then and clears her throat, aware that she is going off track again. She has a habit of doing that, especially when she is nervous.

'Anyway, I recognised her. The girl from the TV. That wee girl they were doing the appeal about, the one that's gone missing.' Jean clears her throat as she gets up from her chair and walks to the sink and points out of the kitchen window to the pathway that runs along the front of her house.

'She was standing just over there.'

'And what time was that roughly?'

'Oh, I can do better than roughly. It was precisely

12.37 a.m. I know because I looked at the clock on the oven and I thought to myself, what a silly girl. Out there on her own at this hour. Wearing that ridiculously short skirt. Anyway, it turns out she wasn't on her own. She had a friend with her.'

'A friend. And did you manage to get a good look at them too?'

'No, sorry.' She shakes her head regretfully. 'It was dark, and from here... well it was more just the silhouette.' She falters, her cheeks glowing a deep red. Wishing she could give him more.

'You didn't have your glasses on? But you recognised the girl?' the officer asks, pursing his lips.

And Jean bristles again, because there is something very patronising now about the way he is looking at her. As if he was somehow bemused at the irony of having a witness who couldn't actually see properly without her glasses.

'I only got up for a drink. I don't need to put them on for that. I know my way down the stairs. Though Harry will tell you different. He often jokes that I'm blind as a bat without my glasses. He reckons my sight has got worse with age. He keeps nagging me to go and get another eye test done but I keep putting it off. It's not nice to admit that everything starts falling apart when you get to our age. Nothing seems to work as well as it used to. Everything aches and creak—'

'But you are certain that the young woman you saw was Kayla Goldman? Did she attempt to fight the person off? Did you see her struggle to get away? Did she seem distressed to you in any way?'

'No. Not really...'

'Not really?' The officer raises his eyes. And Jean picks up on the irritation in the officer's tone as he questions her.

'Well, you see, the thing is, it's been bothering me. What I saw,' Jean says, feeling teary, because she knows now that she'd made a grave error that night, hadn't she? Seeing things that weren't there. Not really seeing things properly at all.

'I can't stop thinking about her shoes.'

'Her shoes?'

'Yes. When her "friend" was helping her to stay upright and led her away, her shoes were dragging across the footpath. I remember thinking to myself how those shoes will be wrecked. Scuffed beyond repair. And shoes can be so expensive nowadays...'

An unsettling feeling of unease rises from deep within her. Rippling through her like waves, as she continues, 'And I keep wondering why she wasn't picking her feet up. Because she was bending down and fiddling with her shoes one minute. Yet seconds later...' She pauses and frowns as she tries to remember exactly what it was that had cast her doubts. 'She could barely stand up. It was almost as if she'd suddenly lost consciousness. God knows how much she must have drunk to get herself in that state. It would have taken me at least ten Martini Rossos.' Jean stares at the officer, waiting for him to put her mind at ease. To tell her she is over-thinking it. That nothing untoward had happened here.

But he didn't say any of that. She can see it on his face, how he thinks it too.

Something isn't quite right.

'Do you think it was her? The girl on the TV that's gone missing?' she asks, her voice breaking as a wave of helplessness washes over her.

The officer doesn't answer. He doesn't need to. Jean can see it written on his face. It was the girl from the TV.

And the chances were that she had been abducted, right in front of Jean. And all Jean had done was stood there sipping her water at the kitchen sink, watching and judging the poor thing on how short her bloody skirt was.

'My Harry is right, isn't he?' Jean's voice is small now and she is shaking uncontrollably. 'I do need to get my eyes checked again.'

'If you could just try and go back and remember, Jean. If you can give me anything at all. Eye colour, hair colour. What the man who led Kayla away was wearing?'

'Oh no, it wasn't a man who was with her. I may not have had my glasses on, so that I couldn't see any of their features, but even I know the difference between a man and a woman. And it was a woman.'

36

'Don't you care?' Sherrie slurs as Richard comes into the kitchen.

Richard had been out all evening. Walking, he'd told her. He needed to go out for air.

Implying that being here in this house meant that he couldn't breathe. That he couldn't get his head straight.

Well, what about her? She needed to get her head straight too.

Only she was forced to do it alone, even now when Richard was finally home, because Sherrie knew that it wouldn't be long until he did another disappearing act and went back upstairs, hiding away in his bedroom for the rest of the evening, away from her, gawping uselessly at his iPad as if it somehow held all the answers to Kayla's whereabouts. That's what he'd been reduced to.

That's how he thought that he would solve all of this. By scrolling through endless news articles about Kayla and the thousands of comments that had been left on social media. Choosing the comforting words of strangers over her.

'Not just about Kayla? About me too? What about me? I

was out all morning driving around, trying to see if I could find her. Knocking on doors. Asking people if they'd seen her. Sticking poxy posters up on lampposts,' Sherrie mumbles. Her words almost incomprehensible as she nods down to the missing posters on the table that she had printed off on their home printer. With her phone number splashed across the top of the page. 'What have you done? Apart from keep disappearing for hours on end, and when you're here all you do is sit on your bloody iPad hoping something will jump out at you. Like that stupid thing is going to give you all the answers. You should be helping me. You should be comforting me. But you can't, can you? Because this is all your fault, and you know it!'

'You're drunk! Again,' Richard spits, not biting to Sherrie's bitter comments like he knows she wants him to. Instead, he stares at the empty bottles that sit at the table beside her. The look of disdain in his eyes. Knowing full well her pattern of old. Have a few drinks and then let the toxic poison spew out.

Aimed always at him.

That would make her feel better, lashing out at someone. Anyone. For this awful situation they were now in. And Sherrie needs to vent. She needs to scream and shout and blame someone for the way that she feels. Empty. Desperate. Beside herself.

She just wants Richard to understand. Even if he can't fix this, she just wants him to show her some compassion. Some support for just once. Only, already he has turned on his heel and begun busying himself in the kitchen, making himself a cup of tea.

One cup, she notices. He's making a hot drink for himself, not her. He doesn't give a shit about her or what she is going through. He should be stepping up and trying to make her feel better. Instead he's moving around the kitchen, acting as if she's invisible to him, as if she's not even there.

Ignoring her.

Sherrie sucks at her teeth, glaring at him then because Richard is so good at that, isn't he? Trying to make her feel like shit by ignoring her. Giving her the silent treatment. *Well fuck him!*

Sherrie pours herself another drink, draining the last of the bottle. Even though she doesn't want it. Even though she feels sick. She knows how much it winds him up, her drinking. How it always used to set him on edge, all those years ago when drinking was pretty much all Sherrie did. Before Kayla came along.

But Kayla isn't here, and Sherrie's heart is broken. Split in half, fractured beyond repair. Right now, all that she wants from him is some kind of reaction. Some sign that he cares. It's the very least he can give her, isn't it? It's the very least she deserves.

But this is Richard's way. This show of passive-aggressive behaviour, so often his weapon of choice. To purposely goad and rile her. It is working.

Sherrie smarts. This is who they are now. This is who they have become. This sad bitter couple sitting in an empty house, clinging on for what?

There is nothing left now.

'You can't just switch off, Richard. You can't just pretend that this isn't happening. That Kayla hasn't gone—'

'I'm not the one pretending, Sherrie!' Richard starts. His voice rising just a few notches higher than he intends, she thinks as she watches him quickly compose himself. 'Of course I care, of course I want to find her. Of course I want to have her home, here and safe. Have you ever thought that maybe this is actually your fault? That you've done this? You caused this. Before you start trying to push the blame on others. On me.' Richard's eyes flash fury then. Having started, he intends to finish.

'Always smothering that girl, Sherrie. You've done it all her life. Wrapping her up in bubble wrap and doing everything for her, to the point where she couldn't breathe. You're too much, Sherrie. You've always been too bloody much!'

'I love her! That's not a crime,' Sherrie screeches defensively.

Richard's words cutting deep. She had just read that in Kayla's diary too. Words straight from her daughter's own mouth. How Sherrie had smothered her. That sometimes she couldn't breathe. Had Kayla voiced it to him too?

Is that what they'd been arguing about in the kitchen that morning she disappeared? Sherrie had felt the tension; she'd suspected that they'd been speaking about her.

'Oh, I see! She told you, didn't she? that she found her passport in my room, hidden in my bedside cabinet. That's what I walked in on the morning she disappeared. The pair of you conspiring against me. I bet you loved that. Kayla making accusations like that. I bet you didn't shut it down either. I bet you made out that it was all me. That I am the one trying to keep her here with me. The only thing I'm guilty of when it comes to that girl, is love.'

'Love? You don't know the meaning of the word, Sherrie. You treat that girl like she's your possession. Like she's so fragile, Sherrie. As if the tiniest thing might break her. As if she hasn't got her own brain, her own mind. When she's more than capable of thinking for herself.' Richard stands and stares at Sherrie. 'Yes, she found it. She knew that you took her passport and hid it from her. She knew,' he says, raising his voice. Angry now.

'And that suits you, Sherrie. That she didn't go. That she had to stay home with you instead. Because that's what you want, to keep her close. And all of this charade you're putting on now. Going on national TV and appealing for our missing daughter, when the truth is, Sherrie, that Kayla probably ran away. She probably couldn't get away from here, from you, faster.'

'You really think that Kayla has run away from home? You really think that she would do that to us?' Sherrie shakes her head.

She doesn't believe him for a second.

Richard isn't fooling her. There is more to this. He knows it too.

This isn't a case of their daughter running away from home, but maybe it is just easier for him to believe than the alternative. He is lying to himself. He is in denial.

And she is about to say all of that to him, only Richard isn't done yet.

'Not to us, no! To you. I don't blame her if she has run away. In fact, I envy her that. Good for her. Good for her for finally seeing through you and your manipulative, conniving ways. I only wish that I had done the same myself all those years ago. I should have run as fast as I could, as far as I could away from you!'

There is silence now.

Sherrie stares at Richard in disbelief, as if she has just been smacked. As if the air has just been punched from her lungs. He really means it. She can see by his eyes. He means every word of it.

So this is how he has always felt about her. She had always known it anyway. Deep down. It had always been there, silently festering between them. Only now, finally, after all these years he is openly admitting it.

But God, it hurt even still. They both know what Richard is referring to. How he'd been planning to leave Sherrie for someone else. For that bitch. The girl he'd cheated on her with. How Sherrie had refused to let him go. She'd refused to accept his rejection of her.

She'd done everything in her power to keep him with her. Whatever it took.

'I only stayed with you for Kayla's sake,' Richard says, the final nail hammered in the coffin now.

Sherrie can't speak. She can't find her voice. The alcohol she'd consumed threatens to rise at the back of her throat. Shocked at the ferocity of the words that spewed from his mouth, for his hatred of her.

She knows that he means it too; he isn't just saying this to hurt her. He means it. He shouldn't have stayed.

Getting up from her chair, Sherrie sags, hunches over, defeated now as she walks from the room, from him.

Kayla has gone.

Richard only stayed because Sherrie had forced him to.

Because of Kayla.

And now she has lost them both.

37

Tessa had slept.

She isn't sure how long for, but when she opens her eyes her head is still fuzzy, still disorientated from the sleeping pills she'd taken, she can see it is dark. She can hear Amelia moving around downstairs. That was something at least, she is still here, she didn't walk out. Earlier they'd had the biggest argument they had ever had, and the truth is that Tessa isn't sure that they can come back from this one.

'How can you ask me that? How can you even think that I could do something like that to an innocent child?' Tessa had said, a shocked expression on her face at Amelia's accusation. She felt as if she'd been slapped.

'After everything that happened to me. Is that what you really think? That I took his daughter to make him pay? You really think that I'm that person? That I'm capable of doing that?'

'Of course I don't,' Amelia said then, only they both heard the waver in her voice. Tessa could tell that Amelia was going back on her words, on her allegations because she didn't want to hurt Tessa's feelings. But it had already been too late for that. It was out there, floating in the air silently between them.

Pushing them both even further apart.

Amelia didn't believe her.

She thought that Tessa had something to do with Kayla Goldman's disappearance.

That she had done this.

That she was as bad as him.

'Of course I don't think that,' Amelia had repeated, and Tessa had seen how she was saying it as much to convince herself. It was as if she was trying to make them both believe it.

'You can't blame me for asking though, Tessa. You have been hiding things from me. And lying to me. And you were there that night, weren't you? Outside his house. The night that his daughter went missing. The police will find out.'

'Find out what?'

'That you have a grudge against this man, that you've been stalking him. That you think he's someone else...'

'That I had something to do with his daughter going missing?' Tessa said, feeling it then. Amelia treading so carefully with her words. She hadn't been outright accusing her, but laying down a warning. The police won't be as lenient. They'll dig deeper. They'll find out everything. Everything Tessa is hiding.

'I get it, Tess. You've been through so much. So much horror, so much destruction and all of it leads back to him. I don't know: if you got the chance to make him feel even an ounce of that misery, wouldn't you take it? Wouldn't any one of us take it?'

And there it was.

The sentence that broke Tessa's heart in two. That there's a tiny part of Amelia that considers the possibility that Tessa is capable of doing something like this, to an innocent girl. That's what hurts Tessa the most. After all this time, these past few years, after everything Tessa had told her, Amelia is still questioning her.

She still isn't certain.

What is worse, Tessa doesn't even know herself anymore.

Had she taken her chance at revenge?

Maybe Amelia is right and she is capable of doing exactly that. Of hurting him, just like he had once hurt her.

Only, part of her wants to believe that she couldn't act so depraved. That she isn't anything like him. She just wished that she could remember those few vital hours from that night, that she'd somehow managed to block out of her mind.

'If you really got it, if you really understood, you wouldn't even ask me that. You wouldn't even think it,' Tessa had said then, shaking her head defensively.

'Then tell me! Stop shutting me out,' Amelia had started crying, trying to justify her doubt. Trying to make things right again between them, desperate to put an end to the madness, to the arguing.

Only this time she can't. They both know that. The void between them is too big.

'You can't have it both ways, Tessa. You can't expect me to believe you, to hang on to every word you say when you are still keeping things from me.'

She was right.

Tessa knew it.

She nodded.

'Okay. I will. I will tell you everything, I promise. But not now. Later. I'm so tired, Amelia. I'm so drained from the past few days that I can't think straight. I need to sleep!' Tessa said, exhausted from it all. From the thoughts that spiralled around and around her head. From thinking non-stop about him. And then from Amelia. From her second guessing her motives. From her questioning Tessa's state of mind. Tessa wasn't strong enough, not yet.

If Amelia kept chipping away at her, she might just break completely. She might just split wide open. Then all her darkest secrets would come tumbling out of her.

And she didn't want Amelia to find out like that.

She wanted to sleep. To rest. So that when she woke, she would feel stronger. She wanted to do this properly.

Now, the bedroom door creeks open and Tessa sees Amelia's face peering in. Checking on her. It almost breaks her again, because she can see from Amelia's expression that she only means well.

That she only cares about Tessa. That she only wants her to be alright.

'I'm sorry! I didn't mean to wake you,' Amelia whispers as she tiptoes in the room and places a glass of water down on the bedside cabinet for her.

'You didn't, don't worry. What time is it?' Tessa asks, realising how dark it is. How there's a strip of light spilling in from where Amelia has left the bedroom door open.

'It's gone eight.'

'Eight in the evening? I slept all day?' Tessa says, feeling disorientated, knowing that she's wasted the day away.

She'd taken two sleeping tablets after the row they'd had. Because she knew that she would never have fallen asleep without them otherwise.

'You clearly needed it. You've been out cold for hours.' Amelia smiles.

'I've been thinking about what you said, and you're right. I don't feel like I'm in a good place right now. In my head,' Tessa says, not knowing where to start. But it was time to be honest.

Amelia nods her head, before sitting down on the edge of the bed. And taking Tessa's hand in hers.

'I'm sorry for what I said...' she begins. 'For doubting you...'

It is Tessa's turn to apologise. 'You have nothing to be sorry for, Amelia. I'm the one who's sorry. For all of this. I think maybe I should make an appointment with my doctor,' Tessa says quietly, feeling her words catch in the back of her throat. Unable to hide the disappointment in her voice because she's come full circle. Somehow, she's landed right back at square one again. Going back to the doctors. Asking for more medication, continuing with counselling sessions. Trying to stop all of this madness.

Tessa doesn't want to be sick anymore.

She doesn't want to ruin what she has with Amelia either.

'You're doing the right thing!' Amelia says, squeezing her hand reassuringly. 'That's brave right there. Asking for help. You're not alone, Tessa, you know that, don't you? I am here with you, every step of the way. Whatever you need, okay?'

Tessa nods her head.

'What's that?' Tessa asks, eyeing the white box that Amelia placed down beside the glass of water.

'Your anxiety medication. I found a pack in the back of bathroom cabinet. They're still in date...' Amelia says gently, still treading lightly.

Because Tessa hasn't taken the medication in months. She didn't need to. Amelia doesn't want to offend Tessa, but she can sense she needs help. 'It's just something to take the edge off it all, until you can get to the doctors. You don't have to take them...'

'No, I will. Thanks!'

Amelia stands up. Trying to make light of the gesture and to give Tessa some privacy so that she can decide what she wants to do of her own accord. They both know that this can only come from Tessa now.

'I'll go and make you a sandwich. You're not supposed to take them on an empty stomach.'

'I can get up, you know!' Tessa starts to protest. Only as she tries to, she realises that she still feels a bit woozy after taking the sleeping tablets. Thinking better of it, she lies back down.

'Rest, Tessa. Properly. Stay right there. I am going to look after you,' Amelia says with sincerity. 'I meant it, when I said I was in this for the long haul, Tessa. It's me and you. No matter what.'

Tessa waits until she hears Amelia's feet on the stairs.

Wincing as she pictures her nose bloody, the deep red scratches on her face from just the other day. Full of guilt that she had done that. She had caused all of that.

There are other things Tessa still hasn't told her, too.

Bad things. Things so unbearable that she could barely bring herself to say out loud.

Amelia is right. The tablets will help until she can get to see a doctor.

Doing as she's told, she takes the tablets and swallows them down. Before taking an extra pill for good measure. This relationship is one of the best things that has ever happened to her and Tessa doesn't want to do anything that might ruin it.

If that means getting help and going back on her medication, then so be it.

38

The smell wakes me from my fretful sleep.

I lift my head and realise it's the smell of food that has woken me. The stench of greasy fried eggs that sit on the tray next to my bed. A sudden violent nausea sweeps over me, and I know that I'm going to be sick. I can feel it. That hot, watery bile that threatens to rocket up from the back of my throat.

I swallow it. Forcing it back down.

But I know that it won't stay down for long. Because nothing stays down for long these days.

I am sick. I am really sick.

The food isn't staying inside of me long enough to fill my belly or for me to feel nourished.

I feel so weak.

Weak and tired, yet all I seem to do all day and night is sleep.

It's as if I have been drained of all the energy that was once inside my body.

Part of me is grateful for the sleep. Because it fills the never-ending monotony of time. Because until now, I had no idea how doing absolutely nothing, just existing, just breathing, would feel so completely exhausting.

I stare down at the tray beside the bed, and eye the food.

Examining the runny yellow centres. The brown and crispy whites pooling with grease at the edges is all too much. I slam my hand over my mouth in a bid to keep the vomit down as my stomach swirls, but it's too late. I'm not quick enough.

Leaping from the bed, I barely make it to the already half-full bucket, when I retch loudly. A trail of spittle hangs down from my lips as I try not to look at the bucket's contents. Not to focus on the pungent, stagnant vomit that's already floating at the bottom of the bucket from the last time that I was sick. At the spray of lumps of food and dripping liquid, splashed all up the sides.

Instead, I focus on the length of my hair as it hangs loosely down over my face. And I'm shocked at how long and unruly it has become. Has it really grown that much since I've been here? How long has it been? I have lost all track of time.

Weeks?

I retch again, staring at my knuckles as they turn a bright translucent white as I clutch the sides of the bucket. There's nothing left inside of me now. Nothing coming out but hot stringy strands of bile.

Still my stomach is cramping. Still my throat feels raw.

Even though I know that I'm empty. That I have nothing left to give.

I need a doctor, I cry out.

Because I know that he is on the other side of the door listening.

He is always out there. Listening.

Creeping around. Skulking there.

I need a fucking doctor, I shout. *Can you hear me? I need help.*

I am screaming. Anger spilling out of me. Because I know that he can hear my pleas. That he is out there, just ignoring me.

I muster all the energy inside me that I possess and stand up, banging my fists against the locked door.

I hear him then. Moving.

And for one stupid minute I actually believe that maybe he feels sorry for me. Maybe he knows that I'm really bad this time. That I'm really sick. That I need help.

He's going to help me.

Only the sound of the TV goes on in the other room. And he turns it up. Loud.

Louder.

To drown me out.

No. Please. You need to help me. You need to get me a doctor.

I'm crying now. Sobbing with all I have left as I slide my body down to the floor and rest my head against the door.

Defeated.

Trapped in here, in this godforsaken room, with this heady stink of pungent eggs and vomit.

I could be dying in here and all he'd do is sit there, on the other side of the door, watching TV and just let me.

I need to make him listen; I need to make him do something.

I crawl on my hands and knees, back to the mattress.

Lying down I pull the blanket up over my head.

An idea coming to me.

What if I get so sick that I came close to death?

He'd have no choice then, would he?

He'd have to call me a doctor then.

That's how I'll do it. That's how I'll get myself out of here.

On my terms.

I'll stop eating the food he brings me; I'll force myself to not eat anything at all. I won't even drink water. The tiniest part of me isn't sure if I'm fighting against him or playing straight into his hands. If ending up dead isn't his plan all along.

It's a risk, but if it means that there's a chance I can get away from here, from him, then I'll willingly take it.

My mind is made up. I pull the blanket up over my head and cry myself to sleep.

39

Opening her eyes, Sherrie stares up at the ceiling. She has slept. That is something. She'd been so drunk she must have passed out, and she's grateful for that much at least. Awake now, the unease lingers with her, and there's a tightness in her chest. Her head feels foggy, her thoughts cloudy, but it hits her all the same, with its full ferocity. The devastating reality that Kayla is gone.

It's groundhog day. Another day waking to relive her nightmare. Each day that she wakes it feels more painful, more brutal than the last. Her tears start to fall as she listens to Richard moving around downstairs. The kettle boiling, cups clanging together noisily as he busies making breakfast.

Breakfast! When was the last time she even ate? She winces, recalling his spiteful, callous words last night. Good old Richard. The trooper. The bastard.

Doing what he does best, what he's spent years doing. Carrying on like nothing's happened. Sherrie despises him for it. For how weak he is. For how pathetic he has become. Staying with her all this time when deep down he just never had the guts to walk away.

Because that would mean walking away from Kayla too.

Sherrie hates him more now in this one moment than ever before. Glad that she no longer has to wake up next to him. Glad that they haven't slept together in years. She is also scared to death of what lies ahead of her. That *this* might be their future, their reality. The two of them rattling around this godforsaken house. This soulless and heartless empty shell of a home, is nothing without Kayla here with them.

Sherrie couldn't bear it. She can't even think about it.

Hearing the doorbell chime, she gets out of bed, grateful for the distraction of having something to do, as she wraps her dressing gown around her. Hugging it tightly to her, listening as Richard goes to answer the front door. The sound of muffled male voices. DI Jenson and a family liaison officer.

There has been an update in the investigation, she hears one of the officers say. From the tones of their voices, she knows that they are not here to deliver good news.

She can feel it in the pit of her stomach, deep in her gut.

They haven't found Kayla.

They don't know where she is.

'Sherrie!' Richard calls, just as Sherrie makes her way down the stairs.

As she passes, she takes in the sight of the montage of framed prints that twist their way down the stairs, the drunken memory of red wine spilling out across the table, flashing inside her head. This is all she has left now, she thinks. The box of treasured photographs of her and Kayla are completely ruined. Kayla's locket is gone, she remembers. Someone took it.

FLASH. Just like a photograph, blink and you'd miss it. That's how Sherrie feels about Kayla's entire childhood. Somehow she'd shut her eyes for just a few seconds and when she'd opened them again her baby was all grown up.

Sherrie had always known that it was coming. That one day Kayla would grow up and naturally want to move on. Become an adult and gain her own independence. Away from home. Away from her. Sherrie had always made a point to try and embrace every moment, to try and soak it all up and stay present.

God, if only Sherrie could have kept her small, because those years had been the very best years.

She stares at the photo of five-year-old Kayla building sand-castles on Littlehampton beach, a smile on her face. Sunshine in her eyes.

If only Sherrie had done better. If only she could have kept her safe.

She'd still be here now.

'Sherrie, DI Jenson is here. I'm just making coffee. Do you want one?'

Reaching the bottom step, Sherrie nods her head. Because coffee would make everything so much better, she thinks bitterly as she follows the three men into the kitchen, aware the place is a mess. Sherrie hasn't touched the place for days.

Usually she would be mortified at anyone turning up and finding her home in such disarray, but today Sherrie no longer cares how her home looks.

Who cares about a clean house, when it is empty and loveless?

Her world has fallen apart; her life is rapidly spiralling out of control.

A tidy house is the least of her worries.

'I've made some eggs, Sherrie. If you want some?'

Sherrie shakes her head. Pursing her lips as she bites her tongue, holding the venom inside that she feels for her husband right now as he busies himself, making his way around the kitchen.

Playing the role of the dutiful, loving husband now that the officers are here. As if last night hadn't happened.

It did though, she thinks as she notices how Richard hasn't

once looked at her since she walked into the room. She hadn't been too drunk or imagining the conversation they'd had last night.

The angry attack he'd launched at her. He had said it, how he didn't love her. That he had never loved her. He'd only stayed for Kayla. This was all an act now, for the police. She was so sick and tired of playing along, of not reacting, or pretending that this was all okay. This was normal. Keeping up this charade of their loving marriage. Hiding their resentment for each other. Concealing the hatred that they felt. They are actors. They've been acting for years. For Kayla's sake.

And maybe that was partly Sherrie's fault. She had insisted that their daughter deserved at least that. A normal family. Clearly they had needed to try harder, because even Kayla had seen through that facade in the end.

'We've had an update on the investigation.' Detective Jenson gets straight to the point. 'I know how important it is for you both that we keep you updated on all aspects of the case.' The detective clears his throat. 'We've had a witness come forward following the appeal that you made, who believes that she saw Kayla being abducted. The last known sighting we have of Kayla was in the very next street at just after 12.30 a.m., Saturday morning. We believe that she had been making her way home.'

'She was abducted?' Sherrie repeats quietly, her voice strained, the sound so small that it is barely audible even to her own ears. Her hands start shaking. Panic flooding through her then.

'No! Oh God no! Abducted? Please no. Did they hurt her? Christ, this can't be happening.' She stares at Richard now, her eyes boring into his, as if pleading with him to tell her that she heard the detective wrong. That this wasn't the case. 'Please tell me that this isn't happening!'

Richard doesn't answer. He looks away, down at the table. Anywhere but at her.

Sherrie is trying to focus on the detective's voice, on what he is saying, only the sound is drowned out by the dull ringing in her ears and the loud pounding of her heart in her chest as her worst fears are confirmed.

'Was Kayla hurt? They didn't hurt her, did they?' Sherrie repeats, unable to control the shaking of her voice or the way her words crack as they hit the air.

She feels the detective's eyes on her, full of sympathy. But she doesn't want sympathy, what she wants is answers.

Her head is spinning, her mind is in overdrive. She watches as the two officers move, realising that Richard must have offered the two men a seat at the table because they both sit down as Richard places the cups down in front of them.

'As far as we are aware, there wasn't a struggle as such so we don't believe that Kayla was hurt in the initial abduction.' The detective pauses, before clearing his throat. 'We believe that Kayla may have not been fully coherent at the time of her abduction. That she may have been under the influence of alcohol and possibly some kind of drug.'

'Drugs?' Sherrie says. Unable to make sense of what they are being told. The shock of what she is now hearing, making her unable to think straight.

'We don't believe Kayla went of her own free will. We feel as if she may have been forced in some way. She may not have been fully conscious.'

'What does that mean? How could she not be fully conscious? You think that someone drugged her? I don't understand.' Richard is speaking now. His voice full of urgency and something else, Sherrie realises.

Panic.

Sherrie looks at him. Properly looks at him and drinks it all in. How his face has drained of all colour. How his eyes are wide with disbelief. That is real fear shining from them. Finally, her husband is showing up, Sherrie thinks to herself. He was in there, somewhere, all this time, hiding underneath all of that facade. Feeling real emotion.

'We don't have enough information at this point to speculate and I'd rather we concentrate only on the cold, hard facts. What I can tell you is that, moving forward, we are going to be focusing our investigation on this new information. I already have officers going door-to-door to see if we can jog anyone's memories and hopefully see if we can gain access to images via local residents' security cameras and CCTV. I know how you both must be feeling, what an awful shock that this must be, but I want you to know that we are confident now that we are on the right track. We are closer now to finding her. It's a lead. It's something.'

'Abducted,' Sherrie mouths again. The word lingering on her tongue, as if she can't get rid of it.

They had all suspected this, hadn't they?

The very worst news. But hearing it aloud, spoken straight from the lead detective's mouth, suddenly made it all very real.

Abducted.

It is stuck there. Just like she is. Sherrie can't move. She can't breathe.

All she can do is stare at the detective. Her eyes fixed on the thin curl of his top lip, how it tilts upwards when he talks, exposing his yellowed coffee-stained teeth.

'She almost made it home? She was coming home?' Richard says quietly as the news sinks in. The illusion that he'd tried to convince himself of, that Kayla had simply run away from home and that any minute now, she'd come waltzing back through their front door of her own accord had been shattered.

Now he knows the truth. Maybe now he would start taking this more seriously. Kayla had been abducted. Someone had taken her. This isn't a game.

Sherrie had known that all along. Right from the very start. Unlike her husband, she'd known differently. That is her superpower. A mother always knows.

This had never been a case of Kayla simply rebelling and not coming home for a few days. Of their daughter hiding out with friends. Of punishing her now she'd found that her mum had hidden her passport. She'd never stay away like this. Not by choice. Not for this long.

'Were sorry we didn't have anything more positive to give you, but I know that you wanted to be kept updated and as soon as I know more, you'll be the first to hear.'

The detective and his colleague both get up, ready to leave.

'I know how difficult this must be for you both. But I want you to be assured that we are doing everything in our power to find Kayla and bring her home to you.'

'That's it? You don't know anything else? Did the witness see who took her? Did they at least have a good description? Maybe whoever it was is known to us? Or to Kayla?' Richard says, still grasping for more.

This can't be all they have. For once Sherrie agrees. If a witness saw something, what exactly did they see?

'I'm afraid we have very little information on the abductor. According to the witness, it was very dark and the lighting wasn't very good. The witness couldn't make out what she had been wearing or what she looked like.'

'She?' Richard says, his voice cracking then as this revelation sinks in.

'Yes, we believe the abductor is female.'

Sherrie stares at Richard. She knows exactly what he is thinking. As his eyes fleetingly catch hers. Full of panic, full of dread. He'd known this all along, deep down. He just hadn't wanted to admit it. Instead, he'd hung on to the idea that Kayla may have just gone on her own account. That she was angry with them, with Sherrie and that she'd run away.

Because the alternative is too much to bear.

'We'll be in touch as soon as we have any updates,' the officers say as Richard stands and shows them out. His movements robotic then as he walks. As he smiles. This is all just an act. He's just going through the motions. Sherrie knows this because she does it too herself. If you pretend enough you start to believe that the lie you live is the truth. This is what they'd always done.

Pretend.

Make-believe.

Only Sherrie doesn't think that she can do it anymore.

She's not strong enough.

It's slipping.

All of it. This life they have built for one another. This family.

When Richard walks back into the kitchen, she is so consumed by the thought of this almighty loss that she almost can't breathe. She can't move. But she forces herself to look at Richard, to stare him in the eyes.

'It's her, isn't it?' Sherrie says. Staring into his eyes as if she can reach right into his soul and pluck out the answers.

She sees it.

The way he falters.

How he tries to think of something to say but his body language betrays him. He seems shifty now. On edge.

'All this time you bloody knew! She found you, didn't she? That's who you think has Kayla, isn't it? Her,' Sherrie spits angrily. 'When the fuck were you going to tell me?'

40

'Tessa? I've got your sandwich here...' Amelia's voice is back in the room. The sound is near, as if she's standing right next to the bed, right next to her, but at the same time it's muffled, as if the noise is coming from inside Tessa's head. Echoing there.

'Tess?'

She wants to answer. To open her eyes and look at her now. To show her that she can hear her, that she is listening. Only her eyelids feel too heavy, as if they are weighted down. And she feels so relaxed. So calm.

SLEEP.

She can see Kayla's face now. That vibrant red hair, all those tiny red freckles. She is back inside the mirror staring out at her. Mouthing the words HELP ME!

I can't! Tessa mumbles, unsure if the words are inside her head or if she is saying them out loud. *I can't help you. I can't help you.*

She must have spoken them out loud, because she hears Amelia's voice then. Laced with concern.

'Tessa? Are you okay? Did you take the tablets already?

Maybe you shouldn't have on an empty stomach, not with the sleeping pills you took earlier...'

'I'm okay. I just wanna sleep...' Tessa mutters, embracing the warmth of her skin as Amelia places a hand on her arm. Shaking her gently. The rocking motion soothing.

So soothing.

She is drifting again. In and out of consciousness. Sinking down, deep down into a blissful sleep.

Only she can't sleep now, because she's not in her bed.

She is back there again, sitting in her car.

Outside his house. Watching them.

You were there that night, weren't you? The words that Amelia shouted during their argument fill her head.

You were there.

She *was* there. Outside their house. Watching them.

When he and his wife had both left the house suddenly in separate cars in the middle of the night.

Stricken looks on their faces. A feeling of urgency about them.

Searching for her.

When they realised that she was missing. When they realised she wasn't coming home.

'I'll stick your clothes in the wash.' Amelia's voice pulls Tessa back to the bedroom. Amelia is fidgeting now, making her way around the room in search of something to do while Tessa slips in and out of sleep.

Amelia could never just sit still. She could never properly relax. She was always fussing and tidying and trying to keep herself busy.

She is tidying now.

Clearing up the bedroom while Tessa slips back inside her dreams.

Tessa hears the drawers from the chest slide open. The

shake of clothes as Amelia flaps them in the air, before folding them and putting them away.

'Spuddy, what have you got?' Amelia chuckles, wrestling to get something off their cat.

'What is that?' Amelia is quiet.

Tessa wants to see, she tries. Her eyes flickering but still she can only see the inside of her eyelids. She can hear Spud though, how his paws scratch at something underneath the wardrobe. His sharp nails scrape against the wood.

He's like a magpie, Amelia often says. Taking little trinkets from around the house and burying them or storing them in little hiding spots. They'd both lost count of how many times an earring or a bracelet had gone missing for it never to be found again.

'A locket?'

Tessa hears the confusion in Amelia's voice, mixed with disbelief.

Even in her drug-fuelled state, Tessa can feel something electric crackle in the air all around them, as she hears the jangle of the chain. The tiny click of the clasp as Amelia's fingers prise it open. Tessa wonders if she's rubbing her fingers over the photos to get a better look at the grainy image of the woman and her newborn baby, just like Tessa had done.

Sleep! Go to sleep.

She tells herself. And she wants to.

Spud has jumped up on the bed now. She feels the warmth of him as he purrs loudly and snuggles into her body.

'This is her, isn't it? This is the girl from the news. The one that went missing? Why is it here? Tessa, why the hell is it in our house?'

Amelia's voice is shrill with alarm, but Tessa can't answer. She can't explain. She can't find her voice. Instead she's holding the vision of Kayla in her mind again. Only this time it's the image of her staring out from a photo.

The photo that Tessa has on her phone. From the night the girl went missing officially.

Because Tessa had seen her.

Tessa feels a dip in the bed as Amelia sinks down onto the mattress. Unable to stand. Unable to convey what she is looking at.

'Kayla Goldman. Fifteenth of November 2006.'

The words are so faint, so quiet that Tessa isn't even sure if she's heard them properly. The girl's name? That date?

That can't be right? Has Amelia taken the photo out from the casing?

'Tessa, why do you have this? Why is this in our house? How did you get it?'

Tessa tries to open her mouth to summon the words that are lodged in her throat, only something is niggling at her. Something bad. What had Amelia just said?

What was it again? She can't think. Her head is fuzzy and she can barely hold her train of thought. The argument flashes inside her mind once more.

'They'll be searching for her, Tessa. They'll be trawling through cameras and CCTV. They'll be noting down licence plate numbers that were in the area at that time. It won't take much for them to lead right back here to you.'

The locket.

The photo.

Amelia is right.

This will all lead back to her.

She was there.

Ducking down in the driver's seat of her car. Trying to stay out of sight.

Waiting. Hiding.

Kayla Goldman tottering up the street in those ridiculously high heels; she reminded Tessa of a gangly deer taking its first steps.

The car door was wide open.

The headlights off. Sitting in darkness.

Then she was gone.

'My phone...' Tessa tries to say, her words slurring now. As if her mouth can't catch up with her brain and it's all she can manage.

Because she needs to explain. To tell Amelia what she remembers about that night. Only she can't find her voice. She is so tired now. So sleepy.

Tessa hears Amelia pick it up, her nails tapping against the glass screen as she accesses her messages. Then her photos. Soon she'll see. Soon she'll know.

'Tessa? What is this?' Amelia says, her words coming out like a cry. A plea. That this isn't what she thinks this is.

Tessa knows that she has seen it.

The photo of Kayla Goldman.

Wearing the same sparkly mini-dress that the reporter had described on the press release on TV. Walking towards her house, in the middle of the night.

The night that she'd disappeared.

The very last sighting of the girl.

'Oh my god, Tessa! What have you done? What have you done?'

41

Something is different. That's my first thought when I awake from my nightmare-laced sleep to the overpowering smell of pungent spices that fill the room.

Disorientated, I sit up and suspiciously eye the steaming hot tray of food that's been left by the side of the bed. I hadn't heard him come in this evening. He'd been quiet, or I'd been completely out of it.

And I'm guessing it's the latter. It feels like days since I last ate anything that he's brought me. I feel weak. I have no energy left inside of me. All I seem to do is sleep. As I look down at the tray I wonder if perhaps I am still dreaming. If my mind is playing tricks on me and showing me things that aren't real. Things that don't really exist.

Because today he has brought me my favourite. An Indian takeaway.

How does he know that? How does he know what food I like?

He does know me, he must.

I stare at the cube-sized chunks of meat in a rich-looking red sauce, with steaming hot rice and a freshly baked naan.

Is it real? It smells real.

My stomach growls loudly as I breathe in those delicious spices. Begging me, pleading with me to give in and eat the food. I have been so stubborn, refusing to eat anything that he brings me. Refusing to eat anything at all.

Resolved to starving myself. Then he'll have no choice, he'll be forced to call a doctor for me. It had felt so liberating at first. So powerful, taking back some kind of control.

Saying no to him.

I thought that he might try and force me. That he'd grab my face and shovel the food in. But he called my bluff and just left me to it. And now he's tempting me with this.

My stomach is aching with a hollowness of hunger that I have never experienced until now. The acid inside my tummy is eating away at my flesh. I'm slowly fading away to nothing. If I carry on like this, not eating, turning his food away, I might die.

He's not going to call a doctor for me. I know it. I am stubborn but so is he.

It feels as if my body is already starting to shut down. My reflexes and movements all feel slower. My brain fogs. A slow, dull pain that has taken over my whole body. I want to refuse it. I want to say no. To pick the tray up and defiantly throw it at the wall. But it smells so tempting, so delicious.

Just a few bites. Maybe if I eat, he'll bring me a crayon and the paper again as a reward. So I can keep writing my letters again to my mum.

God, how I miss my mum.

My mouth is watering now, filling up with saliva. And my stomach is screaming at me to eat. I cave. Sinking down to my knees and scooping up handfuls of the delicious meaty chunks with my bare hands, spooning lumps of chicken tikka masala into my mouth with my fingers. I'm crying.

Not only is it the best, most delicious thing that I've ever tasted, but this means that he has beaten me again.

He has made me play by his rules, and he has won. I can hear him out there. Feeling so smug as he listens in on the other side of the door. Satisfied that I am eating again.

Then he moves.

Clunky footsteps thudding down the wooden floorboards on the stairs, in those big heavy boots he wears. Clomp. Clomp. I hear the sound of the toilet flush. In a room beneath me. Then more footsteps. The sound of something heavy being dragged across the floor. A piece of furniture? A footstool?

Then the sound of the television, blaring loud suddenly that seems to bring the whole place to life. He does this sometimes. Hides out there for hours. In the other room below here.

Usually the door downstairs is shut, his voice is muffled, but today the sound is clearer. He's left the door open, and I press my ear up against the door and strain to listen.

The sound of the TV gives me so much comfort. It's like a portal back to the outside world. To my world before him. My world beyond these four claustrophobic prison walls. I close my eyes today and lap it up. The beautiful angelic voices of children singing and laughing, so careless and free. Oh, to be a child again, back home, and safe.

I picture myself back there, lying on the sofa and watching TV while my mum does her usual and fusses around me. God, how I miss that. How I miss her.

I feel sick with nostalgia and longing, but I won't throw up.

I mustn't. I need to keep it down.

Starving myself isn't going to work with him.

I need to think of a better plan.

Sinking down to the floor, I listen as he changes the channel and the familiar buzzer from the daily gameshow he watches fills my ears. And I listen to his raspy voice as he shouts out and answers the questions.

He is clever. He shouts out and gets most of them right.

Sometimes I beat him to it. But then I guess I don't have anything else to do but sit here and concentrate and play along.

I know so much now because of these game shows; I know all about subjects that I'll probably never use in real life. Geography, literature, sports. Things I should have probably paid more attention to when I'd been at school but that I never really cared for.

What country has the largest population in the world?

'Japan,' he shouts.

China. I mouth. It's all just white noise. None of that matters now that I am in here.

But still, I play along and pretend.

Sometimes pretending is the only things that keep me sane.

Like when I write my letters.

Wrapped up in a world of make-believe that they are getting to my mother, that she is reading them. They make me feel closer to her. I lean back against the wall and fight the urge to cry. What is the point in crying? I have no more tears left to fall and even if I did, I'm not going to waste another single one on him. I won't give him that satisfaction.

He's the only one here that can hear me.

Another question. His voice shouts louder.

I know that voice.

I am sure of it. Certain of it.

Something inside me feels suddenly off-kilter, as if the room is tipping, the ground beneath me slanting unevenly on its axis just as the room begins to spin.

It can't be him!

All this time, he is the one that has kept me here? He is the one who has locked me away?

It can't be true. I must be hearing things.

My mind must be playing tricks on me.

I squeeze my eyes closed as if shutting the thought out.

Refusing to believe it, because if it is him, that changes everything.

It can't be him. It can't be.

I won't believe it. I can't.

Instead, I play along with the rest of the quiz show and wait for the inevitable.

When he leaves, I am plunged back into darkness, all alone again in this silent room.

42

'It's her, isn't it?' Sherrie spits, unable to say the woman's name, unable to even entertain the noise, the shape of letters that it's made up of inside of her mouth. Even after all this time, all these years, it still cuts her so deeply.

Richard's brutal betrayal.

Like a rusty, serrated knife dragging now at her sensitive flesh. Cutting her open, ripping her in two.

'That's who you think has got Kayla? That's what this has really been about all along? Was that why you didn't want me to call the police when she broke in to our house? Because even now, you're still protecting her, aren't you?! After all this time. After all these years.'

Her tone lets him know that she does not require an answer. She watches Richard flinch at the realisation that he's not as smart as he thinks he is.

He sees it then. How Sherrie already knows.

'NO. Of course I'm not... I didn't know for sure... that it was her, not at first,' Richard says quietly. 'You said yourself, nothing was taken. Nothing was damaged. The kitchen window was open. You didn't actually see anyone... I guess I just didn't want to believe that she'd found me. That she'd found us.'

'Christ! She was in Kayla's bedroom, Richard! She was inside our daughter's room. Going through her things. You knew, and you didn't think to tell me? To warn me? You didn't think that maybe you should mention that it was your whore who had been here?' Sherrie screeches loudly, spitting her venom. Anger surging inside her at the thought of her being inside their house. Of her walking around their home and touching their things.

'The second that Kayla went missing, you should have told me. But instead you put yourself first, didn't you?! You put your secrets above the safety of your daughter.'

'No. It wasn't like that. I didn't think that anything had happened to Kayla. She's a teenager, Sherrie. I thought that maybe she was rebelling. That maybe she'd stayed out with friends. I thought that she was angry, that she was trying to teach us a lesson. Teach you a lesson. That she'd turn up. She'd come home. I guess part of me wanted to believe that too, because the alternative was just too much to bear.'

'For who? For you? Don't make me laugh!' Sherrie shakes her head, not falling for Richard's dramatics as she glares at him, her eyes narrowing.

'Did you see her? Did you speak to her?' she asks. Drinking in his reaction. Watching his every move for tell-tale signs of him lying once more.

'No.' Richard shakes his head, but there is no conviction behind the movement.

'You're lying!' Sherrie spits.

'I saw her, once.' Finally, he is telling her the truth. 'Outside the house. At least I thought I saw her. She was sitting in a car, further down the street, watching us. But I couldn't be sure. I made my way to get a better look but she drove off. That was the only time.'

'And still you said nothing?' Sherrie shouts.

'I should have. I realise that now.' Richard starts crying. 'But I was scared, Sherrie. I didn't want it to be true. I didn't want it all to come out.'

Leaning over the kitchen table, his shoulders sagging. His head resting on his hands as big wracking sobs shake his body.

He knows that this is his fault.

He could have stopped it. If he had been stronger, if he had said something.

Well, if he wanted sympathy, he could forget it, because Sherrie isn't finished with him yet.

Let him feel bad. Let him wallow in his guilt. He deserves that much at least; he caused all of this.

'Christ! I need a drink!' Sherrie walks to the fridge and yanks the door wide open with shaking hands, desperately searching for something to take the edge off.

'Where's the wine?'

'It's gone!' Richard mutters quietly.

'You poured it down the sink?' Sherrie bit her lip, fury radiating from her. 'Just to spite me. Classic Richard. You won't even allow me the smallest respite even now!'

Tears form in Sherrie's eyes again. But this time she can't stop them. She can't stop herself from crying. Her life is crumbling right before her eyes and there's nothing that Sherrie can do about it. Her daughter is missing. Her whole world turned upside down. And her husband is a lying bastard.

And what galls her right now is that she is shouldering it all.

Just like she always has.

She is the one who held this relationship together.

She has always powered through.

Sherrie thinks of their sham of a marriage. All the arguments. All the hate that festers between them. All those times that their arguments got physical. How many times tempers had flared.

The hits. The kicks. The beatings.

How Sherrie had tried her hardest to shield Kayla from all of it, especially as she'd got older. But Kayla isn't here now and Sherrie no longer cares if she riles him up and things get out of hand. At least that way she would get something from him. Some kind of reaction. Some kind of response.

Other than that, other than those dark, violent moments between them, there is nothing. It is as if Richard is dead behind the eyes. Like he is only there in body, not spirit.

Because he has to be.

Because he is forced to be.

He has been this way through most of their marriage.

Because of her.

'You actually make me sick! But then you've always been such a weak, pathetic excuse of a man. Spineless. Christ, if you'd been blessed with a backbone, you wouldn't have known what to do with it. You'd have probably thought it was a bloody ornament. I don't know why I expected any different now. It was always me that had to step up. It was always me that held this family together,' Sherrie says, challenging him, purposely goading him as she lights up another cigarette, her hands trembling with rage.

'I knew that you were keeping things from me. I've been through all of this before. You forget that I know you, Richard. I know how you lie. I know when you're hiding things from me.'

Sherrie eyes him, taking a long drag of her cigarette before she finally speaks again.

'When the police confirmed that Kayla had been abducted. By a woman. I saw it flash across your face. Pure dread. You'd been expecting it, hadn't you!?'

Sherrie sneers. Her words loaded with venom.

'This is all your fault. Admit it. Kayla is gone because of you!'

43

When Tessa wakes again the house sits in silence.

She can feel it. A sense of foreboding. A sense of unease as it washes over her like a wave, pushing her back down as if she's unable to lift her head from the deep, murky water.

Something big is coming. Something bad.

Tessa stares at the clock. The day is over, it's late in the evening now.

Why is she still in bed?

She eyes the packets of tablets, remembering then. How she'd willed herself better. Needing to sleep. Needing to stop the anxiety that had been building intensely inside of her.

She'd taken too many.

She must have fallen back to sleep.

She recalls Amelia's voice, warning her that she shouldn't have taken the tablets on an empty stomach. She was right. She shouldn't have taken so many at all. They'd been too strong after all this time without them and, mixed with the sleeping tablets she'd taken earlier, they'd clearly sent her into a comatose state of sleep full of warped, distorted dreams.

Amelia standing over her with the locket in her hand.

Kayla Goldman. The fifteenth of November 2006.

That name. That date. She had dreamt it. She must have.

There was only one way to find out.

'Amelia?' Tessa calls out. Her voice raspy as she shouts. The sound echoing through the house. Tessa doesn't get an answer: she is alone now. She's sure of it, even before she drags her body from the bed and makes her way down the stairs to check the house.

Amelia has gone.

There's a note. Amelia's normally neat handwriting now a hurried scrawl across the piece of paper that sits in the middle of the kitchen table.

I've gone to see Jacqui. I'm worried about you. Stay in bed. REST.

Amelia x

Amelia has gone to see Jacqui? Why?

To dig deeper into her past? So that her aunt would fill in the blanks of the things that Tessa had never had the guts to say out loud herself? Tessa tries to read between the lines, to gauge the tone of the writing.

Flashes of fragmented memories coming back to her now.

She'd been so angry with her when she'd found the locket. When she'd seen the photographs on her phone.

Would she have gone to the police? To tell them that Tessa had been there that night?

What if she thought that Tessa really was ill again and, this time, she tried to get her committed?

Tessa could see how bad it looks.

Kayla Goldman: 15 November 2006.

The words spin inside of Tessa's brain, as if she's trying to compute them; she's trying to register how that could possibly fit in. Though she is sure that's exactly what Amelia had said, as she sank down on the bed next to her. As if the weight of what she had found was too heavy for her to bear now that she'd found the missing girl's locket there in their home.

Only Amelia had no idea of the real weight of any of this.

She couldn't possibly.

Where had Amelia got that date from? Had she remembered it?

Because Tessa hadn't seen it written anywhere.

Had that tiny, vital detail been engraved so delicately on the locket's casing? No, she didn't think so. She'd inspected it closely. She'd rubbed her fingers over it and stared at the images for ages.

The photos. She hadn't taken them out of the locket and taken a close look at them, had she?

Had the date been scrawled on the back of one of the images? The baby one. The one that looked like Sherrie and Kayla's first photo together, taken straight after Kayla had been born.

Kayla Goldman: 15 November 2006.

This is all going to come back on you, Tessa.

It's Amelia's voice again. In stereo now. Replaying inside Tessa's head.

Tessa feels the wave of sickness wash over her as her legs give way beneath her and she grips the stair banister hard, trying to stay upright.

Trying to steady herself.

To focus.

Kayla Goldman is missing. His daughter is missing. And he is out there, a free man. While Tessa is living here, like this. Confused from the medication she's taken, full of paranoia and suspicious. And Amelia has gone and Tessa is alone.

She's not free. She's still his prisoner, even now, after all these years. She can't live a half-life like this, always waiting for him to reappear and destroy everything. Tessa had wanted him to suffer at first, when she'd first found him.

It had been part of her one-woman crusade to make him pay for what he did to her. But not like this. Never like this.

Tessa closes her eyes. Trying so hard to silence the thoughts that have accumulated inside her head. All the things that she'd heard said about her over the years. The muted whispers, the judgemental comments when people thought that she couldn't hear.

She is not in her right mind.

She is not thinking straight.

It's the medication that she's taking.

It's her anxiety.

She. Her.

NO. It was him. It was always him.

Tessa needs to go.

Because Amelia may not have gone to see Jacqui at all. Maybe that is just a ploy, to keep her here. Maybe she has gone to the police, which means that Tessa won't have long. They'll be here soon, and they will arrest her. When they see Kayla Goldman's locket and the photos on Tessa's phone from the night that she went missing.

It will all lead directly back to her, just like Amelia had said it would.

Kayla Goldman: 15 November 2006.

Tessa needs to put an end to this.

She needs to confront him, The Monster.

To face him once and for all.

It's time.

44

'How is this all my fault?' Richard bellows, the force of his voice making Sherrie jump. His face puce. A vein pulsating in the side of his head.

Something about his reaction makes Sherrie feel suddenly alert. Alive. She feels it, how on edge he is, about to lose all control. Part of her relishes it, because it means that finally he is showing her something. Some kind of reaction. Some kind of emotion.

It ignites something inside of her that she still has that power over him.

'Oh, here he is! Finally, he's showing up! Only you're a little too late now!' Sherrie's eyes do not leave his as she forces herself to hold that steely gaze as he stands in front of her.

Towering over her.

Sherrie stands firm. Letting him know that she is not scared of him.

He doesn't frighten her.

He never has.

'Is that why you kept them, is it? The letters. So that you

could blame me for it all if it ever came out?' He is raging now. Seething and spitting with every word that he speaks.

His anger spilling over like red hot molten lava, willing to annihilate everything that stands in its wake. Including Sherrie. Especially Sherrie.

'Kayla found them hidden in the same drawer as her passport. Stuffed down underneath the drawer liner. She showed them to me the morning that she went missing. Though thankfully she had no idea what they meant. No idea who they were from or to, but she was asking questions, Sherrie. She was suspicious.'

'Where are they?' Sherrie bristles.

Richard has the letters. Not Kayla.

He has them now.

'She was starting to work things out, Sherrie. She was saying how weird it was that we had moved around so much when she was smaller. How we never went abroad on holiday. How you rarely let her out of your sight. She was asking questions, Sherrie. Questions we wouldn't be able to answer.'

Sherrie bit her lip, angry. Recalling that morning she'd heard their raised voices from her bedroom. How she'd walked into the kitchen and the pair of them had stopped talking mid-sentence, an awkward silence. It had set something off inside of her. A jealous rage that the two of them were in it together, suddenly. That they were somehow against her.

She'd felt it then and she feels it now, that awful sense of being left out. When all Sherrie had ever done was sacrifice her whole life for them both.

All she'd ever wanted to do was protect Kayla.

To keep her safe.

She loves her. She'd only ever loved her. Fiercely, with everything she had inside of her. More than she loved anyone else in the world. More than she loved herself.

'She will be an adult in a few more years, she'll have her

own life. She'll be able to travel the world then, and go wherever she likes. Or try. How will you control her then? How will you stop her from finding out then?' Richard falters, his voice cracking as if he has only just realised that Kayla is still missing. That she is not here.

That she isn't safe.

He shakes his head.

'This is all on you, Sherrie. Not me. You and your make-believe world of the three of us stuck inside this poxy bubble. This perfect life that you try to portray. This prison.' Richard pauses. 'She was always going to leave you, Sherrie. Eventually. She was starting to see you for who you really are. What will she say when she finally knows the truth? Who will she blame?'

Sherrie flies at him then.

Clawing at his face. Hitting out at him.

'How dare you! This was all you! You and that stupid, fucking bitch. You started all of this! I just picked up the pieces the best that I could. I salvaged something from the wreckage. I cleared up your mess!' Sherrie's voice cracks. Betraying the bravado she is putting on. The raw emotion she feels seeping out and exposing her. How she is still hurting so badly.

She wants him to hurt badly too.

She'd wanted that for their entire marriage.

To make him pay for what he'd done to her.

'And even after all of that, after everything you still stood back and said nothing. When you knew that she'd come back here. That she had found you. She was in our home, Richard. She was in our daughter's bedroom. What did you think she was going to do, Richard? If she could get this close to us. How did you think this was all going to end? And still you said nothing?'

The almighty slap comes from nowhere.

The force of Sherrie's palm against Richard's face so brutal, it sends him flying sideways across the room. The kitchen wall stopping his fall. Richard is momentarily shocked as he presses his hand against his face to ease the heat of the burning pain as it radiates through his skin. Sherrie watches him flick his tongue inside his mouth, as a tooth wriggles free from his gum, dislodging in his mouth.

Blood trickles down his chin.

Sherrie spent years taking her anger and frustrations out on the man. Pounding her fists against his flesh, hitting and kicking him. Wanting to hurt him, to make him feel just an inkling of how she had felt inside after what he had done to her. Making him pay for everything he did to her. To them.

And Richard just took it.

He just stood there and took it as if he was owed every punishment that came his way. As if he just accepted it.

That had always made Sherrie despise him even more. How weak and pathetic he was.

Only today he's not taking it; today he's not going to let her win.

'What could I say? What did you want me to do, Sherrie? How would you have reacted if I'd told you that I'd seen her? If I told you that maybe it was her that had broken into the house. What would you have done about it? Would you have gone to the police? Would you have told them about her? No. Because you knew that they would start digging. And you knew what they would find if they did!'

Richard is pacing now.

'They'd find me. Only now I think that's what you wanted all along. You were going to let me take the fall for it, weren't you? You were going to blame it all on me. Which is why you kept those fucking letters. As proof. They were your insurance policy to use against me so that you can make sure that I was the one who paid. So that you could save yourself and let me take the fall. Haven't I already paid enough, Sherrie?'

Richard is crying now. Sobbing hard, snot trailing down from his nose as he continues to speak.

'You know what, Sherrie, you are right! I am weak and pathetic. For staying with you when I should have left you years ago, because I do not love you. I have never loved you. I should have spoken up back then. And now. I should have done right by Kayla. I should have told the police everything about her.'

Sherrie sees the look on his face, the flash of realisation as it hits him, that confessing to the police is exactly what he must do. If he wants to fix this, what other choice does he have? It's not too late. He can still end this.

'That's what I'm going to do. I'll tell them everything,' he says, his voice robotic again. 'If it will help to find Kayla, then so be it. If it means that she will be found, that she will be safe. No matter what the outcome for me. I'll suffer the consequences. And if you really love her like you say you do, so will you.'

'No chance!' Sherrie says, stepping forward now. Letting Richard know that she isn't going to back down. That if he wants to do that, he'll have to go through her first.

'You're not going to do this. You're not going to ruin our lives. Mine and Kayla's lives. Not when you started it. Not when it was all your fault. You owe us.'

That's when Richard sees the flash of light hit the blade of the knife.

Sherrie's fist clenching around the handle as she holds it between them. The serrated point is aimed in Richard's direction.

'Ruin Kayla's life? It's already ruined. We need to do this, Sherrie. We need to find her.'

'You really are completely clueless, aren't you? You still haven't worked it out?'

45

'I'm one step ahead of you, Richard. I always was!' Sherrie says. Stepping closer. Her eyes still fixed on his.

Though he isn't looking at her now.

He is looking at the knife between them.

His eyes resting on the pointed blade.

'You forget that I know the tell-tale signs. How you lied to me before. I knew back then and I knew this time too, that you were keeping something from me. So I checked your iPad. After you'd gone out looking for Kayla that day she went missing. After the break-in. I went down your search history on that poxy thing that you always seem glued to. And what did I find? Her name. Her face. That bitch. You were looking her up, because you'd seen her here. And you thought she had broken in,' Sherrie spits. 'Did you look up all those old newspaper articles that were written about you back then too? A reminder, was it, about what you did to her? A monster? That's what they called you! What a joke!' Sherrie raises her voice then. Relishing in the fact that she has already worked it out.

That she had known what he was hiding from her; he will never get the better of her.

'If only they could see you now, eh! Such a big, brave man, aren't you! Willing to put your own safety first, to protect yourself ahead of your daughter. That's the only reason you didn't say anything. To me, to the police. You were too busy trying to protect yourself. So don't stand here with that sanctimonious look on your face. You did this. You did all of it.' Sherrie edges towards him still waving the knife.

His eyes are on the kitchen doorway, as if assessing how quickly he can get there. If he could make it out of there, and outrun Sherrie.

Sherrie shakes her head. Jabbing the knife out in front of her as if he should heed her warning.

'You know that I'll do it,' she warns, noting the look of terror spreading across his face, the fear that beams out from his eyes. He knows she is more than capable of doing it.

Of plunging the sharp pointed blade into his flesh.

Of standing over him and watching him bleed out all over their kitchen floor.

They both know.

How Sherrie is more than capable of a lot of things, if it means she gets what she wants.

And she always got what she wanted. She had expected Richard to step back. To stand down from the confrontation; only he is standing taller, more defiant. Not cowering away from her like he usually did when she attacked him or lashed out at him.

It is as if something snapped inside him. As if he somehow no longer cares about his own fate. As if he is challenging her.

And part of her is mildly impressed that her darling husband has finally dared to stand up for himself.

'Do it! If this is what it takes to save yourself. That's what you're really good at, putting yourself first. Making sure that you're happy no matter what. Over everyone else around you. No matter whose life you ruin. Well, I'm not doing it anymore.

Kayla's gone, and if I need to blow this all up in order for her to be found safely, then so be it. Without her...' Richard eyes her, a look of disgust on his face. Pure hate radiating from him. 'There's nothing left to live for. She is why I stayed. She is why I'm here. You know that. I would have never chosen you, and deep down you know it. But I would never have left her with you either.'

Sherrie falters. This is not the Richard she knows. The Richard who has always shut up, who did as he was told. The Richard that Sherrie controlled.

'Go on, put me out of my misery!' Richard says as Sherrie lowers the knife; she isn't in control now and it feels unnerving.

'Either way, this is over, Sherrie. I'm not doing it anymore. I can't. No more pretending. I'm going to confess everything to the police. All of it. Kayla deserves to know the truth. She deserves to know what we did. *We*, Sherrie. Not just me.'

Richard is braver now. Sure that Sherrie won't do it.

That she can't bring herself to harm him.

Not like this.

Only Richard is wrong.

Sherrie moves fast then. The knife out in front of her again.

They struggle.

The blade piercing flesh.

Blood spilling out all over the floor.

A deadly silence descends on the house.

46

I'm sitting on the floor, listening to yet another quiz show as it finishes, waiting for the inevitable. When I'll be plunged back into my own silent, lonely world with only the make-believe voices in my head for company again.

Only today when the quiz ends, he doesn't switch the TV off straight away and I wonder if he's going to stay here for longer. He does that sometimes. I hear him. Moving around. Watching his shows. Flushing the toilet. He hasn't moved from his chair though; I can hear him. He's still there, still watching the TV.

I hear my name.

At first I convince myself that I haven't, that it is impossible. I'm sure it was just my mind playing cruel tricks on me, because my mind does that a lot these days. I shake my head wildly to dislodge the make-believe voice inside my head that I know is taunting me.

Only I hear it again.

A woman's voice, and she's speaking my name. Her tone is serious. And she slowly annunciates each word clearly.

It's a news reader.

She is louder, clearer this time. The sound isn't coming from inside my head, or inside this room. It's real. It's a news bulletin. And they are talking about me. I am on the TV.

Hope fills me.

He is listening too, because the TV suddenly gets louder as he turns the volume up. Good, I think. Let him listen. Let him realise that they are out there looking for me.

That I am not forgotten.

The woman's voice on the TV says how it's been fourteen weeks now, and I wonder what she's referring to. What's been fourteen weeks?

Three and a half months missing, she says. I frown and narrow my eyes.

She must be mistaken. Me? Does she mean me? That I've been missing for three and a half months? Panic floods me. No. That can't be right. But it could be. It feels like I have been here for an eternity.

Is it possible? Have I really spent all this time trapped inside this bloody room?

So far, search parties and the authorities haven't found any leads on the young woman's disappearance, the voice continues.

No. They still don't know I'm here. They are no closer to finding me.

He'll hear that too.

He'll think he's got away with it.

He has got away with it.

I falter, tears cascading down my face. Search parties.

People had looked for me, that was something. Because I had started to believe that no one was looking. That no one was coming, because it had been too long.

The funeral will be held on Thursday...

WHAT! NO! I hold my breath. How can they hold my funeral if I'm not there? If there is no body. I am not dead.

I'M NOT DEAD! I want to scream.

But I mustn't, because if he hears me, if he knows that I'm listening, he'll turn it off.

I clamp my hand tightly over my mouth. I need to listen. I need to hear what they are saying about me. Only they are talking about me as if I no longer exist.

But I am here. I am alive.

They have no body. No proof that I am dead.

If they declare me dead, I'd be stuck here with him forever.

There will be no reason for him to ever think that he has to let me go.

The room starts to spin. The walls closing in and I gulp back the burning, acidic bile that rises at the back of my throat.

I feel so sick.

It's a tragedy, the news reporter continues. *A grieving mother passing away so suddenly with no answers as to where her missing daughter is...*

A grieving mother passing away.

A mother?

My mother?

No. NO! It can't be.

The woman on the TV is wrong. She is lying.

Or is he the one lying? Is he doing all of this? Playing his sick twisted games. Punishing me again.

They are all liars. The woman on the TV. Him.

I refuse to believe it.

It can't be true.

Only I hear another voice then, a voice sounding just like my mother's. A similar tilt and the sound is both beautiful and devastating all at once.

It's Jacqui. My auntie. It's really her and she's on the TV. And her voice is thick with emotion as she talks about her dead sister.

Oh God, Oh God!

It's true. It's true.

My mother really is dead.

It's a tragedy, Jacqui says. *The cause of death was a heart attack, but my sister died of a broken heart. Broken through grief and the not knowing where her daughter is. What happened to her. Her soul was tormented.*

Click.

He's switched the TV off and we are both plunged into silence. I can hear the stool being dragged across the floor again.

He's just going to leave me here. After hearing that.

After knowing that my mother is gone.

That I'll never see her again.

She never got the letters that I wrote to her. She didn't know that I was here all along. That I was still alive.

He never sent them to her like I hoped. Like I'd silently prayed.

I feel the rage as it swells and rises through my body. My silent tears become huge wracking sobs. And suddenly I've lost all control. I can feel everything and nothing all at once.

He did this. HIM. He killed my mother.

There's a strange tingling sensation rising from my toes, buzzing at first then turning into a violent tremble as the wave of shock rushes up through me.

I feel as if I'm outside of myself looking in.

I've reached a point of no return.

I can't do this anymore. I can't be here anymore.

I need to get out. Because while I've been slowly dying in here, my mother had been tortured out there.

By him.

I won't let him kill us both. I won't let him kill me too.

I am going to take control and end this now, myself.

Standing up I throw myself against the door.

Knowing the risk it holds as I slam my stomach into the wood, smashing my skull against the solid door frame.

Bashing it repeatedly. Thud. Thud.

The pain explodes in my head, but I want it. I want to feel it. MORE. This isn't enough. It isn't anywhere near enough.

I smack myself and punch myself so hard, so furiously that when the pain finally takes hold in my very core it's brutal. Final. The guttural scream that leaves my mouth comes from somewhere so deep. And it's so visceral, so unrecognisable that I don't even register it as my own.

It sounds like that of a wounded, dying animal.

I hear the clank of the lock as the door is pulled open.

A look of horror spreads across his face.

And that makes it all so much more worth it.

I'm glad.

I am glad when I place my hand down there, between my legs and I feel the warm, sticky sensation of blood.

Pouring out from me.

I hold my hand up and stare at the blood. My blood.

He's too late.

My mother is dead.

And now the damage is already done.

47

It's late.

His street sits in darkness as Tessa turns the engine off and steps out of the car, eyeing the warm lights that pool out from the windows like beacons as she approaches the house. She sees the family are still up, not yet in bed.

But it's only when Tessa reaches the door that she feels something is amiss. A narrow stream of light seeping out from the frame, the door slightly ajar. Tessa pushes it open a few more inches, so that she can hear inside. Straining for voices or the gentle hum of the TV. But there is nothing. Just an eerie silence enveloping the house, and a feeling of unease.

Something is wrong. Tessa can sense it.

The same heaviness weighing her down since she woke up earlier this evening and found that Amelia had gone. Tessa wonders if they will be looking for her now. The police and Amelia. If they'd gone back to their home and found her gone. Would they come here next?

Would this be where they assume she'd come? Because Amelia could prove to them that she'd been here before, couldn't she? And how could Tessa explain any of this without sounding crazy? How could anyone on the outside looking in believe what she was saying, when part of her still wasn't sure herself?

They hadn't before, and they wouldn't now.

Tessa knows that from experience – that her word isn't enough: she needs proof. She needs something to show them for certain that this is the monster who destroyed her life.

That it is him; he is living here with his perfect life, in plain sight.

A man whose daughter is now missing.

Kayla Goldman. 15 November 2006.

That she might have been there the night his daughter had disappeared, but Tessa hadn't taken her.

She is almost certain of that.

Tessa shakes her head as a noise floats out from the kitchen.

It's faint at first, and Tessa has to strain to listen until she hears it again. A mild whimper, like that of a maimed animal, writhing in pain. Someone is in there. Someone is hurt.

An awful thought enters Tessa's head then.

What if Amelia didn't go to the police at all? What if that wasn't what her note meant? What if she came straight here instead? To see this family for herself. To see him. Because that's the sort of thing that Amelia would do.

She'd try and smooth things over for Tessa. To make things better for her, to explain that Tessa wasn't well: she'd try and get her out of trouble.

Maybe she had brought the locket back too, because when Tessa woke it had gone.

It wouldn't have been too hard for Amelia to find his house. She had been on Tessa's phone; she'd seen the name of the street on the sign in the background of one of the photos that Tessa took. Amelia would have seen the other photos she'd taken too.

Photographs of his house, of his car. Of him.

Photographs of his daughter, the night she went missing.

Amelia?

Tessa moves fast then.

Her fear heightening as soon as she steps into the hallway and her eyes go to the bright red smudge in the middle of the white tiled floor. An outline of someone's shoe, a footprint stamped in blood.

Blood?

Her heart pounds as she continues to walk towards the kitchen, where the groaning sound continues on the other side of the open kitchen door, unsure what she will be faced with.

The groaning is louder now.

And as she steps inside she sees the figure in the middle of the kitchen floor. Covered in blood.

48

'I'm so sorry for turning up unannounced like this, at this time of the evening, but I didn't know where else to go,' Amelia explains as she steps into Jacqui's house and follows her through to the kitchen. Having already declined her offer of a cup of tea. Amelia has made it clear that she isn't here for a social visit.

'It's Tessa, Jacqui. I'm worried about her.'

'What's happened? Is she okay?' Jacqui narrows her eyes as she sees the red jagged scratches down the side of Amelia's face, which are illuminated now under the glare of the bright kitchen light. 'What happened to your face?'

'Oh, this! It's nothing...' Amelia starts, raising her hand as if to conceal the marks that she'd forgotten all about in her haste to get here. She realises now that she must look a sight.

Turning up out of the blue, her face etched with worry and bruising.

'It doesn't look like nothing!' Jacqui raises her brows. She isn't stupid and the stern look on her face tells Amelia that she doesn't have the patience for games.

'She didn't mean to do it.' Amelia closes her eyes, admitting the truth finally. 'She had a panic attack and I guess she just blacked out. For a few minutes it was as if she wasn't there. She didn't mean to hurt me. She'd never, ever do something like this to me intentionally.'

Amelia takes a deep breath, knowing how hard this would be for Jacqui to hear. Because Jacqui has been like a mother to Tessa since she lost her own mum. Jacqui loved and worried about Tessa just as much as Amelia did, if not more. This isn't going to be an easy conversation.

'She's been getting bad again, Jacqui.'

'Bad as in how?' Jacqui asks, though her tone indicates that she'd expected as much, giving Amelia's unexpected visit. It is the first time that Amelia has ever turned up here alone, without Tessa.

'She's been hiding things from me...' Amelia starts, not sure where to begin. Because it is all so much worse than just a few secrets. So much more than just a few white lies. 'She is back there again, in her head. Fixated on him. Claiming that she's seen him. The first time was at our house, where she was convinced that he'd found her. She was so scared that she barricaded herself in the bathroom and I had to call the police. That's when she did this to my face. She thought I was him.'

'Christ!' Jacqui shakes her head, sadly. 'I had no idea.'

But there is worse to come and Amelia knows that she just has to say it. She needs to be honest with the woman and tell her everything she knows. Because this is too big for Amelia to deal with alone. She needs help. She needs someone who has Tessa's best intentions at heart and can tell her what to do for the best.

Because Amelia has no idea what the best thing to do with Tessa is anymore.

'It gets worse.' Amelia shakes her head. 'Christ, worse doesn't even begin to cover it. It turns out that it wasn't the first time she'd seen him. The reason why she thought he'd found her was because she had found him first. She'd been stalking someone. She'd followed this guy home and she sat outside his house. Watching him. Watching his family. I had no idea because she kept it all from me. I've only just found out.

'She broke into his house, Jacqui. She stole this from him. I found this in our bedroom.' Amelia holds open the locket and gives it to Jacqui so she can examine it for herself.

'Who is that?' Jacqui asks, a look of vague recognition sweeping across her face as she takes in the sight of the pretty teenage girl staring back at her from the tiny photograph.

Amelia can see the cogs whirling inside the woman's head. How she has seen that face somewhere before. Somewhere recently. Only she can't quite place where.

'That's his daughter: Kayla. She went missing a few days ago. It's been all over the local news.' Amelia pauses then, gathering herself. Willing herself to say the next part out loud. Because once she says this, there will be no going back.

It will be out there.

Amelia knows that this is the only way. That Tessa needs help that she isn't capable of giving her. She needs professional help, and there will be consequences for Tessa, now. For her behaviour.

She might end up committed. Or worse, they might arrest her.

Though Amelia can't even bear to think about any of that right now.

Tessa needs help.

'Tessa was there, Jacqui. She had been there the night that his daughter went missing.'

'No. She wouldn't do something like that...' Jacqui purses her lips. Her skin pales as she realises the severity of what Amelia is implying.

Grabbing at the chair closest to her, she slumps down into it, as if her legs physically give way beneath her.

'She wouldn't. She isn't capable...'

Jacqui stops talking then, as if she didn't believe the words herself, before she starts to cry.

'She wouldn't do something like that. Not after everything she went through.' Her eyes go to Amelia's, as if pleading with her to tell her that it couldn't be true. That Tessa couldn't be in any way involved with this young girl's disappearance.

Only Amelia can't give her that answer.

'He broke her,' Jacqui says a few seconds later, after she'd fought to compose herself. 'When she came back, when she finally managed to escape from him, she wasn't the same person. Gone was the happy, playful niece that I knew and loved and in her place was this empty shell of a being. Riddled with panic attacks and nightmares. They were the worst years of Tessa's life. They were the worst years of my life too. Tessa was grieving. But I was grieving too. She had lost her mother and I had lost my sister.'

Jacqui paused then, clearing her throat.

'She fought him off. Did you know that? That's how she got away from him. She stabbed him with a pair of scissors. She was found in the woods by some young boy, covered in blood. His blood mainly. But some of it was hers. You'd never get over something like that, would you? Being taken like that by someone she thought she loved. Someone she trusted. Being held captive in a tiny room for months. Feeling so vulnerable and helpless. And then worse, learning of your own mother's death in that way. That had been the catalyst you see...' Jacqui winces as if she can't continue.

But her eyes tell Amelia that she knows she must.

That she has to say whatever it is that she's bottled up for all these years, for Tessa's sake.

'He has haunted her, for her entire life. She's never been free of him, not really.'

Amelia nods.

She knows first-hand what Jacqui is saying, how even all

these years later, Tessa still fought on a daily basis to keep herself together. To try and maintain some level of sanity. Despite everything that had happened to her.

'They never caught him. That's the worst part, they never even got close. The police investigation went on for months, but he somehow managed to get away. It was as if he just disappeared into thin air.' Jacqui is talking quietly now, as if speaking to herself. As if trying to justify Tessa's behaviour.

'And she was left to pick up the pieces. But he was always there festering underneath the surface. He was always there tormenting her. And I didn't think that she'd ever be capable of finding love after that. After him. I didn't think she could ever trust anyone again. But she has with you. She trusts you, Amelia. But you're right, she is hiding things still. And part of that is my fault because I stupidly, naively went along with it thinking that I was doing the right thing, when I should have insisted that she told someone. The police. The councillors, someone. Because it was too much for Tessa to bear, burying a secret like that for all these years. But she begged me. She pleaded with me never to tell a soul. And part of me understood that too, because I saw it. The way the media had a field day with her story. How they'd shared every tiny detail of her harrowing ordeal with the whole wide world. She didn't want that for him too... She said that he deserved better than that. She said that she owed him that much at least.'

'She *owed him*? Who? Nick Reading?' Amelia didn't understand. 'Why would Tessa owe that man anything after everything he'd done to her? After he'd destroyed her life.'

'No, not Nick.'

Jacqui shakes her head sadly.

'Tessa's son. Tessa had a son, with him.'

49

I am dying. I must be because I have never felt a pain quite like this.

But all I can do is stare at his face.

'It is you?' I say, my voice trembling as I start to cry. He forgot to put his mask on. In his haste to get in here and stop me from hurting myself, he forgot to hide his face.

I see him now, but deep down I had already known that it was him doing this to me.

I'd worked it out weeks ago.

Same height. Same build. Those same steely eyes staring back at me.

Of course I had known. Only I hadn't wanted to believe it.

Because he had been kind. He had been good.

Until he wasn't.

A flashback of the day I was taken. It had only been a few days after I'd told him my news. *Our* news. How he'd gone silent at the mention of a baby.

And that's what this has been all about. Him keeping me here like this.

Locking away his filthy secret from the prying eyes of the world.

Saving himself.

That night, in darkness, walking down a street. A noise behind me. A hand clamped around my mouth to silence my screams.

And when I'd woken, I was here. I have been here ever since.

The pain grips me again then and I roar.

'I need a doctor,' I beg him, the pain so intense that there's no way that I'm going to survive this.

He looks terrified, I hear the panic in his voice as he picks up his phone. Shouting at someone to come. To hurry. He's saying that I am bleeding. That there is too much blood. That there is something wrong.

And there is something wrong, I realise as I register the horror that shines from his eyes as he hangs up and looks down at the floor, to the blanket from my bed that's been placed down on the floor.

To the blood.

My blood.

'Here. Drink this,' he says, purposely ignoring my pleas as he holds a bottle of water to my mouth. To shut me up, to buy himself more time to think.

I don't argue this time. I just drink it back gratefully because my throat is dry and raw from screaming out in pain, and my entire body feels as if it's burning from the inside out. I savour the coolness of the water as I greedily gulp it down.

Sweat drips from my hair. My skin is soaked in it.

He is rendered useless. He doesn't know what to do. He can only focus on the blood on the floor, mopping it up as if it gives him something to do.

And I focus on the door.

It is open. If I could only get up. If I was only strong enough to try, I could make a run for it.

Only even as I sit up, another wave of pain hits me and the room spins violently. The pain so acute it's consuming me entirely, my eyes, my ears. Setting fire to every single cell in my body.

It's as if he reads my mind, second-guesses my thoughts. 'Rest, before it comes again,' he says as he guides me back down to the floor.

I don't fight him this time. Because I know that for once he's right.

If I'm going to survive this, I need to do as he says. I need to conserve every ounce of my energy. The next wave comes so quickly that I don't have time to think or to speak or to panic.

It takes me wholly. Squashing me with its enormity, and I have no choice but to give in to it and ride it out. I shrink inside of myself, and my body automatically takes over as if it knows what to do. The next pain is complete agony, an explosion, and the entire time I'm looking at him. Focusing on the horror on his face at what is unfolding.

This is bad.

I feel as if I'm being ripped in two. A hot, burning pain.

I look down between my legs and see the blood-soaked tiny human that is being expelled from my body.

50

It's her. His wife.

Lying in the middle of their kitchen floor, clutching at her side, as blood pools out from the gaping wound.

'Oh my god!' Tessa says as she instinctively rushes to the woman's side, crouching down and pressing her hand tightly over hers to help to stem the bleeding.

'I'm going to call an ambulance for you! You're going to be okay.' Tessa grabs her phone from her pocket and enters the emergency number.

'No! There's no time!' The woman pants, clambering into a sitting position as she reaches for Tessa's phone and knocks it out of Tessa's hand, shaking her head, hysterical.

'He has got her. He has got Kayla. I need to stop him...'

Tessa falters. As she realises what the woman is saying.

He took Kayla?

'Did *he* do this to you?' Tessa says, her voice quieter now.

The woman nods.

A look of something Tessa can't quiet register flashes across the woman's face. Sympathy. A knowing.

'You know who I am, don't you? You know what he did to me?' Tessa asks the woman quietly.

'I've only just found out. I didn't know until now. Until I found out about Kayla. Please, we have to hurry.'

Sherrie slowly stands up, her body bending forward as she holds on to the kitchen side for support. Tessa can see the pain that is etched on her face. How unbearable it must be and there is so much blood.

All down her clothes. Pooling at her feet.

She's gone so pale that her skin looks almost translucent. Her lips are tinged with blue.

'We need to get you to a hospital...' Tessa begins, only she is silenced by the woman's words.

'There's no time. He won't let her live. He's trying to cover it all up, like he did with you. First me, then her. We need to get to him. We need to stop him.' Sherrie winces, doubled over, her hand cupping the wound. In a desperate bid to stem the bleeding as it pumps through the gaps in her fingers.

'Where is she? Where is he keeping her?' Tessa asks, her voice a small strained squeak as if she's too scared to ask the question, afraid of the answer.

Her mind racing, a sick feeling swirling wildly in her stomach. Because she already knows where Kayla Goldman is being kept.

But she needs to hear it.

Sherrie stares her straight in the eyes before she mouths, 'He's got her locked away in the same place that he kept you.'

51

Tessa is back there. Back at the one place she'd spent the last sixteen years trying to erase from her memory.

Back at the house that he kept her locked up in all those years ago.

Though Tessa has no recollection of the dark country lane that the house sits in, no memory of the exterior of the house at all. Directions are the only words that Sherrie has spoken the whole journey here. Sitting with her head back, resting against the passenger seat headrest, her face twisted, contorted with pain, she only spoke to give Tessa the precise information she needed to get them here. Conserving the little energy she has left.

Tessa wouldn't have known this place otherwise; she would have simply driven past it.

Because she has never seen it.

It had been late in the evening and dark, the day she'd been abducted. And she could still recall that sense of being watched, followed. Then that feeling that someone was creeping up behind her.

The last thing she'd felt had been a hand clamped around her mouth.

When she'd woken up, she was inside a house. Locked inside a room.

In this house?

The house he'd kept her in for months.

'Are you sure this is the right place?' Tessa asks. Eyeing the place and how derelict it looks. Hidden behind the overgrown foliage and hedgerows, set back from the main road. How it sits in complete darkness.

She sees the paint peeling and flaking in places around the rotten wooden frames of the windows. No lights beaming out of them.

It doesn't look like there is anyone here.

And now she can see it properly, apart from the fact that it must have stood empty for years, it doesn't look like the sinister place she'd imagined in her head, any time she had thought about it.

It just seems like a normal house.

Un-lived in, unloved.

'Yes. This is it.' Sherrie nods with certainty. Hobbling still, walking slowly behind Tessa, as they both make their way down the pathway, towards the front door. It's only then that Tessa sees it.

The glass on the front door has been smashed. Jagged spikes of glass fan up like icicles. There is a brick on the ground, surrounded by tiny fragments of broken glass. A smear of blood all across the doorframe.

She wonders if someone cut themselves in the process of reaching inside and undoing the lock.

Maybe he really is here, after all.

'Go!' Sherrie nods at Tessa, indicating at her to go inside.

And she does, creeping now, quietly. Aware of the

impending danger. That they are no longer alone. Someone is in here.

He is in here.

A noise chimes out from somewhere upstairs. A scape of furniture being dragged across the floor. Footsteps.

Tessa forces herself to continue, following the sound as they make their way quietly up the staircase with Sherrie walking closely behind her. Eyeing the dark abandoned hallways and the rooms that lead off both landings, until they reach the very top.

Another noise then, the sound coming from above them, and it's only then that Tessa notices the thin, narrow stairway that twists itself up towards the attic, to the loft room in the roof of the house.

To the room that she was kept in.

Tessa's heart is pounding, beating wildly inside of her chest as if it's trying to be free of her body, as the walls start closing in on her.

Her breath is sparse; her chest is wheezing.

The signs of another panic attack as she has a flashback.

She's treading so carefully, feeling her way down this same narrow staircase with the sole of her foot; his hand is on her arm as he guides her. The blindfold he pulled so tightly around her face, digging into her skin.

The memory is gone as quickly as it came to her.

She can't do this.

She can't go up there.

She can't go back into that room.

She's not strong enough to face him.

She needs air. She needs to get outside so that she can breathe.

Only when Tessa turns to Sherrie, she is shocked at how ashen Sherrie's skin looks now, a sickly pale, her eyes bloodshot. Yet her expression is fixed. Pure determination across her face.

She is still climbing, she is still making her way up these stairs, for the sake of her daughter.

Despite her injury. Despite her agony.

And she is right.

Because there is a girl up there, in that room, in trouble, just like Tessa had once been.

A girl who needs their help.

Tessa couldn't go back now. She couldn't give up.

Even if she wants to.

And she wants to. She really wants to.

BREATHE! Taking a deep lungful of air, before she continues walking. Tiptoeing, creeping quietly until they reach the single door at the top of the landing. It's shut but the narrow strip of light as it runs across the gap underneath the door tells her that there is movement the other side of it.

Tessa can hear that noise again.

The scrape of something heavy like furniture being dragged along bare wooden floorboards. Tessa places her hand on the door handle and the realisation is not lost on her. She is back here where it all started. Only this time he is inside and she is the one on the outside of the door.

But to make sure that Kayla is safe, Tessa is going to have to go back inside that room.

She was going to have to confront him. To face her monster once and for all.

BREATHE!

Tessa pulls at the handle, and pushes open the door.

The gaudy bubble-gum pink painted room flooding her vision first.

Then that same musty smell. The familiarity of it all pulls at her. And in an instant she is right back there again. Back in this room on that very last day.

Her mother is dead. The words radiate out from the TV. She'd been standing right here, her ear pressed up against the door, listening, as he'd watched his TV show. Her mother is dead. That's how she had found out. And it had triggered something visceral inside of her. She'd wanted it all to stop.

Him, keeping her here against her will.

The baby that had been growing inside of her.

His baby.

Tessa looks down at the bare floor. To the very spot where the baby had lain after she'd given birth.

Ten little fingers. Ten little toes.

A son.

Banished from even the darkest recesses of her mind because of the chronic, agonising pain it caused her.

She couldn't bear to think about the baby, not for a second, not for a single moment.

How he wasn't crying. He wasn't breathing.

The movement in the room pulls her back from her most harrowing thoughts. Tessa bristles now, knowing before she looks over that it's him.

He is standing by the bed, his arms wrapped around his daughter as if he's trying to lift her, trying to move her, while the girl lies limp in his arms.

Her head flopping back. Her eyes closed.

Not crying. Not breathing. Not a sound. Dead.

Tessa lets out a bloodcurdling scream.

52

He runs from the room.

I am left alone with this thing. This tiny alien that is covered in a sticky, milky residue and speckled with blood. Born from my body, splayed out on the floor in between my legs. Its red face contorted with anger at the injustice of having been pushed out into the world. As if it has been forced here against its will.

And it has.

This is what it has been all about.

This is the reason I am here.

But then I guessed that already.

I've known for a while that this is why he brought me here, that this is why he has kept me locked inside this room. All the while his child was growing inside of me. Violating my body. He didn't want anyone to find out about it. He didn't want anyone to know that the baby exists.

Because it would destroy his career.

Sleeping with his student.

He'd crossed the line, violating his position of power.

It didn't matter that I was almost eighteen. It didn't matter that we loved each other.

Had he even loved me or had that all been a lie too?

Because he'd told me he'd leave his job and his girlfriend for me. He told me that he wasn't happy with her and that he wanted this baby.

And then he'd locked me away.

He'd locked me up in this very room as if I was nothing more than a dirty, sordid secret.

That's when I had started to disassociate with this thing that had been growing inside of me. I had become detached, unable to bear the thought of even touching the small mound of my belly, because it had felt as if it was contagious, that it was a disgusting disease that was killing me.

And now it's here. On the floor.

As I think about reaching for it, he is back in the room.

A bag in his hand and a fresh towel.

He's standing over us, his eyes fixed on this blood-soaked tiny human.

He takes charge, reaching down, wrapping some wool around the cord against the baby's stomach before he takes out a pair of scissors and cuts at the umbilical cord, before wrapping the baby in the towel.

I'm glad that he knows what to do, because all I can do is stare.

Two little eyes. Two little ears. Ten tiny fingers, Ten tiny toes.

The child is so small. Too small, I think as he lifts the baby to him. Holding it against his chest.

I see a look cross his face, a look of panic.

And it's only then that I register the sudden silence in the room. So quiet that it's deafening.

The baby is making no sound at all.

'What's wrong?' I say, my voice stricken.

He doesn't answer, instead he gets up and leaves the room. Locking the door behind him.

Leaving me here.

And I am quick. Seeing the scissors he's left behind, I pick them up and scramble across the bedroom floor, tucking them down underneath the mattress, before going back to the spot on the floor that's covered in blood and goop. I wait for him.

For the baby.

He must be taking it to a doctor I think, he must be getting it some help.

When he comes back he is all alone. He walks into the room, and for the first time he looks down at the floor, unable to look at me.

'Where's the baby?' I ask, and he shakes his head.

'WHERE'S THE BABY?' I scream then, terrified of the answer. Because I already know. Even before he tells me.

'The baby is dead. He was too small.'

He. *He* was a boy. I had a son.

I shake my head to push the words back out, as if to dislodge them from my ears. And I laugh then. A deranged cackle leaving my lips. He doesn't really mean it. He's saying it to hurt me.

To taunt me. It's another one of his sick and twisted games.

I don't believe him.

This is all just another one of his cruel, wicked games that he likes to play with me.

I have been so good. Waiting here so patiently for him to come back. Glad that at least the baby managed to get out of this godforsaken room, and its sickly pink walls and the constant smell of shit. Even if it was only for a few seconds, or minutes.

Only the baby hasn't come back.

'He was born too early. He didn't make it.'

Dead.

It's just one little word but it is so final.

I picture myself slamming into the wall. Wanting it out of me. Wanting to purposely expel it from my body.

The baby is dead.

I did that. I did that!

'He was too small. Too fragile.'

And then he shrugs.

That single gesture like a slap to my face.

How he simply shakes his words off, just like that.

As if the baby's life doesn't matter. As if my life doesn't matter.

'You need to go to the hospital,' he says, looking down at me now, and I look too. That's when I realise that I am still bleeding.

There is blood on the floor and trailing down my legs.

I walk to the bed and pull my jumper on, then I wrap the blanket around my lower body, as if trying to cover myself up and protect my modesty, as I slip my hand down underneath the mattress feeling around for the scissors that I hid there when he first left.

I grip them in my fist and think about running at him now, plunging them into his neck.

For that shrug.

I eye the door behind him, ajar. I might make it if I run.

Blood drips down my leg and I feel weak. Queasy.

Something is wrong.

He's going to take me to a hospital.

He is going to get me help.

I push the scissors up inside my sleeve.

He walks towards me as I glance around the room one last time.

Eyeing the bloody towels that are heaped in a pile on the floor. The stinking bucket that sits in the corner.

The bed behind me that I have slept on for the past few months.

I stand obediently as he wraps a blindfold around my head, covering my eyes.

And I tell myself that whatever happens next, at least I know that I did finally make it out of this room.

53

'Put her down.' Sherrie's voice is as hard as it is cold, and her eyes flash with malice as she steps towards Richard.

It's only then that Tessa sees the knife in Sherrie's hand. She must have brought it with her; she must have taken it from the house and concealed it somewhere, so that Tessa wouldn't see.

Had she planned this all along? Did she know what awaited them? That she was going to need to protect herself from this monster. She was going to need to protect her daughter from him too.

'Move away from my daughter!'

Sherrie says it again, lurching forward, her tone firmer. One hand still clutching at her side, pain etched on her face.

The knife is pointing straight at Richard.

Showing him that she will use it if she has to. If he forces her to.

Heeding her warning, Richard does as he is told.

Carefully, he lays Kayla back down on the bed, before he steps away from her, holding up his hands as if he is surrendering.

'Sherrie, I can't do this anymore. I can't...'

Kayla is not dead, Tessa realises, flooded with relief as she sees Kayla's eyelids flicker. Such a tiny movement, as if she is in there listening. Aware of everything that is going on around her.

She's not dead. She's unconscious.

She's been drugged.

That's how he has done it, Tessa thinks, that's how he has kept her here against her will.

What kind of a sicko drugs his own daughter and locks her away?

And why?

Was this how he got his cheap thrills? By locking young women away like his prisoners, because hadn't Tessa only been a few years older than Kayla when he'd done the very same to her too?

But he had kept Tessa here for a reason: to hide his sordid secret from the world.

The baby. Their son.

He hadn't wanted anyone to know that he'd slept with his student and got her pregnant. He hadn't wanted anyone to know how he'd abused his position of trust and taken advantage of Tessa.

Did Kayla have a secret he wanted hidden too?

Tessa felt sick at the thought of what it might be. What this man might be trying to cover up this time.

Only this time he won't get away with it.

'I said, move away from her. Move away from my daughter,' Sherrie commands, her voice steady now, focused, fully back in control despite what he did to her.

She is losing blood, a lot of blood. Tessa can see it seeping through her fingers as she clamps them over the gaping wound in her side.

'You're still going to do this? After everything, Sherrie?'

Richard says finally, raising his eyes as he stares back at Sherrie then, almost challenging her to answer him.

Now that he is standing right here in front of her, Tessa can't take her eyes off him. She had been right all along. It really is him. Except, he is older now. His face is fuller. His hair has greyed. But this is him.

The monster.

And it feels almost surreal, as if she is still stuck inside a bad dream, that they are both back here in this very room, after all these years.

'Tell her what you did,' Richard says. Breaking Tessa's trance.

He's talking about her, Tessa realises. He's telling Sherrie to tell her. Tell her what?

Whatever it is, his eyes don't move from Sherrie's as he shouts. He is angry. His face growing red. His expression unhinged. Spital sprays from his lips as he bellows. 'Tell her what you did, Sherrie. Go on, tell her. Because this is all over for us, Sherrie. There's no coming back from any of this. And I am glad. I want this to be over. I want to be done with you! TELL HER THE TRUTH! ALL OF IT!'

'Don't you dare!' Sherrie thunders.

None of them move. 'Don't you fucking dare. After all I have done for you. After all I have given you. And all you have done is lied. You ruined this family. All I did was try and hold it all together. I tried to fix the mess that you caused. You destroyed us!'

There is silence now. Until finally Richard's voice cuts through the air.

'It was her.' He looks directly at Tessa then, and it's the first time that he's looked her in the eye since she stepped into the room.

Almost as if, until now, he has been unable to face her. He has been unable to look her in the eye.

He forces himself to now.

His eyes fixed on hers, full of tears, his voice cracking with emotion.

'She knew about us. She knew about you and the baby. She set you up. Abducted you. She got the medication to drug you off the dark web. Always so obsessed with true crime, weren't you Sherrie! Because the life you were living was one.'

Tessa shakes her head. She has no idea what Richard is telling her.

She saw him. In this room. Every day that she had been locked in here. Bringing her food. Emptying that stinking bucket.

He'd been here when she'd had the baby.

It was him. Only him.

He was lying.

'She followed you, abducted you. She put you here in this room.' Richard is crying now. His words drowned out by his loud sobbing as he breaks down.

'He's lying.' Sherrie shakes her head. Still she doesn't shift her gaze from his. Hate radiating from her. 'He is a pitiful, weak, pathetic excuse of a man. He always was. He always will be—'

'I was!' Richard cries. 'I was all of that and, God, so much more. Because she punished me too. If I didn't go along with her. She'd beat me, or kick me or bite me. And in the end I was forced to go along with it all. Because I am all of the things that she says I am. But I thought she would let you go. I thought after a few days that she'd realise the madness of what she had done. She'd see how she wouldn't be able to get away with it. Only she did get away with it, and the days turned into weeks and by then I knew how unhinged she was, how much she wanted to make you suffer. How far she was willing to go. And that's why I stayed.' Richard shakes his head sadly. 'I was just her puppet. Here every day like your jailer, but really I was too frightened to leave you here with her alone. Because I thought that she might kill you. And she would have, had you not been pregnant. I'm sure of it. The baby was the only thing that saved you.'

'Liar. Liar. Liar,' Sherrie shrieks.

Tessa can't move. She can't breathe. As she drinks them both in, their expressions, their body language. Seeing the pure fire and determination on Sherrie's face to save her daughter, while he is oozing desperation. He is cornered. Like a scared animal clamped inside a trap, trying to gnaw off its own limbs in a bid to escape.

He is an actor.

He is lying.

That's what he's always done.

He'd tricked her then and he is trying to trick her now.

'I didn't do that!' Richard says, pointing to Sherrie's wound. To where the knife had pierced her stomach. To the patch of blood spreading out, expanding across her clothes. 'She lunged at me. She attacked me. She tried to kill me because I found out that she had been keeping Kayla here. She knew that you had found us, and she said that she wanted to keep her safe. To keep her away from you,' Richard continues. 'We've been living a lie. It's all fake. Christ, even the colour of her hair isn't real! She dyes it red so that they look the same. She's done it since the day Kayla was born.'

'That's a lie!' Sherrie shouts now, pursing her lips. 'You did this. Just like you kept her here too. You did all of this.'

Richard shakes his head.

'I let you go, Tessa. Don't you remember? I let you go...' Richard says, searching Tessa's eyes for the memory. For the realisation that he hadn't wanted to harm her. He hadn't wanted to hurt her.

Not like that.

He needs her to remember.

She has to remember.

'After the baby, she wanted you dead. I was the one who told you to run!'

Tessa shakes her head again, remembering how he'd tricked her and told her that he was taking her to the hospital when he had driven her to some woodlands instead. That impending feeling that something awful was about to happen to her.

Blood everywhere.

Scissors plunged into his leg.

That's how she'd managed to get away. She had run through the woods, covered in his blood. In her hair, in her mouth, on her skin.

He hadn't let her go: she'd escaped from him.

He is lying now.

He is lying still.

'I loved you,' he says finally. 'I loved you and she knew it. She knew that I was prepared to lose everything for you. My job, my life. Her.' Richard is pleading with Tessa to believe him. 'The only reason I stayed with her was because of her. The baby.'

Then Sherrie lunges at him.

54

'I am sorry,' he says.

He's taken off my blindfold and the harsh sunlight streams in through the windscreen and almost blinds me with its brightness.

We are in a large gravel carpark, surrounded by trees.

'I thought you were taking me to a hospital?' I whimper.

We are in a park or a nature reserve, I'm not sure which. But we are alone. There is no one else around and I can feel that something really bad is coming.

Something awful. Something final.

'Are you going to kill me?' I ask, wondering what he is saying sorry for.

For what he's already done to me, or for what is coming.

He doesn't answer and he won't look at me.

He can't bring himself to look at me.

'I didn't mean for any of this to happen to you. I never meant for any of it. Please, God. Forgive me!'

He is crying. Big fat tears roll down his cheeks as his face crumples and he starts to sob.

I wonder for a second if he expects sympathy from me.

Compassion? But I have none to give him. Whatever I once felt for him is gone and I feel nothing for him now at all.

I'm numb to him.

I clutch the scissors, hardening my grip.

One strike, a stab, and I could end this. I could end him. And that's what he deserves.

To suffer like I have. To feel some pain.

And I deserve it too, don't I? My revenge.

Only I can't do it. I want to, but I can't move, and he sees them. As the sunlight hits the metal blade of the scissors and reflects up at him.

He knows what I'm about to do.

'Do it!' he shouts. 'DO IT.'

Calling my bluff. Challenging me to execute my plan. To plunge the scissors into him.

Only I can't.

I freeze, and it's only for a fraction of a second. A heartbeat in time. It's long enough for him to lunge at me and grab the scissors from my grasp. I was too slow, too weak, too pathetic and now once again the power is his.

'I am sorry!' he says, and his words linger in the air between us. I eye the trail of snot that hangs down from his nose. The scissors still in his grasp.

And I accept my fate.

That this is how I'll die.

I am ready.

My mother is dead. My baby is dead. This is my only way to get away from this monster.

Everything happens so quickly I don't have a chance to register what happens or how it happens. Or what any of it means.

The car door clicks. And then there is so much blood.

I look down and the scissors are plunged deep into his leg, though I have no memory of doing it.

Blood pools out across his lap.

'RUN.'

Was that his voice? Did he say that?

I don't wait.

I am out of the car, running. Ignoring the searing pain as the sharp spiked ends of twigs and broken branches imbed themselves into the soft soles of my feet.

The piercing sting of brambles, the serrated scratch of thorns, ripping my skin to shreds as I run further into the dense woodlands.

I am running for my life.

Until my lungs feel as if they might burst inside my chest.

Until I can't run another single step.

Then I hide.

55

Richard is lying on the floor, the knife beside him, blood pooling out from the stab wound on his chest. His eyes are shut and from where Tessa is standing he doesn't look as if he's breathing.

He is dead, she realises.

The monster is finally dead.

Part of her should feel free at last. Elated. That justice has finally been done. Vengeance is hers.

But something about this moment feels so wrong.

Her head is spinning. The room is spinning.

And all she can think about are his final words.

I stayed because of her. The baby.

Her.

Tessa eyes Sherrie as she goes to their daughter.

'It's okay, my darling. Mummy is here.' Her voice is hoarse. Her skin has gone a muted shade of grey, her eyes too.

She looks weak, as if she has aged ten years since they have been in this room.

There is something about her demeanour, the way she seems so deranged and demented as she drapes her arms around her unconscious daughter like she's a possession.

'Mummy loves you. Mummy is here.'

The words pour out of her like a mantra, like she's stating her claim on her. Like she is saying the words to comfort herself more than she is saying them for her daughter. All the while her husband lies dead at her feet.

And Sherrie hasn't so much as flinched.

'He's dead!' Tessa says, her mouth releasing the words as if she can no longer hold them in. As if until she says them out loud, she can't actually believe it. Tessa had seen it with her own eyes, as if it had played out in front of her in slow motion. Sherrie's actions almost robotic as she'd plunged the knife into her husband's chest. Showing no emotion at all as she'd ended his life.

Richard hadn't fought her.

He had just stood there and taken it.

And now he is dead.

He stayed with Sherrie for the baby.

That's what he just said. He stayed for her.

Her.

Kayla Goldman: 15 November 2006.

The day that her baby was born. The day that Tessa escaped.

A daughter?

Tessa hadn't given birth to a baby boy at all.

He'd lied to her.

The baby hadn't died. *She* lived.

'Mummy's here, my darling,' Sherrie coos. Fussing now, wiping strands of Kayla's hair away from her face. Kissing her forehead, before she starts to sing.

'You are my sunshine, my only sunshine, you make me happy when skies are grey...'

Her voice is strained and unhinged as she looks up at Tessa. Her glare unwavering.

It hits Tessa, a jolt of electricity shocking her system, the horrific realisation of what this woman has done.

He wasn't lying.

He had been telling the truth.

She did this.

Sherrie was the mastermind behind it all. That's why Tessa had been taken here and held in this room. It had been about the baby all along.

Sherrie had set out to destroy Tessa by taking everything from her. She had taken her baby and made Richard lie to her.

She'd made him tell her that her little boy was dead.

Then she had taken her baby from her and brought her up as her own.

Richard hadn't killed her, like Sherrie had wanted him to.

Richard had let Tessa get away.

He'd tried to save her. To spare her.

Was that why she'd put Kayla here? Why she'd hidden her away in this room?

Why she had drugged her own daughter?

Because Tessa had found them, found him, and Sherrie thought that she had known. That she had worked it out and that she had come back for Kayla.

For her child.

'No!' Tessa mouths, her voice lost. Suddenly the air is sucked from the room and she is on the floor, her vision blurring as she frantically wheezes for breath. This isn't a panic attack. This is far worse than that, she thinks as her throat closes in, a crushing sensation inside her chest.

She's having a heart attack.

She is dying.

Right here in the very spot where her baby was born.

Tessa's eyes flicker open, and she sees Sherrie, crouching next to her. Her eyes manic, her lips twisted into a smirk.

The knife is in her hand.

'We're the only ones left. When you're gone, no one need ever find out the truth.'

Sherrie holds up the knife. And Tessa can't fight her.

She can't stop her.

And suddenly she doesn't feel scared anymore. Instead of fear, she feels a strange sense of calm, as if she's accepted her fate and she's waiting now for the inevitable to come.

For the blade to strike her, for the last breath to leave her body.

For darkness..

Then she hears a voice. Amelia's, from somewhere far off in the distance. Bringing her some comfort in her final moment as Sherrie slams down next to her.

Only Tessa doesn't feel any pain.

She doesn't feel anything at all.

But she can hear noise. Lots of noise and commotion, and it's all coming from behind her, by the bedroom door.

Sherrie is just inches away from her. Her body lying alongside hers, and it's only then that Tessa realises that her head is being pushed into the carpet. Another hand is prising the knife from Sherrie's fingers. Her legs are being restrained as she lashes out.

'Tessa, baby! You're going to be okay. I tracked your phone, the police are here.' Amelia's voice cuts through all the noise and the chaos, and Tessa finally allows her tears to fall. 'They are not who they said they were. You were right. We checked the dates. We checked the birth records...'

And Amelia doesn't need to say anymore.

Because she knows. They both know what Tessa had been holding back.

What it had really been all about.

Tessa turns her head.

Her eyes lock on Sherrie's.

The two women lying side by side.

As Tessa summons up every last bit of energy she has within her. Every last bit of air she can pull into her lungs. This woman has already taken so much of her life. Tessa had thought her baby had died. The saying was true: Death doesn't change you; it reveals you. She had heard that expression before, but she hadn't realised the actual weight of the meaning it held until now.

She had tried to be strong for so long, when really all she had done was push it down. The trauma of losing her baby had tainted her whole existence. The thought that she had played a part in killing her own child.

She'd pushed it down so far, so deeply, that sometimes in her darkest moments she'd questioned if it had even been real.

She wondered at times if it had really happened at all.

Tessa knows the truth now. Finally. And she will not allow this woman to destroy another second of her life.

Tessa is taking it back.

'You were never enough,' Tessa says quietly then, her words loud enough for only Sherrie to hear. Her tone full of pure determination.

A finality to it.

It is over now.

She is taking her power back from this woman. This monster.

'You were never enough for him or for her. And you can't have her. Kayla doesn't belong to you. She is mine.'

56

Sweeping her hair up into a ponytail, Tessa turns her head to the side to admire her profile before frustratedly shaking it back out again and combing her brush back through it, before sweeping it to one side.

'That's about the tenth hairstyle you've given yourself this morning!'

Amelia's voice startles her as she eyes her reflection in the mirror. Standing behind her, her back against the wall, as she holds Spud in her arms. A silly grin on her face.

'I take it that you are feeling nervous?'

'How did you guess?' Tessa admits, rolling her eyes before turning to face Amelia. Her voice small as she adds, 'What if she doesn't like me. Or what if we just don't get on? If we don't, I don't know, feel a connection?'

'Tessa! What's not to like? You are an amazing woman. And from what we've heard, Kayla is too. You've both been through so much. You already have a connection. I know how scary this might feel for you, Tess, really I do, but can you even imagine how scary this must feel for her? I can't even comprehend how traumatic this has been for her. Her father murdered by the woman that she thought was her mother for all these years. Finding out that she was taken as a baby. That her whole life had been a lie.'

'I know. I know!' Tessa says, realising that Amelia is right, and she needs to shift the focus.

Kayla had reached out to her. She asked Tessa to meet with her today. So that they could both have the opportunity to get to know each other.

Without the police. Or social workers.

Without the pressure of being mother and daughter. Not yet. Neither of them were ready for that.

But as friends.

As two women who had been through trauma.

Amelia is right. They have both been through so much. But at least Tessa knows now what had happened to her. Kayla had been blindsided. That girl had grown up living a life that had been nothing more than a lie. Her parents' names weren't even real. Kayla hadn't even known her real age. It would take years for the shock to subside, if ever. And Tessa knows all about that.

How hard the journey ahead of her would be, how much time and healing she'd need.

'You're right. It's going to take time. But I'm ready for that. I want to help her. I want to make this right. Especially with Sherrie's sentencing coming up. They're not going to be lenient with her, are they? Not after everything she's confessed to?'

'I don't think so, no,' Amelia says, wrapping her arms around Tessa, reassuring her. 'And you will make it right. You are both going to be just fine, I promise. Baby steps, okay. Just be yourself, because you are enough, Tessa. You are more than enough and that girl is going to need you as much, if not more, than you need her. Especially once Sherrie has been sentenced.'

Tessa nods, a single tear running down her cheek.

Despite everything, the lies and the confusion and the drama of it all, Amelia is still here.

Just like she always told her she would be.

She still has her arms wrapped firmly around her, she's still here holding her up. Tessa feels eternally grateful that Amelia believed her in the end. That she and Jacqui had gone to the police to get Tessa help. That they had turned up at the house when they had. Just as Sherrie had been about to end her life too.

'Er, babe, what's that awful smell?' Amelia says, stepping back as a plume of smoke floats above them, streaming in from the kitchen doorway.

'Shit! The cakes!' Tessa says, panicking, running to the oven and turning it off. Before she frantically waves a tea towel around the room, and indicates to Amelia to open a window just as the doorbell rings.

'Jeez, Tessa. I know I said be yourself, but maybe it's a bit too soon to be pushing your "baking skills" on the poor girl just yet.' Amelia giggles, and Tessa starts laughing then.

'I'll get the door.'

57

Sherrie's hand trembles as she holds the letter. Eyeing the familiar handwriting that is scrawled across the front of the envelope before she pulls it open.

Hope.

She sobs uncontrollably at the sight of the small grey rabbit holding out a bunch of pretty pink flowers, the words *Happy Mother's Day* emblazoned across the top.

Kayla sent her a card for Mother's Day.

The first and only contact she has had with her daughter since she was arrested three weeks ago. Placed on remand, in prison, whilst awaiting her sentencing, her solicitor had warned her that the judge wouldn't be lenient with her.

Meanwhile, Tessa and Kayla's story had become a media sensation. Mother and daughter reunited after all these years.

The likelihood is that they will make an example of Sherrie. She stands to get a life sentence. To be locked away for a long time. The thought of being here, kept from her daughter, had been the worst pain Sherrie had ever felt in her life. Worse still since Kayla had refused all contact.

Until now.

Give her time, her solicitor had said, and he had been right.

Sherrie has hope now.

Even though part of her knows that she doesn't deserve it, Kayla reaching out to her like this, after all that she has done.

Richard is dead, and Kayla's life had all been a lie.

But the truth is, Sherrie isn't sorry.

She'd do it all over again if she had to. If it meant that she got to be Kayla's mother, because the past sixteen years were the best days of Sherrie's life.

Sherrie loved and protected Kayla from that very first day she was placed in her arms as a baby.

When Kayla couldn't sleep at night, it had been Sherrie who had stayed up late into the night reading her favourite books to her. Sherrie who had been the one to wrap her arms around her and hold her tight whenever she had a nightmare. She had been the one she had laughed with. Played with. Loved her.

Sherrie had never had that.

Her own mother had never shown Sherrie any kind of affection or anything close to love. She had always acted as though Sherrie was a nuisance. As if she was always in the way, always holding her back from doing something better.

Leaving Sherrie her childhood home after she had passed away was the only decent thing her mother had ever done for her.

An empty gesture of bricks and mortar. A house void of loving memories. A home missing a beating heart.

Though it had its uses in the end. It had brought Kayla to her.

Sherrie had never known the feeling of unconditional love between mother and child, until Kayla had come into her life, and Sherrie would treasure the precious memories always.

Kayla must feel that too.

How Sherrie only ever had her best intentions at heart.

How they might not be bonded by blood, but she still loved her more than anyone else in the world.

Running her finger over the embellished writing of the beautiful Mother's Day card, Sherrie decides she will pin it to the cell wall. To cherish it forever.

She will make this work.

She'll send Kayla a visiting order, so that she could see her every week if she wanted. They could write to one another. They could call.

Having Kayla back in her life is going to get her through her darkest days, and Sherrie needs that more than ever.

She has a reason to live again.

Sherrie opens the card and shuffles back on the bed, before she scans the neat handwriting. The letters joined so beautifully. Remembering how she'd sat for hours each day with Kayla as a child, doing her spellings with her, making her flash cards, reading her favourite stories to her over and over again.

Kayla had excelled in her classes. She'd always been ahead of the others. So advanced. And that wasn't just because she was actually a year older than they'd told her either. Kayla is smart.

She is really clever.

Sherrie likes to think she got that from her.

Mum,

I want to say thank you for all you did for me. For loving me. For protecting me.

Growing up, you were the light of my life. You were my bestest friend.

The best mother.

I would like to say all of that, but none of it was real.

Our life together was nothing more than a lie.

And I don't think I can forgive you for that. I don't think I can ever forgive you for what you did to me. Or for what you did to my real mother.

But I hope that one day you can forgive yourself.

Kayla

Her *real mother*.

Sherrie drops the card. Those three words cutting her like a knife.

Her hands shake violently, bile burning at the back of her throat at the thought of Kayla, out there right now, playing happy families with that bitch.

The walls feel as if they are closing in on her.

Up off the bed then, Sherrie slams her fist against the locked door.

'Let me out. Let me out of here!'

She is trapped, all alone in this tiny cell.

In this prison.

She has lost her beloved Kayla forever.

Tessa has won.

A LETTER FROM CASEY KELLEHER

Dear reader,

I want to say a huge thank you for choosing to read *Only Child*. If you enjoyed the book and you would like to keep up to date with all my latest releases, just sign up at the following link. Your email address will never be shared and you can unsubscribe at any time.

www.bookouture.com/casey-kelleher

This is my third psychological thriller, and I have to say I thoroughly enjoyed the dark, twisted turns that this book took as I started to write Tessa's story. As always with my books, I started the writing process with such a small seed of an idea.

Only Child started with the idea of someone being held captive in a room. I had no idea who they were, or why they were being held against their will, but I knew immediately that there was a great story there. I hope you agree. Once again, those readers who have followed me from my change of genre from the gritty gangland reads, thank you! I hope you enjoyed the change of pace, and that you still got your fix of darkness.

I'd love to hear what you thought of *Only Child*, so if you have the time, and you'd like to leave me a review on Amazon it's always appreciated. (I do make a point of reading every single one.)

I also love hearing from you, my readers – your messages

and photos of the books that you tag me in on social media always make my day! And trust me, some days us authors really need that to spur us on with that dreaded daily word-count.

So, please feel free to get in touch on my Facebook page, or through Instagram, Twitter or my website.

Thank you

Casey Kelleher

www.caseykelleher.co.uk

 facebook.com/officialcaseykelleher

 twitter.com/CaseyKelleher

 instagram.com/caseykelleher

ACKNOWLEDGEMENTS

Many thanks to my amazing editor Susannah Hamilton. This book was a crazy journey for me from start to finish, for a million reasons. After two years of working through the madness that's been going in the world, this was probably the hardest writing experience I've had to date. *Only Child* really wouldn't be the book that it is today without your kindness, patience, and expertise. And for cheering me on, all the way to the finishing line.

It's been a pleasure working alongside you and I'm already looking forward to getting stuck into the next one!

Special thanks as always to the amazing Noelle Holten – PR extraordinaire! And to all of the Bookouture dream team, and to all of the fabulous authors in the lounge.

Special mention to Emma Graham Tallon and Victoria Jenkins. You girls are the BEST and I just want you to know that there's no one else I'd rather be locked inside a haunted library and drinking cocktails with at one in the morning. Looking forward to our next trip!

Thanks as always to my bestie, Lucy Murphy, who has always been so super supportive of everything I do. And to my sister-in-law, Laura Cooper. I can't tell you how nerve-wracking it is to have people reading my books for the first time. So, I'm super grateful to you both for not only being so supportive but for also being super speedy and not making me wait too long!

Huge thanks also to Colin Scott and for the Savvys for all your fantastic advice and support.

And to all the lovely readers in Gangland Governors (Not-Rights), TBC, UK Crime book club, Bitchy Bookworms, Psychological Thriller Readers – and so many more groups! For reading, reviewing and sharing my book! I really appreciate all your support.

As always I'd like to thank my extremely supportive friends and family for all the encouragement that they give me along the way.

The Coopers, The Kellehers, The Ellises.

And to all my lovely friends.

To my beautiful niece Kayla, thank you for allowing me to pinch your name for the main character! I hope you read this one and that you enjoy it.

To Alex Besley for winning Fit With Marlene's FitMas Challenge prize of a named character in the book. Ethan made the first page!

Finally, a big thank you to my husband Danny. My rock!

By the time this book is published we will be celebrating twenty years together. I can't wait for all the adventures ahead of us in the next twenty.

Much love to my sons Ben, Danny and Kyle. I'm so proud of the men you've grown into.

Not forgetting our two little fur-babies/writer's assistants, Sassy and Miska.

And to you, my lovely reader,

I say this often, because it's true.

You are the very reason I write. Without you, none of this would have been possible.

Casey x

Printed in Great Britain
by Amazon